Silvaria

Witch Haven Cozy Mystery - book 14

K.E. O'Connor

SILVARIA

ISBN: 978-1-915378-41-5

Written by: K.E. O'Connor

Preface

The Witch Haven series has been created so you spend time with four amazing witches:

Books 1-3 tell Indigo's story: Spells and Spooks, Hexes and Haunts, Curses and Corpses

Books 4-6 tell Luna's story: Muffins and Moonlight, Cupcakes and Cauldrons, Pancakes and Potions

Book 7-9 tell Odessa's story: Hauntings and High Jinx, Hauntings and Havoc, Hauntings and Hoaxes

Book 10-12 tell Storm's story: The Case of the Screaming Skull, The Case of the Poisoned Pumpkin, The Case of the Cursed Candy

And there are two bonus origin stories to enjoy:
Fire Fang and **Silvaria**

Chapter 1

"I hope we won't talk about dead bodies all night." My tall, broad-shouldered, classically handsome fiancé, Emory Farr, adjusted his high-starched collar, inching a finger in between the fabric and his neck.

"Aunt Ruby will expect some discussion about corpses. It's only polite." I smoothed the pale pink silk of my new corseted dress over my knees. It had a charming sweetheart neckline, long lace sleeves, and the hem brushed the floor as I walked. Aunt Ruby was old-fashioned in every sense. Too much flesh on display, and she wouldn't talk to you.

"Not all of us find the dead as fascinating as your family." Emory stopped tugging at his collar and settled into the plush red velvet cushions in the carriage as it trundled toward my aunt's estate on the edge of Briar Pass.

"Marry me, marry into the Digby's world of the undead." I tried to make light of my family's long history as cemetery guardians, but it wasn't for everyone. Including me. Many found our work morbid, and controlling corpses wasn't an ability

I'd ever wanted. But some things in life couldn't be chosen. They just were.

Emory's sigh sounded like he was in pain. "Silvaria, darling, I do understand. And I'll fake an interest and talk to the old girl about dead things, but change the subject as soon as you think it's polite."

"Of course." I reached over and adjusted his pink silk cravat. It matched my dress.

He gently pulled my hand away but kept hold of it. "Stop fussing. I've handled worse dragons than your aunt Ruby."

"She can be difficult, and this is the first time you've visited her estate. Aunt Ruby is old and set in her ways. And we mustn't be late. Dinner is on the table at six sharp."

"We won't be late. I don't know why you're so intent on impressing her. It's not as if you need her money."

"Emory! That's not why we're visiting. She's my only living aunt. I like to check in on her and make sure she's well. She's become isolated as she's gotten older and spends more time with the corpses than anyone else."

"Isn't that your family's motto? You prefer the dead to the living. *Vivos praeferre mortuos*?"

I swatted his arm. "Don't tease. And it's not that. It's *Memento mori*. Remember, we all die, so we treat the corpses with respect because we'll become one eventually."

He placed an arm around my shoulders, sending a small thrill down my spine. "I'll be on my best behavior. Even your frosty old aunt will be enchanted by me by the end of the evening."

"She said she won't come to our wedding." I leaned into his embrace. I felt so lucky to have such a handsome, clever man to marry. It wasn't easy to find someone who accepted my unusual, and unwanted, ability to control the dead. Many people found my family's talent as cemetery guardians creepy. Some actively avoided them. But we were an essential part of the magical community. If the dead weren't cared for, they rose and rioted.

Emory had seen past all of that. Of course, he'd been wary when we started dating, but he was comfortable with my heritage. Me, not so much.

"If your aunt doesn't want to come to the wedding, she can stay in her manor house and dance with the corpses if she likes. Nothing will spoil our big day," Emory said.

"I would love her to be there, though. Perhaps that's what she needs, a break from the morbid life she's built. Well, it's more like a morbid half-life. She talks about the bodies more than she does her family."

"If your aunt Ruby causes problems for us, we'll distance ourselves from her. We'll both be ridiculously wealthy soon enough, so we can do whatever we want. You already have your trust fund, and my business plans are on the up, so it's not as if we need to fake charm the old lady out of her fortune."

I sat up straight and glared at him. "I hope that was a joke. Aunt Ruby may be rich, but that's not the reason I keep in touch."

He arched a thick eyebrow. "Then you're better than most. What do you get out of this relationship? She browbeats you every time you visit, and her default position is to complain."

I clasped my gloved hands in my lap. "Aunt Ruby was different when she was younger. I even remember her playing with me when I was a child. I can't imagine her doing that now. It's the power, you see. It drains you."

Emory chuckled. "She'd probably feed you to one of her pet corpses if you were still small."

"She does not have pet corpses in the house." He got another smack on the arm for that comment.

"Darling, I'm teasing. All I meant was, even if your aunt doesn't approve of what we're doing, we'll still be blissfully happy. We have the world at our feet. We could move to another country, build our own enormous manor house in the countryside, or buy a home somewhere warmer."

"And fill those homes with children?" I'd always wanted a big family, and Emory was the same. We'd talked for hours about how we'd create a household full of laughter and brimming with life. It was something I'd never experienced when growing up.

"Of course. Whatever your heart desires."

I sighed and rested against him, smiling at the future within reach. My childhood had been surrounded by groaning corpses and the restless dead. It wasn't something I'd recommend to anybody.

All I'd wanted when I was younger was to be loved and included, but my parents were as obsessed with corpses as Aunt Ruby. They definitely lived by the family motto of preferring the dead to the living and were quick to remind me of my own mortality.

When we started our family, I'd make sure none of my children ever felt unloved or uncertain about their place in the household.

"We're almost there." Emory looked out the window as the carriage turned and the horses passed between two large, open black gates.

"Aunt Ruby will grow to adore you almost as much as I do. Just give her a few hours to thaw. She won't be able to resist you for long, especially since you look so handsome in your new suit."

"It is an excellent cut. You spoil me, darling. I didn't need another suit. You bought me two last month."

"You said you liked the tailoring when we stopped to look in the Saville's storefront. And you had to look your best. Aunt Ruby would expect nothing less. Besides, I enjoy treating you." I smoothed his cravat again.

He pressed a soft kiss against one of my powdered cheeks. "You're a sweetheart. I'm so happy we have each other."

So was I, and I still had to pinch myself to be certain this was real. Emory could have had his pick of the ladies, but he'd chosen me. When we'd met at the Countess of Eden's winter ball six months ago, everything had fallen into place. He'd only danced with two other ladies that evening and spent the rest of it with me. I'd left the ball giddy and hopelessly in love. Our relationship had only gotten better from there, and our future together would be amazing.

The carriage pulled up after a slow meander along my aunt's gravel driveway. Despite living alone, she maintained one of the three family manor houses as her private residence. The house was a pale sandstone detached building with a dark roof, elaborate chimney stacks, and twelve bedrooms.

I'd suggested she downsize, but she'd dismissed my comment. Family values had to be maintained, and everyone knew the estate belonged to the Digbys. That would never change.

I'd learned to keep quiet with my aunt and my parents over matters of propriety. They were sticklers for formality and reputation. Nothing was more important. Not even the happiness of their only daughter.

Emory climbed out of the carriage and held out his hand to allow me to disembark. My silk dress was stunning but difficult to move in. There was a large bustle on the back, and the fitted long shift under the dress meant I could only take tiny steps to avoid toppling, so I was grateful for Emory's arm as we headed to the black front door with its brass knocker.

The door opened on its own, and we stepped inside. The entrance hall had a cold marble floor, and several urns containing former cemetery guardian ashes stood on either side of the door.

Emory's gaze was full of interest as he looked around the high-ceilinged hallway. "It must cost a fortune to keep this place warm."

"It does, but my aunt prefers it chilly." I coughed delicately into my hand. "She often has undead visitors, and they decay slower if it's cold. It's why

I told you to wear a thermal layer underneath your suit."

"Does she often have corpses visit?" Horror flickered in his eyes for a second.

"More often than she should." Approaching footsteps had me looking up, and Aunt Ruby strode toward us.

Despite her advanced years, having survived three hundred and fifty of them, she had a firm, steady pace, and her back was straight. Her skin was paled and lined and her purple eyes watery, but the power radiating off her tingled against my skin.

She stepped forward to greet me first with two light air kisses on either cheek, making sure not to smudge my makeup or disrupt my elaborate dark curls. "You have stayed away too long, niece. I barely recognize you." Her gaze ran over me several times. "You look thin."

"I want to look my best at the wedding."

She glared at me as if I'd said something stupid and then did a thorough visual inspection of Emory. "He's too handsome for a plain Jane like you. I never trust a face so perfectly symmetrical."

Emory softly cleared his throat. "It's a great honor to meet you again. I've heard so much about your incredible work from Silvaria. She treasures your talent with the... dead."

My aunt harrumphed. "I doubt that very much. My niece has yet to take to her role as a cemetery guardian, but time will mature her, and she'll see this is the only path. This way. Dinner is about to be served."

I raised my eyebrows at Emory, my cheeks hot with embarrassment at being talked about as if I wasn't present, but his smile was calm, and it reassured me as we headed into the dining room.

The room was an austere work of art, with a mosaic floor that had been removed piece by piece from a Roman amphitheater and reconstructed inside the manor house. Original tapestries from the reign of Queen Hilda covered most of the walls, depicting countryside scenes and the occasional bloody battle. A large black dining table dominated the center of the room. There were twenty chairs around it, but my aunt always sat at the head of the table and her guests in the seats closest to her.

She stood by her seat and waited for her butler to pull out the chair. Once we were settled, three servers came in with plates covered in silver domes.

They presented my aunt with her food. She glared at it as if it had done something wrong to her then cut off a small piece of chicken and tasted it. "It's dry. Tell Cook to be more careful."

"Shall I take it back?" The serving girl's hand shook slightly.

"It's fine. Leave us." My aunt glared at the servers until they'd left the room. "Emory, pour the wine."

He hopped from his seat and filled our glasses.

My aunt took a sip and winced. "Sharp. I need to clear the wine cellar and start again. I'm sure it's not being stored appropriately. The servants don't know what they're doing."

I took a small sip from my glass. "It's good, and dinner looks lovely."

My aunt ignored my comments, took several small bites, and then pushed her plate away. "I have no appetite for bland fare. I should get someone who knows what they're doing in my kitchen."

"It's excellent food," Emory said.

My aunt turned an acerbic look on him. "Silvaria tells me you're in trade."

"No! Not trade. Emory is an entrepreneur. He has many business ideas. Wonderful ideas," I said.

"Ideas? Do you have any form of employment?" My aunt peered down her long, thin nose at him.

Emory carefully set down his knife and fork as a gentle pink flush spread up his neck and onto his cheeks. "I've tried several businesses over the years but have recently settled on property development. There will always be a need for people to have safe, warm places to live. Just today, my new business partner and I visited a potential site for future development."

"I didn't know about that. How exciting," I said.

Aunt Ruby didn't look impressed. "That's an occupation of sorts. Of course, when you marry Silvaria, you will assist her. My first husband was my assistant. He gathered the grave dirt, met with the families who were having troubles, and dealt with the paperwork."

"Oh, no. That won't work!"

Aunt Ruby silenced me with a sharp look. "And my last husband, Yanez, had an affinity with the dead. That was useful. Do you have any natural ability with our clients, Mr. Farr?"

Emory shuffled in his seat. "My magic is more a secondary concern of mine."

Alarm flickered in my aunt's eyes. "You have power, though?"

"He does. Emory is incredible with people and makes everyone feel comfortable in all situations. It's a real talent," I said.

Aunt Ruby pushed her food around the plate with her fork. "Silvaria's always been socially awkward. Having a natural charmer by her side should smooth over her stiffness."

My cheeks flushed again, and I busied myself with cutting into some tender stem broccoli. I struggled in the company of others but tried hard to fit in. People gossiped about my ability with the dead, and I'd even had a few individuals ask if I could provide them with a corpse for entertainment. What a dreadful thought.

"Have your parents chosen you a cemetery yet?" Aunt Ruby said. "I have several suggestions if they're struggling to settle on one."

I almost choked on my broccoli and took several sips of wine to help regain my composure. "Not yet. They're still considering my options."

"They've kept you coddled. You must take up the mantel of guardian. I was eighteen when I took on my first cemetery. If you don't have a placement soon, you'll forget how to look after the dead."

"We were planning on finding a situation close to my first development project," Emory said. "That way, Silvaria can tend to her cemetery guardian duties while I work."

"Putting your future husband's needs before the dead is unwise," Aunt Ruby said. "I married five times and picked my partners because of their affinity with the dead. You should marry a half-vampire, Silvaria. They like the quiet of the night and would enjoy their time in the cemeteries you tend to."

I gulped down my panic. I hadn't yet had the courage to tell my family I didn't want to be a cemetery guardian. The dead left me cold in every sense. I hated everything about being born into a guardian family. I hated the headstones, the eerie silence as I walked among the crypts and sarcophagi, the stench of rot and decay, the dirt, and the ever present feeling of something stirring beneath my feet, waiting for a command.

Being a cemetery guardian was a dismal life, and having parents who were guardians had ruined my childhood. I was only awkward because we kept to ourselves, and when another child found out what I could do, they ran away and didn't want to be friends with a corpse tender.

Aunt Ruby clicked her fingers. "I've always loved the power and control. When a corpse misbehaves, I'm there to take them in hand. Show me what you've got."

"I'm sorry?" I said.

She clicked her fingers again, and the door leading out to the herb garden opened.

Emory lurched from his seat with a yelp as a bedraggled corpse missing an arm appeared.

"Calm yourself, boy. You'll have to get used to this if you're marrying into the family."

"Aunt! No corpses in the dining room. We're eating." I jumped up too, alarmed at Emory's panic.

He'd seen plenty of corpses when he was with me, so he shouldn't be so startled.

"If you want the corpse gone, you deal with him," Aunt Ruby said, a sly smile on her face.

Emory backed away. "Silvaria, do something. It's looking at me strangely."

I pleaded silently with my aunt, staring at her and clasping my hands, but she wouldn't acknowledge me. She sipped her wine and gave me another cold smile.

I held out my hands, grimacing as the cold flood of power ran through me. "Return to where you came from. Your presence is not wanted."

The corpse groaned, turned, and ambled back into the herb garden.

I rushed over and slammed the door shut. I whirled toward my aunt. "What are you doing with bodies in your backyard? He had fresh dirt on him. Does he sleep here?"

She gave a small shrug. "It's always good to keep your hand in, and I like to have subjects close by. The walking dead are a valuable asset."

I shook my head at her. My family was unbelievable. No wonder everyone gossiped about us.

"Don't look so scandalized." Aunt Ruby gestured at my chair. "This is your destiny. Marry a tradesman if you must, but your cemetery guardian duties will always come first."

I returned to my seat after checking Emory wasn't about to collapse in shock.

Aunt Ruby was wrong. I made my own destiny. And it didn't involve dead bodies at the dining table.

Chapter 2

"Thank you for a most interesting evening." Emory bowed at the waist in front of my aunt.

"Next time, let's see if you don't run away when a corpse appears," Aunt Ruby said. She gave me another round of air kisses, and we left the house.

"Emory, I'm so sorry and so embarrassed. I didn't know Aunt Ruby would do that. Can you forgive me?" I clutched his arm as we waited for the carriage to stop beside us.

He helped me inside and climbed in, settling in the seat next to me. "It's something I'll have to get used to. It amazed me how easily she summoned that corpse. Was that creature waiting outside the whole time we were eating?"

I shook my head, falling back in my seat as the carriage pulled away. "No, it's something we can all do. If a corpse is nearby, we only have to think about them, and it summons them. They move at alarming speeds when they're called, especially the newly dead. And the more powerful the cemetery guardian, the quicker they come."

"Do you have a family plot here? Is that why the corpse was so close?" His eyebrows rose. "That wasn't one of her husbands, was it?"

"No! It's a mystery how she managed that. I'll have to speak to my parents about why Aunt Ruby is burying bodies under her herbs. It's not acceptable. And it's illegal. If the Magic Council hears of her behavior, she'll get in trouble."

"She probably killed a few people to have them on hand when she needed entertaining."

I sighed. "Aunt Ruby is an eccentric, but she's not a monster."

Emory patted my clenched hand. "Darling, you must admit, your family's ability is scarily unique. Not everyone will understand if you embrace all aspects of being a cemetery guardian."

I turned in my seat to face him. "You do, don't you? I have to know you're on my side."

He brushed a stray curl off my cheek. "I do. But it doesn't mean I want corpses shambling around our house. Keep the corpses in the cemetery where they belong, and we won't have a problem."

"I want nothing to do with them." I sighed dramatically. "With the corpse showing up, and Aunt Ruby forcing me to deal with it, I didn't tell her my plans. If I can get her to understand being a cemetery guardian isn't for me, I should be able to convince my parents, too."

"You're not still going on about becoming a dancer, are you?" Emory took my hand and kissed the back of it.

"Of course. That's my passion. And dancing led me to love. Thanks to your fleet of foot, we spent an evening dancing together at our first meeting. You knew then how much I adored dancing. Nothing has changed."

"Dancing is perfect for social events but not as an occupation. It's not appropriate."

"There are highly respected professional dancers. Madame Tatiana's Belly Dance Academy is renowned throughout the world."

Emory snorted a laugh. "No wife of mine will become a belly dancer and shimmy her delicate body in other men's faces."

I pulled my hand away. "Belly dancing is an ancient and respected form of dance. Magic flows through those dancers. It's astonishing and so beautiful."

"Absolutely not. I forbid you to become a belly dancer."

"You forbid me?" I crossed my arms over my chest.

"Yes! I'll be a laughingstock if my wife takes most of her clothes off and dances."

"Even if it makes me happy?"

"How can making me miserable make you happy?"

I huffed out a breath. "I didn't say I wanted to belly dance. I love Latin dance. There's something about salsa that sends me to another realm. A place where there are no shambling corpses or unruly relatives to deal with. The music brings my feet to life, and I could move all day. My tutor says I'm a natural."

Emory stiffened in his seat. "You didn't tell me you'd hired a tutor. Who is he?"

"Don't get jealous. He's a respectable older man and won a world championship for his routine. Magic sparks off his heels when he dances."

"Don't waste your money on dance lessons."

"It's not a waste. It's an investment in my career."

Emory was shaking his head, an unattractive stubborn set to his jaw.

"I will dance if I want to, and there's nothing you can do to stop me."

"I could tell your aunt your secret. I'm sure she'd have something to say about it."

"Don't you dare! Let me handle my family. I'll know when the time is right to inform them I won't be taking up my guardian duties."

We glared at each other before Emory finally sighed.

"Darling, I admire your spirit and your love of dance, but it's almost impossible to have a respectable career as a professional dancer."

"It is possible, though."

"But unlikely. And dance magic isn't in you." He took my hands in his. "And your impeccable reputation in the magical community is one of the reasons I adore you so much."

"That's all you care about? That my social standing will help you?"

"No! But you know my situation. When I fell in love with you at the ball, I didn't know your background. Then I learned you were a Digby, and the stars aligned. We were meant to be. I'll cherish and look after you, and you'll help me restore my family name. Your family has such a respected reputation, and it's something I wish for my own family again." His gaze dipped. "It's not been easy for me, losing so much and having to work so hard to get it back."

My indignation faded. Emory's family had once been hugely wealthy. His late father had been a baron but lost his fortune after being duped by a friend. It left the family's reputation in tatters. His father died and his mother soon after from a broken heart and shame. My sweet fiancé had worked to restore their reputation ever since. I shouldn't hold it against him that he was concerned my passion could cause him a setback.

"I spoke too hastily. I don't want to make you unhappy. I just want to dance and be with you," I said.

"I know. And it's not that I don't admire you for having an interest in something other than your family duty. We should all have that. But consider what it would do to your family if you abandoned your role. Would that make you happy?"

"You know that's what I've always planned. You were the first person I confided in about not wanting to be a cemetery guardian." I looked at our entwined hands. "I thought you'd encourage my plan."

"I don't want any corpses in our house, but you must fulfil your obligation. You're a responsible adult, and you'll be responsible for an even greater fortune once your parents are gone. You'll be a society lady with estates to manage."

"You mean, cemeteries?" The Digby family were elite guardians who looked after hundreds of acres of final resting places. Every other cemetery guardian looked to my family for guidance. It was a huge burden to carry.

"Those cemeteries provide you with an incredible status and a role you can't turn your back on."

"Even if that makes me miserable?"

"I understand your work is unsettling, but it is your role in life." The look in Emory's eyes suggested he did not know my stomach churned every time I thought about a long, cold life as a guardian. "However, I have been thinking..."

"You know a way I can keep the corpses out of my life?"

He turned my hand over and traced the veins on the inside of my wrist. "Not so much. But have you considered using the cemeteries for something else?"

"What else would I use them for other than housing the magical deceased?"

"There's more money to be made in bricks than bones."

I stared at him, my mouth open. "You want to build on my cemeteries?"

"Don't dismiss the idea. Many cemeteries are redevelopment hot spots. There's a cemetery in every average-sized town. You could move the bodies, and then we'd use the land to build my business."

"I can't decide if you're joking or not. You don't move the dead from their final place of rest." I shuddered in horror. "I may not love corpses, but we make a solemn vow as cemetery guardians to protect their resting place."

"There must be a way around that. And it would be a win for both of us. You could find a place to put the corpses where they wouldn't trouble you or anyone else, and once the cemeteries are cleared, we grow the empire."

I breathed so shallowly, I grew dizzy. "Emory, that'll never happen. I'll protect those corpses with my life. When they buy a plot in a cemetery protected by a guardian, they get a guaranteed eternal rest. The bodies in my cemeteries aren't those of ordinary magic users."

He sank back in his seat. "Sure, sure. You've told me about the plots, the magic, and all the work your family does to stop the dead from going rogue."

"Don't sound so flippant. We care for some of the most powerful individuals who have ever walked this earth. Strong weather witches who could destroy a town with a tornado, witches with the ability to slow time, goblins who turned stone into gold, and warlocks who healed with a single touch. Their corpses could never be moved into a basic grave and left unmarked and unprotected."

Emory's expression grew sullen. "Then encase the bones somewhere they can't get out. Bury them under concrete."

"Absolutely not! Chaos would ensue. The magical community would fall apart. I will not stand by and—"

"Relax! It was just an idea." His gaze hardened, and he turned his head away from me. "I don't understand you. You constantly complain about your role as a cemetery guardian, and now you're protecting them. You want to be a dancer, but the second I give you an alternative option for the cemeteries, you lash out. You need to decide what you want from life."

I bit my tongue to keep my anger in and allowed his words to sink in. I was conflicted. I hated my future, but I felt it edging around me like mold in a poorly sealed coffin. Soon, I'd have no option but to accept my path into the graveyard. But to destroy the sacred cemeteries. No, it would never happen.

"I'm sorry," I whispered. "I know you're trying to be helpful, but even though I don't want to be a guardian, I'd protect the cemeteries if they were at risk."

Emory looked out the carriage window and didn't speak for a moment. He finally turned to me. "No, I'm sorry. I forget how deeply intertwined you and death already are. When you tell me you don't want any part of it, I believe you, but I suspect you'll take on the role, anyway. You'll always put the dead first."

"No! Not before you. My aunt was wrong. You'll be my priority when we marry. Even if I find myself in the role of cemetery guardian, our happiness will come first. I won't be like my parents, and I definitely won't be like my aunt, complaining about everything and trusting no one, taking husbands because of their power and usefulness."

His eyes grew moist. "I want to believe you, darling. I see an incredible future for us, but only if you find the right path. We deserve to be blissfully happy."

"We will! Nothing will prevent that from coming true." I stroked his cheek. "We're made for each other. And you're so clever at getting me to consider the options. I'd never have thought about relocating the corpses and building on the land. But you did. You're astonishing."

Emory dipped his head. "Could it ever happen? You'll own the land once your parents are gone. Maybe it's time to shake things up. I could do research for you, see if there's a safe way to store the bodies."

My protective instincts flared to life again, and I gently shook my head. "The ground is sacred, and I must look after those who could cause others harm. That will never change."

He sighed. "You think I'm stupid for suggesting it."

"You're perfect." I nuzzled his cheek with my nose. "It might be possible to modernize the cemeteries, though. They're such dreary places."

"Well, they are full of the dead."

I arched my eyebrows at him, and he chuckled. "I want them to be places people enjoy. Somewhere they can seek comfort, rather than have to look over their shoulder in case a corpse has crawled out to eat them. You could help with that."

"A warm, welcoming cemetery? Maybe add a cute cafe in one corner?"

My nose wrinkled. "And offer free cake with a side order of grave dirt?"

"It could work."

We shared a smile, and the tension became a wisp of a ghost and drifted out of the carriage.

"There must be a way I can have the things I love and perform my duty to my family," I said.

"There will be. And of course, I'll be beside you to make sure you get things right."

"Which is why I adore you." I lightly kissed his mouth.

"And I you. I got you a gift." Emory pulled a velvet box out of his pocket and opened it. Inside was a beautiful silver necklace, sparkling with diamonds.

"It's stunning. It must have been expensive."

"You're worth it, my love." He put the necklace on me. "It sparkles almost as brightly as you."

"You're so good to me. I'd be lost without you."

"I feel the same." He admired the necklace for a second. "I've been thinking, and I'd love your input on my business. I'm serious about getting into development, and I want our marriage to be an equal partnership. If the worst happens, and you take a guardian role, I want you to have something in your life you can enjoy."

"Emory! That's wonderful. I'm flattered, but I know nothing about property development."

"We all have to learn. I want you by my side, and your involvement is important to me. I'd also like you to meet my new business partner. You'll get along wonderfully. He's my ideas man. Clever as a fox."

"Of course. I'd love that. And I'm happy to help in any way I can." I kissed him again, forgetting our tiny tiff. All couples bickered, but that was natural. Our relationship was still idyllic.

With Emory beside me, and my involvement in his business, we'd be the golden couple. We'd have a successful empire. I'd manage the corpses without them taking over my life and turning me into a cold drudge, and we'd discover a happy compromise where I could dance.

My life was complicated, but I could still find my path to happiness. Moldering corpses and all.

Chapter 3

"I've been thinking about my birthday." My best friend, Olivia Sibley-Wood, sat opposite me at the breakfast table the next day, while we dined on a feast of almond croissants and cherry muffins. Well, I watched her eat the delicious treats. I had to keep my figure trim for my upcoming wedding.

"You have? Such a surprise. It's been at least thirty seconds since we discussed it." I sipped my black coffee.

She poked her tongue out at me. "I was thinking we could have an all-day event. I'm sure your servants won't mind a small amount of extra work. After all, you're only twenty-five once."

"A whole day!" When I'd agreed to host her birthday party at our manor house in Shady Pines in two weeks, I'd expected a genteel afternoon tea with scones, fresh cream, and some bubbly.

"Why not? Oh, say yes. You don't want to let me down, do you?" Olivia fluttered her long lashes and giggled. "I'd do the same for you."

"Like last year, you mean? You were a month late bringing me my gift."

"That's not fair! I was sick."

"Did that sickness make you forget my address? Someone could have brought my parcel."

"Oh, don't hold a grudge. It makes you look ugly. I promise, next year, I'll host you an incredible birthday."

I sighed. Olivia could be forgetful, but she had a good heart. "I want to make your special day perfect. The house is empty, so it's all yours. We agreed on thirty guests. Is that right?"

"Oh, no. I'm inviting everybody. The thirty named are my closest friends, including you. And they'll be staying the night before, too." Olivia tilted her long neck to expose porcelain skin. "Perhaps you should let them have the rooms for the next night, as well. We may have a few who drink too much, and we don't want them to come to any harm on their way home. Can they all stay?"

"Rooms for thirty guests? There's space to fit that many, but it'll take some organizing."

"It makes sense to offer accommodation. Some of them are coming from such a long way, so they'll need a place to rest and freshen up. We don't want them to be uncomfortable, or they won't enjoy themselves."

"Of course. I may need to hire extra help, though. I thought I'd borrow two servants from here, but if the beds need changing to accommodate party guests staying—"

"There are always people in town looking for work. It'll cost you barely nothing to hire them for a few days. You may need to keep them around for the cleanup, too. You know how my parties get out of hand." Olivia raised her cup of coffee. "It'll be amazing. You're such a good friend to spoil me like this."

"It's always a pleasure." Although I hadn't meant to spoil Olivia quite so much, but it wouldn't be a problem. I had a generous weekly allowance, so I had money to hire extra help and could always dip into my trust fund. I'd ask Arthur, our house butler, for advice.

"How are the party favors coming along?" Olivia cut open a muffin and pulled out the cherries.

"Aren't you arranging those?"

"You're funny. I love having a best friend with such a good sense of humor. I can't arrange my own party favors. I don't want to be stressed before my birthday in case it gives me more wrinkles." She leaned forward. "I'm considering going to the apothecary and getting a spell to remove fine lines."

"Olivia, you're so beautiful, a few wrinkles won't do you any harm."

She dropped her knife. "Are you saying I'm haggard and lined?"

"No!" I peered at her forehead. "Maybe you have a few tiny lines, but you're perfect. Don't dabble in anti-aging magic, or you'll end up looking oddly plump."

"I might have to if I'm enduring sleepless nights worrying about party favors. The last time we spoke, you said you knew someone who did that sort of thing and you'd make the arrangements. Don't say you forgot."

"No, no, I didn't. I'll look into it." I didn't remember having that conversation, but Olivia wouldn't lie to me.

"Pick colors to go with my pink and cream flowers."

"Yes, the flowers. I need to order those, too."

"Silvaria! Typical you, you leave everything to the last minute."

"I've been busy."

Her delicate nose wrinkled. "With the shamblers?"

"No. Well, sometimes with the walking dead, but also my wedding plans and... other things. How many party favors?" Few people knew about my ambitions to be a dancer, and I needed to keep it that way until I'd convinced my parents it was the right thing to do.

"Order enough for three-hundred and fifty guests."

"My goodness! That's a lot more than thirty. Do you even have that many friends?"

"Don't be mean. I have lots of friends. Just because everyone is too scared to get to know you—" Olivia pressed her lips together. "Sorry. That wasn't kind. It's just... it's the bodies. They unsettle people."

I focused on my fruit salad. "I'm grateful you've remained friends with me. What would you like in your party favors?"

"Make sure most of the contents are edible. That way, if there are any left over, we can enjoy them." She sighed and leaned back in her seat.

I finished my chilled fruit salad as I made a mental to-do list of all the things for the party. If I asked Arthur nicely, he'd arrange the whole thing. I wasn't good at planning, but I wouldn't let Olivia down.

Although I was certain we hadn't agreed to such an extravagant affair. It was no matter. Everything would work out, and Olivia deserved a beautiful birthday. I owed her that.

When all the other children had been calling me the Queen of Creep, Olivia had stood by my side and told them to leave me alone. We were friends for life.

"Fill me in on the gossip. How did Aunt Ruby like meeting Emory again?" Olivia said.

"It went as well as I could expect."

"Emory didn't charm her? He must be losing his touch. Although he still gets all the ladies fawning over him at the dances."

My eyes narrowed. "Not anymore, he doesn't. And he doesn't attend dances without me."

"Oh, you know what I mean. He's still the best-looking man for miles. It's no surprise you've gotten some rivals jealous. Even I'm a little jealous, and I have the gorgeous Jeremiah desperate to marry me. It's just a shame..."

"What's a shame?"

"Emory isn't bringing much to your marriage."

I bristled and sat very straight. "He's bringing plenty to our marriage. And he wants me to join him in his new business venture. Property development."

Her eyes sparkled with amusement. "What do you know about building houses?"

"Plenty more than you once I've helped Emory establish himself. I'll be overseeing things and making... recommendations." I hadn't thought through the details of my role in the business, and Emory had been vague when I'd quizzed him.

"Oh, Silvaria." Olivia neatly folded her napkin and set it beside her plate. "I hope you've thought this through."

"What do you mean by that?"

"You're a sweet girl, but people never come to you for information or help."

"I'm planning your birthday party. That's a big help to you, so you don't get more wrinkles!"

She arched a perfect eyebrow. "You'll give that job to Arthur the second my back is turned. I mean, you're not practical. It's something I love about you. You always lead with your heart."

"Is there anything wrong with that?"

"Well, no. I just don't want you making a fool of yourself by pretending Emory trusts you with his business."

"Are you suggesting I'm lying?"

"No! But Emory is the world's best flatterer. When you think about it, what could you offer him? Business is about practical matters, paperwork, and things like that. Is that the life you want?"

"I can lead with my heart and be practical. It's not as if I'll be doing the office filing."

"What will you do?"

I flustered for an answer. "Support him. Talk over his ideas. And houses need to be beautiful. I can help with that. The design. Yes, I can make things look perfect."

"My dear friend, given your heritage, isn't that beneath you?"

"It'll be more than that. Emory said we'll be equal partners. He respects me and wants me involved in all aspects of his life." I huffed out a breath, too hot in my yellow day dress. "Besides, if I'm working alongside him, I can fend off those jealous women you've just told me about."

Olivia's laugh tinkled out of her, and she delicately shrugged. "I'm sure you'll be blissfully happy."

A silence settled around us that was as uncomfortable as a pinching pair of shoes. Olivia was only trying to help, but it left me with a bad taste in my mouth. Maybe the melon was overly ripe.

"I'm looking forward to my next bridesmaid's dress fitting," she said softly.

I wasn't ready to take her tiny olive branch. "The wedding is soon after your birthday party, so make sure you don't eat too much cake."

She pursed her lips and set down her cup. "My figure is exquisite. Now, if you'll excuse me, I'm going present shopping with my father. He promised me I can pick anything I like as an early gift."

"Lucky you." On my last birthday, my parents had raced off to quell a corpse uprising on the other side of the country. I'd been left with a three-tier birthday cake and no one but the servants to share it with. I'd had a stomach ache for a week.

After showing Olivia out, I settled in for a morning of letter writing, while reviewing a written tutorial of my last salsa lesson. Every time I reviewed the dance steps, I got a tingle up my spine. Salsa was so vibrant. It was the opposite of what my family had planned for me. I couldn't spend my days in some dreary, drab cemetery looking after bones, when there was a world of dance out there.

And I had a plan to reveal how important dance was and how well I could perform.

Emory didn't know about this yet, but at our wedding reception, I'd surprise him with a dance. I'd dance in front of everyone. My salsa tutor had agreed to be there on the day to lend me some last-minute advice, and I'd been practicing, so I'd be perfect. Once Emory and my parents saw me, they'd agree giving up my cemetery guardian role was the right thing to do.

There was a knock at the study door, and Molly Tomkins looked in. "Sorry to bother you, Miss Digby, but you've got your appointment with the cake designer. She'll be here in half an hour. I thought you might like to get changed."

"Thank you. I lost track of time." I hid the tutorial notes. Molly had seen me reading the dance steps several times and had even asked about them, but I'd kept quiet, even though she was more than just a servant to me. Her loyalty lay with my parents. They paid her wages, so she'd be on the lookout for anything unusual to report to them. It was expected of all household servants.

After I'd sealed my letters and left them to be collected, I headed to my dressing room with Molly. "I was thinking the blue silk with the red hem edging."

"And jewelry?" Molly was a year older than me and adept at outfitting me splendidly. She had an eye for detail to make sure I was impeccably turned out.

"My new diamond necklace and the teardrop diamond earrings. Two silver rings. You pick which ones," I said.

Molly got to work, laid out my dress, shoes and gloves, and then took a moment to select my accessories. She released me from my day dress, and I slid out of it.

She carefully placed the blue silk fitted dress by my feet, and I stepped in. She wriggled it over my hips and fastened the back before lacing me in. "This gets easier to do every time you wear it. You need to eat more."

"Everyone tells me that, but with my wedding coming up, I need to watch my figure. Emory won't want me turning chubby and lazy because I have his ring on my finger. I want to be the perfect wife."

"A few extra curves would still make you the perfect wife, if you don't mind me saying," Molly said. "My gentleman friend says he likes something to grab hold of."

I turned a shrewd eye to her. "You have a gentleman friend?"

Her cheeks flushed, and she ducked her head. "No! I mean... I know we're not supposed to date while we're employed here. Your parents consider it a distraction."

"They do. But I'm intrigued. What's his name?" I waited until she'd finished fastening my dress and then turned to her. "Molly, I won't say anything about you dating. I want you to be happy. I've never been happier since settling with Emory. I feel lucky to have found him."

"Mr. Farr is a catch, Miss Digby. Handsome, too. I often see him about when I've finished work and am going home."

"Where do you see him?"

"He's usually heading into some restaurant. The expensive ones."

"Oh, I suppose he must use them to do business. He's looking for the perfect office venue. Emory's going into property development and is already looking at sites. It's exciting."

"It sounds expensive, Miss. It's not cheap to build a house."

"No, I expect it isn't. But he's so clever, he'll figure it out. And I'll be helping. Look at me, a businesswoman. I feel so grown up."

"Well, you are. You've changed a lot in the last five years." Molly fastened my belt and handed me my gloves.

"So have you. We've grown up together, I suppose."

She smiled. "We have. I joined the household when I was seventeen. I was so scared of what your parents did for a living, and all those dead bodies and the cellar full of creepy bits and bobs. My knees shook for an entire week."

I turned wide eyes on her. "You never told me. I had no idea you were terrified. I hope you aren't now."

"Oh, no. I'm used to seeing corpses wandering about. I don't even mind going down to the cellar when it's full of coffins or pots of grave dirt. I can walk right by, get the supplies I need, and even give the corpses a cheery wave if there are any down there."

I carefully adjusted my gloves, not looking at Molly. "Would you ever consider leaving? Finding somewhere without too many corpses in the house?"

She chuckled. "I'm fine with them. They were once people, too."

I teased my gloves into submission and looked up. "I... I was hoping to talk to you about joining my household after I marry. It would mean the world if I could keep you. And I promise, my cellar will be full of wine and preserved goods, not bodies."

Molly's eyes widened. "I don't know what to say, Miss Digby. I'd thought about what I'd do once you left. I've always looked after you and wondered if your parents wouldn't keep me if it was just them and the corpses."

"You're interested?"

"I am!"

"Of course, I need to speak to my parents, but I'm certain they won't mind you joining my household." I gently took her hand. "Things will be different, though. We won't live in such a grand place, but since Emory is getting into property development, we can build our own house, so everything will be new. No creaking stairs or gaps in the windows."

"That sounds wonderful. I'd be honored to join your household." Molly's smile stretched across her face.

On impulse, I hugged her. "Then it's settled. I must give you something. A show of companionship and respect."

"You don't have to do that, Miss Digby. I enjoy working for you. I feel privileged you want me to stay with you."

"I insist. It'll be our silent agreement until I get my parents' permission." I sorted through dozens of necklaces I'd been bought or gifted over the years. I pulled out one of my favorites. It was a long silver necklace with tiny stars set on the chain. "This is the one. It'll go with the ring I gave you a few months ago."

Molly thrust her hands behind her back. "I can't accept. It's too much."

"You don't like it? Did I pick the wrong one?"

"No, it's beautiful."

"It is the right one, isn't it? It will match the ring?" I walked over to her and held out the necklace. "I noticed you haven't been wearing it."

She shook her head, her cheeks pink. "My fingers are too small, so I need to get it resized."

"I didn't think about that when I gave it to you. How silly of me. Well, you take this, and the next time you step out with your fancy man, you can stun him with your beautiful jewelry."

After a second of hesitation, Molly took the necklace and stared at it in awe. "I'll look after it."

"Make sure you do. My parents gave that to me."

Molly's eyes widened in horror, and she tried to give it back.

I laughed and pushed her hand away. "That necklace belongs to you now. Don't fear what my parents will think." They probably wouldn't even remember gifting it to me.

Molly looked like she wanted to keep protesting, but a knock at the door stopped her. She hurried over to open it.

"Miss Digby, there's a man outside. It's the coffin delivery your parents have been waiting for," Arthur said.

"Oh, I'd forgotten they were arriving today. Give me a moment." I made sure Molly tucked the necklace in her pocket. "I'll deal with this. You get my hair accessories sorted. I won't be long." I dashed down the stairs and met a tall, ruddy-faced man outside. "Good afternoon. You're not our usual deliveryman."

"Ah, no. He's coming in a bit." The man shuffled his feet, a cap gripped in his hands. "I've got some coffins on the back of my truck. Lending a hand, you see."

"What's the problem with our usual deliveryman?"

"No problem. He was just late arriving. I thought I'd drop these off in case you needed them and collect the payment. You'll get the rest later." He scratched his balding head.

"Fine. Haven't you already been paid, though? I thought my parents had an account with you." I peered at the poorly stacked coffins on the back of his rusty vehicle.

"No. New arrangement. I was told to pick up the full payment before offloading the coffins."

I looked at his van and then over my shoulder. My parents had been clear they needed the coffins stored before they got back. They were handling some tricky corpses and needed to house them in the cellar for several nights to get them stable.

"Sorry to hurry you, miss, but I need to get to my next job."

"I'll get your money. The cellar entrance is to the right of the house, through those blue doors. Arthur will meet you on the other side and show you where they need to go."

"Right you are." He dashed off and opened the back of his van.

After the coffins had been unloaded and I'd paid him, he sped away from the house, his tires spitting up gravel. He must have been late for his next delivery to be going so fast.

I went to my room in search of Molly, but she wasn't there. I had been longer than expected, since the man hadn't had a clue how to handle coffins, and I'd had to stop several from falling off the back of his van.

I was heading down the stairs to find her when a scream froze me in place. A yell followed it. I headed in the direction the scream had come from and into the kitchen. A small group of servants stood by the back door. "What's going on? Who screamed?"

Arthur dashed over and stood in front of me. "I'll deal with this."

"Deal with what?" I stood on my tiptoes and looked over his shoulder but couldn't see into the courtyard. "I insist on knowing what's going on. That's an order."

He gave a soft sigh. "This way, Miss Digby. Make a path, please."

The small group of servants separated in front of me. As they stepped back, my heart dropped into my stomach. Molly lay on the cobblestones.

She was dead.

Chapter 4

I couldn't breathe as I stared at Molly splayed on the ground, one arm above her head and her sightless eyes open and unblinking.

I staggered but was prevented from falling by Arthur's steady hand holding my elbow. "Come away, Miss Digby. You don't need to see this."

"What happened? Molly was upstairs recently helping me dress."

"I'm not sure. Lucy found her."

Lucy Brooker was sobbing in the arms of our second kitchen assistant, Amanda Smeeton. Both girls had tears on their cheeks.

I shook my head, my gaze drawn back to the horrible sight. "Did Molly fall and hit her head? Did she have a seizure? She seemed so healthy."

"We'll get that looked into," Arthur said. "Please, come inside and sit. You've had a shock."

I took a few wobbly steps but then stopped. "What time are my parents returning?"

"Late. They sent word they had trouble locating all the corpses. I'm not expecting them until gone midnight."

The last thing they needed after a day of corpse wrangling was to discover this tragic situation. If Molly had been taken ill, I could deal with this. I took several deep breaths, deeply regretting picking this dress, since the lacing and corset made it so hard to breathe properly.

I gently removed Arthur's hand from my elbow. "Thank you, but I'm all right, and I'm in charge of this household until my parents' return." I looked at Molly, and tears clouded my vision, but I held them in. It would do no good falling apart in front of the servants. They expected me to know what to do.

"I really think you should come inside, Miss Digby," Arthur said. "Cook will make you some tea."

"No, no tea."

"Some warm milk? Or a nip of brandy? Something to help you with the shock."

"Maybe a small brandy." I clapped my hands, and everyone jumped. "Please, pay attention. I know this is terrible, but I need to know what happened. Lucy, you found Molly?"

She nodded, her cheeks blotchy and her dark eyes red from crying. "I came out with a bucket of food waste, and she was just... there."

"Did you check on her? We're certain she's dead?"

"Yes, Miss Digby. It was the first thing I did. I was so shocked, and for a second I thought she was having a laugh with me. I called her name several times, but she didn't respond. That's when I realized it was serious." Lucy wiped her eyes on the sleeve of her dress. "I checked her pulse, and when I didn't find it, I screamed."

"I also checked her pulse," Arthur said. "I can confirm Molly is no longer with us."

"Who came out next?" I said.

"Me and Cook," Amanda said. "We were inside, working on the evening meal, when we heard Lucy holler."

"Did any of you see what happened to Molly?" My gaze went around the assembled group.

Lucy shook her head, along with Amanda. Cook stepped forward. She was a short, round woman, with a large nose and bright beady eyes. "I was last out and thought the girls were messing around. Then I saw Molly and the marks on her neck. Someone did this to her."

"Marks? Let me see." I strode over to Molly, brushing away Arthur's protests. I couldn't bring myself to look at Molly's sweet face too closely, so I focused on her neck. Cook was right. There were several red marks around her throat. "Do you think someone strangled her?"

"Let's not get ahead of ourselves, Miss Digby." Arthur joined me, his expression forlorn.

"Molly wouldn't have done that to herself. You don't get marks like that from a fall. And if she tripped and hurt her head, there'd be blood. There are no signs of any other injuries." I turned back to Lucy, Amanda, and Cook. "You definitely didn't hear or see anyone out here? Molly was with me until recently, so this has only just happened."

"Nobody. She came down after looking after you and said she had good news. She was giddy and excited and kept talking too fast," Lucy said.

"So I sent her out here," Cook said. "She was distracting the others from their work. I told her to calm herself and then come back in. Oh dear, I sent her out, and the poor little thing died. Some madmen crept into the yard and killed her."

"We don't have mad men running around here. This is a respectable area." I looked at the gate leading into the formal rose garden. "Has anyone checked to see if that's locked?"

Arthur hurried over and tried the gate. It opened.

"It's not unusual for it to be unlocked during the day," Cook said. "We get deliveries coming in all the time, so it's easier to have it open for the tradespeople. Otherwise, we keep having to stop and see to them. Then they expect a mug of tea and a chat. No time for that."

"Whoever got to Molly must have come in that way." I opened the gate and looked around. The rose garden was empty. I shut the gate and walked back to the servants. "Molly was well-liked and respected, so I can't imagine anyone she knew wanting her dead, but are any of you aware of any problems she was having?"

No one spoke.

I studied each of them. Amanda and Lucy were a couple of years older than Molly, but I knew they were friendly with each other. Cook and Arthur had been with the household since before I was born. I trusted everyone here, and they had no reason to dislike Molly or want to strangle her.

I tried again. "Did Molly talk to you about someone she feared? Was she in trouble?"

"She said nothing to me about trouble," Cook said. "And Molly talked a lot. I know she sometimes argued with her sister, but everyone fights with their siblings."

"What about the gentleman she was dating?" I said.

Lucy and Amanda stared at me with wide eyes.

"Molly told me about him. I was wondering if they'd argued. Perhaps he confronted her, and she tried to end things. It could have turned nasty. Has he ever visited here while she was working?"

"We know nothing about that," Lucy said swiftly. "We're not supposed to be in relationships while we work for the family. And we know to inform Mr. and Mrs. Digby if anyone breaks that rule."

I sighed. Of course, my parents had everyone too scared to tell the truth. "I'm not my parents, and I won't be angry if you have a life outside of your work. It's to be expected. Please, there's no point in keeping information from me. It could be useful to help figure out what happened to Molly."

"If you don't mind me intervening, Miss Digby," Arthur said, "we need to let the Magic Council know about this. There'll need to be an investigation."

I put my hand over my mouth and then lowered it. "I wasn't thinking. Of course, they need to know. Contact them immediately. Tell them to hurry."

"Very good." Arthur dashed off.

I paced the yard in front of the servants, still not able to do more than glance at Molly. She was so young and should have had her life ahead of her, but it had been stolen. It was unfair, and I was appalled it had happened in my home.

After steadying my nerves, I looked down at Molly, and a single tear trickled down my cheek. I'd always assumed I knew her well, but she must have been having terrible troubles to end up like this. Troubles I'd had no idea about. I'd been so busy with my upcoming marriage and figuring out my career that I'd missed the signs. She may have needed to talk, and I hadn't given her the chance.

The gate leading into the courtyard opened, and Ralph Little, our part-time handyman, strolled in. He stopped dead, his cheery smile fading as he took in the scene. He looked at Molly, and his mouth dropped open.

"Ralph, come in quickly and close the gate," I said. "Where have you been?"

He sputtered several words before following my orders. He set down the small stepladder he carried as he kept staring at Molly. "What happened? Is she..."

"We have a situation. And we must act quickly. Do you know anyone who'd want to hurt Molly?"

He blinked several times, the color gone from his face. "No. I like her. I mean, I liked her. Everyone did."

"Someone didn't," I said. "I thought you were supposed to be here all day. Why did you leave?"

"I... I, well, I do other jobs when I'm not busy." Ralph rubbed the back of his neck. "Lord Talbet had an emergency, so I dashed over to help. Sorry, I know I was supposed to be here, but there was nothing that needed doing."

"There's plenty that needs doing. You're just never around to do it." Cook's tone was sharp.

"I do the important jobs! And I'm only paid for ten hours a week."

"Let's not worry about that now. Tell me everything you can about Molly," I said.

Ralph looked startled. "There's nothing to tell. She was a sweet girl with a nice laugh. She was always sneaking me cups of tea and slices of bread and butter when Cook wasn't looking. I would have starved if it weren't for her."

"You get the meal you're owed when you're around," Cook said.

"You skimp on the portions," Ralph said. "Molly looked after me. What happened to her?"

"That's what I'm trying to find out," I said. "By the marks on her neck, I think someone strangled her."

His mouth fell open again. "Someone here?" His gaze turned hard as he looked at the small group.

"It wasn't anyone here," Cook said. "We all liked Molly, too."

I tapped my fingers together. I was certain it was no one in this group. I was around the servants more than my parents, so I knew them. Molly had been popular and always made friends rather than enemies. And Cook was telling the truth. They all liked her. So had I.

"Oh! The man with the coffins. I didn't recognize him, and he was behaving strangely. He raced away as if he needed to escape. What if he did this to Molly?" I said.

"I don't like to contradict you, Miss Digby." Arthur stepped out from the kitchen. "But you were with him most of the time, and then I assisted him to arrange the coffins. In fact, I wanted to speak to you about that delivery. The coffins are of poor quality."

"They looked fine to me. The delivery man could have snuck away and hurt Molly."

"I don't think he did it. He wouldn't have had the time."

"We must still question him. Even if he didn't do it, he could have seen something important."

"Did he say when he'd return with the rest of the delivery?"

"He won't be back at all if he killed Molly." I huffed out a breath. I couldn't think about coffins. I needed to find that man.

Arthur cleared his throat. "Miss Digby, if you didn't recognize him, what's to say he'll return?"

Why was Arthur being so irritating with these irrelevant questions? "We should contact the company and find out more about him."

"I'm sorry to press the issue, but a note has just arrived from the supplier. The delivery has been delayed until later this evening."

"We both saw the coffins." I chewed on my bottom lip then stopped. My parents scolded me every time I used that bad habit. "They're all paid for."

"Did that man ask you for money?"

"Of course!"

Arthur pressed his hands together. "We always pay in advance. He shouldn't have taken any money."

"But... the coffins. Why would he ask for money if he didn't need it?"

"Perhaps next time, let your parents handle the coffin deliveries," Arthur said. "Or I can do it in their absence. Don't concern yourself. I'm sure this will work out."

"Perhaps... call the company, just to be sure everything is as it should be. This is a misunderstanding."

Arthur bowed his head. "Of course."

"But if the delivery man wasn't who he claimed to be, perhaps he was here for Molly. Or after offloading the coffins, he hid and Molly found him and confronted him. She may have known him if he lives around here. Or she saw he'd taken money when he wasn't supposed to and tried to get it back." I was warming to the idea that the delivery man was involved. "They argued, and he strangled Molly to keep her quiet."

"How would he have known how to get into this yard?" Arthur said. "And why come back here?"

"I don't know, but we must find him. He hasn't been gone long. If we hurry, we could catch him."

"Miss Digby, perhaps you should stop." Arthur's attention had shifted to the kitchen, but I was pacing again, too lost in my thoughts to pay him much attention.

"We can't stop now. Molly deserves justice. I must know who killed her." I turned and discovered a strange man standing in the doorway. "Oh! Who are you?"

His dour expression and plain black cloak and hat showed he was from the Magic Council. "I'm here to discover how your servant died. Although it sounds as if you've already done my job for me."

Chapter 5

Although his clothing was drab, the stranger in the doorway had bright blue eyes and a firm, clean-shaven jaw. He was in his late twenties, so not a senior member of the Magic Council. Trust them to send someone junior to do such an important job.

He stepped into the yard, his attention on me. "I'm Detective Tristan Noir. You're in charge of this household?"

"Yes."

His eyes narrowed a fraction. "And your name?"

"Miss Silvaria Digby."

Detective Noir nodded once, a flash of recognition entering his eyes. Everyone knew the Digby family. If there was ever a problem with a corpse, people came to us.

"And you discovered the body?" His gaze shifted to Molly.

"No, that was Lucy, one of our kitchen assistants."

Lucy sniffed up tears and nodded. "I was coming out with some food waste. I must have just missed it happening. I'm lucky I didn't get murdered, too."

"Molly's been strangled," I said.

Detective Noir's attention returned to me. "How would you know that?"

"Look at her neck. It's clear what happened."

"The only thing clear to me is you're all contaminating a potential crime scene."

"I've barely touched a thing. And Molly was my friend. I had to make sure there was nothing we could do to save her." I wasn't letting this man bluster in and make unfounded accusations.

"A friend? She didn't work for you?"

"Yes, she did, but she was also my friend." I battled with tears for a second.

"You were considering a reanimation?" he asked.

"No. It was impossible to know her time of death, and a person must be reanimated within a minute of their demise, or you create a ghoul or trap their spirit and it'll attach to you or the house. I wouldn't have wanted that for Molly."

Detective Noir gestured for me to move away from Molly.

I took a step back but held my ground. This was my house, and these were my servants. I wasn't letting this stranger take over. The Magic Council needed to know about Molly's murder, but we'd been making excellent progress without Detective Noir and his cynical looks and snide comments.

"Miss Digby, your cooperation would be appreciated. I know what I'm doing. This isn't my first dead body," he said.

"And neither is it mine."

His cheeks flushed. "You deal with the dead. You don't deal with criminal activity. Allow me to begin my investigation if you want to find out what happened to your servant."

"I want justice for Molly." More tears flooded my vision. I really had considered Molly so much more than a servant, but I'd been so busy figuring out what had happened to her, I'd kept my emotions pinned in place like one of the uncomfortable hats my mother insisted I wore to cemetery gatherings. Now I had a moment to process, everything wanted to pour out in an embarrassing mess in front of this stranger. I couldn't let that happen.

I took a few seconds to compose myself, straightened my shoulders, and looked Detective Noir in the eye. "Molly was murdered. There is no question about that."

"Then let me find out who did it," Detective Noir said, a touch of unwelcome sympathy in those brilliant blue eyes. "Your butler told me the basics when he contacted the Magic Council, but I need to gather all the information quickly."

"Yes! The killer won't be far away," I said. "Molly's body is still warm, and she was alive less than an hour ago." Tears threatened again, but with willpower, I kept them in check.

Detective Noir let out a sigh. "Where are your parents? It would be better if I dealt with them."

"You'll deal with me. I'm in charge of this household in their absence."

"Even so, they should come home. They need to be informed of what happened."

"They can't be disturbed. They're at Longview cemetery. The corpses have been restless and must be taken under their care."

"You didn't go with them? You're not a cemetery guardian, too?"

"No. I'm training to be a dancer," I blurted out, my cheeks growing warm as I realized I'd just revealed a long held secret.

The servants didn't comment or flinch, and Arthur's expression remained stoic. Perhaps my secret wasn't such a secret after all.

Detective Noir's surprised look turned to amusement, and his indulgent smile suggested he considered me a child who did not know what I wanted. Irritating man.

I wished Emory was here. He'd get this mess sorted. But the servants were looking at me to keep a level head and make sure Molly was done right. I'd handle the situation on my own.

"Detective Noir, the Magic Council has an obligation to investigate what happened," I said.

"I'm aware of that."

"So why are you questioning who's in charge, rather than looking at the crime scene, which is right under your nose?"

"Because there are people here who shouldn't be contaminating evidence. If there was any useful information about how Molly died in this yard, it's been trampled underfoot."

"Nothing has been trampled. We were all careful."

"Careful! Please don't tell me you moved the body."

"Of course not! Molly is just as she was found. Isn't that right, Lucy?"

Lucy sniffed again. "I checked her pulse in several places, but I didn't move her. Was that the right thing to do?"

"Of course it was," I said before Detective Noir spoke. "You were trying to help your friend."

"Miss Digby, please. Move your servants into the kitchen. I'll look at the scene, and then I'll need to question all of you."

"Shouldn't you get people looking for the strangler?"

"If and when I have a description of this so-called strangler, that's what I'll do, but I can't send my people out without a clear idea of whom to arrest. Now, remove everyone from this area so I can look around unimpeded."

I bit my tongue. I would have problems with this gentleman. Still, the servants didn't need to stay and watch us argue. And I was distressed at seeing Molly growing cold on the ground, so they would feel the same.

I turned to the quiet group. "Everyone take a break. Make tea, and I'll be in shortly once I've assisted Detective Noir with his inquiries."

"You, too, Miss Digby," Detective Noir said.

"I can be useful to you. I know about dead bodies."

"I need to assess things with no interruptions. I'm sure you understand. There can be no distractions. If there are, I may miss something important." He stood in front of Molly, shielding her body.

After a few seconds of tense staring, I gave in. "Oh, very well. But I'm only doing this for Molly." I followed the servants into the kitchen.

Nobody spoke as water was boiled and tea brewed. I remained by the window, watching Detective Noir as he kneeled beside Molly. He checked her pulse, spent several minutes looking at the marks on her neck, then carefully looked at her hands and face. He stepped back, remaining still as he inspected the yard.

"Here's a cup of tea. There's a dash of something strong in it, too." Cook handed me a flowered patterned china cup and saucer. "Don't worry yourself. The detective will figure out what happened."

"He'd better, or I will." I sipped the welcome hot liquid. I hadn't realized I was shaking until I almost missed my mouth and had to dab tea off my chin.

I took a step back from the window as Detective Noir came to the door. He nodded thanks at Cook when she handed him some tea. "It appears Molly suffered fatal injuries to her neck. It's likely her windpipe was crushed."

"By someone's hands," I said. "The marks look like long red lines, suggesting fingers, not a rope or a garrote."

"And how would you know about marks and murder weapons?"

"Do I need to keep reminding you of my parents' occupation? As of this moment, we have twelve corpses in our cellar. Not all of them expired after living a long and healthy life. Some met messy ends, and those ends leave clues."

"I imagine few were strangulations." Detective Noir sipped his tea.

"Maybe not, but I've witnessed similar markings before." Now my senses were no longer rattled with shock, my many years of being around bodies was proving useful.

"Slice of cake?" Cook said.

"No, but thank you," Detective Noir said. "I'm sure this is a shock for all of you, but I need to get the facts in order. Who was the last person to see Molly alive?"

No one seemed keen to speak, so I started. "She was dressing me for an appointment. Oh, Arthur, we must put off the wedding cake tasting. She'll be here any second."

"I've already sent word, Miss Digby, after contacting the Magic Council," Arthur said. "I rescheduled the appointment for next week."

"Thank you." I could always rely on him.

"You're getting married?" Detective Noir said.

He didn't need to sound so surprised. I was an attractive, eligible single lady with a large fortune. "I am."

"Congratulations. So, Molly was with you, and then what happened?"

"This will be of interest. A man claiming to be delivering coffins arrived. I was instantly suspicious because he wasn't our regular delivery man. He also wanted full payment, when he'd only provided half the load." I wasn't being completely truthful, but I felt too foolish to admit a conman had possibly duped me.

"Why would that interest me?" Detective Noir said.

"Because he could have killed Molly. I didn't know the man, and he assured me he'd bring the rest of the order. It's not here."

"You believe this man posed as a coffin deliverer to get to Molly and strangle her in your yard?"

"It's a solid theory, and none of us wanted Molly dead. We all loved her."

"It's not usually a stranger who commits such a violent act," Detective Noir said. "What motive would he have for killing Molly?"

"She saw what he was up to and questioned him," I said. "He panicked and killed her."

"There are simpler and less risky ways to kill someone. Even so, you'd better give me a description." Detective Noir scribbled the description I gave him on his notepad. "So, the coffin delivery was made. Where was Molly during that time?"

Lucy raised a hand. "She came down from Miss Digby's room at about one o'clock. She was in a good mood and had something to tell us but said it was a secret."

"Does anyone know what the secret was?" Detective Noir said.

"I asked Molly to join my household after I married. I hadn't meant to make the proposition so soon, but Molly was concerned she wouldn't have a place here after I moved out."

"Molly never said a word to us about leaving," Amanda said.

"She probably thought it best to keep quiet until we finalized things."

Amanda didn't look happy. Perhaps she wanted to join my household, too.

"Where was Molly when you had this conversation?" Detective Noir said.

"We were all in this kitchen," Cook said. "I was working with Amanda and Lucy on the evening meal."

"All three of you work only in the kitchen?"

"Just me and Lucy," Cook said. "Amanda and Molly do a bit of everything. They sometimes help with the food preparation but also cleaning and assisting members of the family."

I nodded. "Only three of us live here, so we don't need a large retinue of servants. And of course, we have Arthur. He ensures the household runs smoothly. And we have Ralph, our handyman, who works with us part time."

"I wasn't here when it happened," Ralph said.

Detective Noir raised a hand. "Let's get the facts in order before I take statements. Where did Molly go after she told you she had a secret?"

"She went upstairs to get fresh bedding then came back into the kitchen and was chattering again. It gave me a headache." Cook looked down at her clasped hands. "I passed her a list of supplies to collect from the outside store. We keep the nonperishables in the cold store. I didn't need them right away but wanted her out from under my feet. How was I to know there'd be some crazed person waiting to strike?"

"This wasn't your fault," I said.

Cook's lips were pressed together, but she nodded.

"How long was Molly outside before you became concerned about her?" Detective Noir said.

"Not long. I didn't expect her to be gone for more than twenty minutes," Cook said. "When she didn't come back straightaway, I assumed she was tidying. She was good like that. A neat girl. Responsible."

"No one went looking for her?" Detective Noir said.

"No, Lucy took a full bucket of food waste outside, and that's when she saw her," Cook said.

Detective Noir turned to Lucy. "And? What did you see?"

"Molly was lying there, as you saw her. It didn't take me long to realize something was wrong. That's when I screamed," Lucy said.

Detective Noir made more notes on his pad. "Where were you, Arthur?"

"Hold on a moment. None of my servants hurt Molly," I said. "They're loyal to the household, and they all adored her."

Everyone was swift to nod their agreement.

"I need everyone's alibis so I can discount them," Detective Noir said.

"That's easy. Cook, Lucy, and Amanda were together in the kitchen," I said. "I was outside dealing with the fraudulent coffin man, as was Arthur, and Ralph was out on another job. It wasn't any of us."

Detective Noir looked like he was biting his tongue. "I need to hear their alibis, not the ones you've created for them."

"I created nothing! You just heard the truth." Perhaps Detective Noir had taken a course in how to be a belligerent idiot. He wouldn't get any help from this household if he kept being so stern.

"From them, not you." Detective Noir caught hold of my arm and moved me to the open back door. "Let me do my job and I'll catch the killer faster. You're causing an obstruction."

"I'm being helpful."

"You're talking for people. I understand they're your servants, but I must hear their alibis from them. Otherwise, I won't get an accurate understanding of what happened."

"You don't believe my word?"

"It's protocol."

"You're wasting your time with nonsense protocol. My servants are trustworthy. They wouldn't work here if they weren't."

"Then humor me by allowing me to do my job and follow my nonsense protocols. Let me speak to them without you being in the same room, and then I'll find you and let you know the outcome. If I don't cover all the bases, I'll get in trouble."

I'd heard the Magic Council was sticklers for rules. "You're worried your boss will think you're doing a bad job?"

"Something like that." He spoke through gritted teeth.

I didn't want to show the man up. Providing he proved he was competent, I'd allow him to continue. "So long as you find Molly's killer, I'll put in a good word with your superior. We're regular dinner guests of the Commissioner, so I can speak to him."

"How kind. Please, leave the kitchen."

I didn't want to, but I wanted Molly's killer found, and even though Detective Noir was wasting his time quizzing the servants, perhaps he'd find a clue to lead him in the right direction.

I considered going into the yard, but Molly was out there. Corpses may be my parents' day-to-day normality, but I had no intention of it ever being mine.

I took my tea and paced the hallway as Detective Noir questioned the servants. I listened at the door several times, but he was speaking so softly, it was impossible to hear what was being said.

Where was Emory? He'd know what to do. He'd set Detective Noir to rights and then send a group to hunt down the killer. The murder would have been solved by now if he'd been around to assist.

I checked the time and sighed. If Detective Noir didn't hurry, I'd have no choice but to solve Molly's murder on my own.

Chapter 6

I dashed away from the kitchen door as firm footsteps approached and hurried into the parlor at the front of the house. I settled in a pale pink day seat with embroidered silk cushions and pretended to study something fascinating out the front window.

Someone tapped on the door.

"Come in," I said.

Detective Noir entered and glanced around the room. "Did you hear everything I said?"

I pretended to be scandalized by the suggestion. "I can't imagine what you're referring to."

"You kept stopping by the kitchen door as you paced the hallway." Detective Noir arched an eyebrow. "I assure you, I treated your servants fairly when I questioned them."

"I don't doubt you did. People who work for the Magic Council always play by the rules."

"Usually, we do."

I wasn't sure what to make of that comment. "Did you discover I'd lied regarding their alibis?"

"Everyone was where you said they were at the time of Molly's death."

"What about the man with the coffins? He must be your prime suspect."

"May I?" He gestured to a seat. "It's been a long day."

"Of course." I was forgetting my manners, but this was a unique situation, so Detective Noir would have to forgive my small social hiccup.

He settled in the seat with a sigh. "I didn't say anything in front of your servants, but what you described with the coffins is a regular trick. It's a local gang. They learn the delivery schedules of wealthy households and exploit them."

I blinked rapidly and frowned. "How do they exploit them?"

"They pose as a new delivery driver but only bring some of the goods ordered. If they're questioned, they pretend the usual driver is off sick or busy. Then they collect full payment, offload the shoddy supplies, and are never seen again. They rely on the household being too embarrassed by their error to report the crime."

"Oh! Well, I suppose if I have made that mistake, I'd be feeling embarrassed, too." I didn't want to admit that was exactly what had happened. Even Arthur suggested all wasn't well with the delivery. "Does that mean someone has been watching this household?"

"It would appear so. And we've had three reports of similar criminal behavior across the city. I'm certain there are more that haven't come forward. You're their latest victim."

I was leaning forward, equal parts annoyed and intrigued by this information. "Was anyone killed in the other households?"

"No, they simply wanted cash. They're clever. They steal goods from one part of the city, deliver it to another with their fabricated story, and then take the money. I suspect the coffins you were given were stolen from an undertaker."

"Not from one of our regular undertakers. According to Arthur, they're shoddy quality."

"We know who the key players are in this gang, so I'll speak to them. They're always a step ahead of us, though, and quick to hide the money, so we have no evidence to charge them with anything."

"What about Molly? You don't think the man delivering the coffins hurt her?"

"They're thieves, not killers. Even if Molly confronted him because she was suspicious of his behavior, he'd have threatened her to keep quiet or scared her. They're not a violent gang, just greedy and sly."

"I demand you tell me their names. They stole from us. And even if this thief didn't hurt Molly, he could have seen the killer running from the house."

"No, Miss Digby. That's my job. Molly's murder is my priority."

"You do believe it was a murder?"

"You were right about the marks on her neck. Nothing else could have made those impressions. I've seen a few strangulations, so I recognized the injuries."

"I'm sorry you've had to witness such atrocities."

"It's a part of the job."

"With my parents' line of work, I've almost become immune to such darkness." I gave a slight shudder.

"But not quite? If you want to be a dancer, you won't have corpses in your life for much longer."

"Keep that information to yourself. I shouldn't have said anything about my desire to dance. My parents believe I'll soon take up the family business." My heart gave a sad, slow thud. "After all, people die every day and will always need guarding and looking after. Most corpses are silent and well-behaved, but magic users with significant power need eternal care. And there are those who'll always remain restless. They not only need care, but companionship and education. Being a corpse is a difficult transition to achieve. Not all go quietly."

"It sounds like you don't think your vocation is so terrible. You're helping those in need and keeping everyone else safe."

"Perhaps. But it's not my passion." I tilted my head, my gaze running over Detective Noir. My initial judgment of him had been too harsh. When he wasn't chiding me, he was an interesting man. "How did you know you wanted to join the Magic Council?"

His eyebrows rose slowly, but he smiled. "A bit like you. It was a family tradition. My father, my grandfather, and my great-grandfather held prestigious roles in the criminal division of the Magic Council. From a young age, stories of their daring deeds surrounded me as they tracked criminals and brought them to justice. I thought I might like to do that, too."

I noticed the way his tone dipped as he finished speaking. "But now you're not so sure?"

He straightened in his seat. "What makes you say that?"

"You're not old, but you seem burdened."

"Dealing with murder and criminals every day can get to you," he said. "Is that why you don't want to be a cemetery guardian? You think being surrounded by death and disquiet will affect you?"

I pressed my lips together. It was rare I talked about my doubts, but sitting with someone who was also on a path that didn't bring them joy lowered my defenses. "It's always been assumed this is what I'll do. Corpses have been in my life since I was a baby."

"That must have been frightening."

"Not really. My parents have always brought the unruly ones here to educate them. They care for them more than anything or anyone else in this world. I've lost count of the number of times I sat at the top of the stairs and watched as they coaxed an angry or scared corpse into submission. Their energy goes into their careers." A small sigh slipped out. "There is little left for me."

"And you've grown to resent the corpses?"

"Yes, I did. I still do. I'm getting married soon, and I've only had five brief conversations with my parents about my wedding day. Of course, they're paying for everything and will be there, and my father will give me away, but they're disinterested in my life. That'll change when I become a cemetery guardian. Until that happens, I'm of little importance to them." I swallowed to dislodge the lump in my throat. My parents loved the dead more than me. It was a hard confession to make.

Detective Noir nodded slowly. "And you want to be known as more than a corpse whisperer?"

My top lip curled. "That's an insulting term. Corpses maintain a little of what made them alive. The magic that flowed through them so vibrantly is still there, although it's more of an echo. And we don't whisper at them. We talk to them, we take time to understand them, and we console them. They aren't wisps of ghosts with fragmented thoughts. They understand everything."

"My apologies. I'm just trying to find out more about your work. People talk about cemetery guardians as if they're mythical creatures and can control armies of the dead with a click of their fingers." Detective Noir chuckled. "That would be a sight to see."

"I could do that if I wanted to." I raised a hand as his expression grew alarmed. "But I don't. We know our duty, and we always uphold it."

"Except you. You want dancing, not death."

Was he questioning me because he was interested in my life or seeking a flaw to exploit in regard to Molly? "Perhaps. But who knows what my future will bring? Everything could change in a heartbeat. Molly had plans, and her life was about to change in so many ways. She was leaving here and would have been given more responsibilities in my household. It would have been exciting for both of us. And she had a young man. That could have gone somewhere."

Detective Noir took out his notepad and flicked through the pages. "Lucy mentioned Molly was seeing someone, but she knew nothing about him. Do you?"

"Today was the first I heard about him. My parents forbid servants from being in relationships. When the girls marry, they inevitably have families and then resign. My parents have lost several excellent servants as a result of them falling in love, so it's in their contracts."

"That's surely illegal," Detective Noir said.

"I don't doubt it. But the pay is excellent, the conditions are good, and my parents aren't demanding employers, once you get past the corpse issue. And they're rarely here to check on the servants, so any position in this household is ideal. Cook and Arthur have worked here longer than I've been alive."

He remained silent, so I had no choice but to fill the disquiet.

"When I learned Molly was seeing someone, I was happy for her. I can't tell you anything about the person she was involved with, though."

"I'll ask around. Someone will know something about their relationship. Two young lovers are rarely discreet," he said.

My cheeks flushed. "I'll take your word for that. You don't think any of my servants are guilty, do you?"

"None of them seemed nervous or behaved as if they were hiding anything." Detective Noir opened his pad to a blank page. "I need to confirm what you were doing."

"I've already told you."

"One more time."

I held in a sigh. Detective Noir was only doing his job, no matter how annoying that made him. "After dealing with the coffins, I went upstairs to find Molly. She wasn't there, and I was coming down the stairs when Lucy screamed. I rushed outside, and there was Molly."

"You were on your own the whole time?"

"Well, yes. But it was a matter of minutes."

"Did you have any problems with Molly?"

"Since I'd just invited her to join my household once I was married, you can assume the answer is no. I was fond of her."

"I'm just checking the facts. And your other servants supported your alibi."

"Of course they did. Besides, how could I have gotten into the yard without someone seeing me, strangled Molly, gotten back upstairs, and then faked my innocence?" I held up my hands. "And look at these. They're hardly big enough or strong enough to strangle someone."

"You'd be surprised what people can do when motivated."

"What is my motivation?"

"That's for me to find out."

I tutted at him. Detective Noir was being ridiculous again.

"I'm covering all possibilities. And you know this house better than anyone, since you've lived here all your life. Maybe there are sneaky ways in and out I don't know about."

"Don't look at me as a suspect. It's a waste of your time."

He put away his pad. "I'm not. But I can't afford to miss anything. All the bases must be covered."

"As you're so fond of saying." I smoothed my dress over my knees. "What will you do next to find Molly's killer?"

"Visit your parents. I need to inform them of this situation."

I pressed a hand against my stomach. "They won't be happy to hear this news."

"I'll also bring in a small team to take Molly away. I've posted a man out there, so no one can go into the yard."

"Be gentle with her. She was such a happy young thing, and it's so unfair she had such a brutal end to her life."

Detective Noir stood and nodded. "Of course. I'll treat the dead as respectfully as you do. If you think of anything else that could help in the investigation, here are my contact details." He handed me a small white card.

I tucked it away then showed him out.

Once he was gone, I swiftly gathered the servants in the parlor. "You're all innocent, and I told Detective Noir that. He knows none of you are guilty."

"Thank you, Miss Digby," Arthur said. "It's a shock for all of us."

"It will be for my parents, too. What we need is a distraction. Detective Noir is off to tell them what happened, so I was thinking a wonderful dinner will improve their mood when they return. I don't want them dwelling on what happened to Molly."

"I was already working on tonight's meal, but I can add two extra courses," Cook said. "And I was only doing a fruit salad for dessert, but maybe a Pavlova? It's Mr. Digby's favorite."

"Yes. Make them something delicious. The rest of you, if you need a little time off, take a break. Shock can make you feel terrible." I already had the beginnings of a headache I was trying to ignore.

"I think the best thing is for everyone to go about their business as normal," Arthur said.

"If that's what people want, then I'm happy." I nodded at Arthur. "Detective Noir said there was someone looking after Molly."

"A man arrived a few minutes ago. He's outside the kitchen door. He said there were more people coming."

"To remove Molly. Thank you, everyone. This has been a difficult day. Off you go. Get back to work," I said.

Everyone left, apart from Lucy, who hung back from the group, her gaze flicking to the door and then to me.

"Is everything okay?" I said to her. "You don't have to return to your duties if you don't feel up to it. I'll understand."

"I... I didn't want to mention this, but you already know about Molly and her fella, so I figured it wouldn't hurt to say something."

I eased the door closed. "I know a little. What can you tell me about him?"

"It was Jack Solstice. He works at the Marriage household."

"I don't know him. Of course, I know the Marriages. We dine there regularly."

"Molly kept it quiet because she'd get in trouble with your parents." Lucy wrung her hands together. "I shouldn't say anything else."

"You're safe with me. Is there something worrying you about Jack?"

"Molly didn't say much, but things were bad between them. Jack's a charmer, but he's got a temper, and he was pushing Molly to get wed. She asked me what I thought about getting hitched, and I told her she was too young. Jack was her first serious boyfriend. How did she know he was the right one?"

"She was considering ending things with him?"

"She already did. Molly came in late one morning last week. Her eyes were red, so I could tell she'd been crying, but she wouldn't talk about it. She just told me things were over with Jack. I think she feared him. She kept jumping every time the gate in the yard opened. I reckon she was expecting him to barge in and keep fighting with her or demand she changed her mind and took him back."

"Did you tell Detective Noir this information?"

"I said she was in a relationship, but I didn't want Jack to get in trouble. I like him, you see. I didn't think he was right for Molly, but he's no killer. Although, with his temper..." Lucy played with a loose thread on her sleeve. "I thought you could speak to Jack and see what happened between them. I could be getting things wrong and he had nothing to do with this. Of course, if you think he did it after speaking to him, you could report it to the Magic Council. With all your connections, you'd know who to speak to."

"Thank you, Lucy. Yes, I'll look into it. Off you go now." I bit my bottom lip as I considered my options. I had my first genuine suspect in Molly's murder, and I needed to investigate.

Chapter 7

I dashed away from the front door and ducked into the front parlor just before my father opened the door. I didn't want my parents to know I'd been waiting for over an hour for them to arrive home.

"We'll do hourly checks on our guests." Father stepped into the hallway. He was a tall, imposing man with pale skin and dark eyes. He always dressed in black and wore a fresh red rosebud on his lapel.

My mother was right behind him. "I'll take the first shift." She was the opposite of my father. Small-boned, only brushing five feet tall, and pale, from her hair to her almost invisible eyelashes.

They were both as cold as a snow witch's grave.

I stepped out of the parlor door in the pretense I'd been in there, occupied with a book. "It's good to have you home." I didn't hug them.

My father glanced at me. "You're up late."

"You should have been in bed hours ago." Mother brushed past me, the scent of dirt and death clinging to her clothes, and took off her long, black cloak.

"I thought... well, given what happened..."

"Ah, Molly," Father said. "That shouldn't concern you."

"It does. I grew up with her." I hurried after my parents as they strode along the hallway. "I considered her a friend. And she'd loyally served the household for years."

My mother's pale gaze flickered over me as she paused by the study door. "If you consider a servant your friend, then we haven't done our job. Why aren't you associating with the students in your classes?"

I held back a shudder. I was forced to attend a weekly half-day training event for future cemetery guardians. The location changed every week, but they always held it in a cemetery of some renown. The other students who attended were macabre and obsessed with death. Every time I'd engaged someone in conversation, all they'd talked about was my ability, my family legacy, or how many corpses I'd successfully mastered. What was wrong with talking about dresses, or the next ball, or even my upcoming marriage?

"Answer your mother. A servant isn't a friend. They're paid to be here," Father said.

"Sorry, Father." I trailed after them as they set down equipment, removed their boots, and walked into their study at the back of the house. "Molly was a kind person. I wanted to make sure neither of you were unsettled by her passing. After all, it happened in this house."

"In the yard." Father glanced up from the stack of post left on his desk.

"Molly died outside. Don't be concerned about her haunting us," Mother said.

I was about to say I wasn't when Arthur appeared in the doorway.

"Good evening. There is a meal prepared whenever you are ready."

"Thank you. We'll dine straight away. The corpses will need our full attention tonight." Father's gaze shifted to me, and it looked like he'd seen something he didn't approve of. "Will you be joining us?"

I nodded, although I was already wishing I hadn't waited up.

"If you're staying up so late, I don't want you surly in the morning," Mother said. "If I hear you complaining once about being tired, that'll be the end of this break from routine. Routine is everything when you're a trainee cemetery guardian. The corpses sense weakness, and that puts you and the cemetery in danger."

"I thought you'd like me here to welcome you home. It's hardly been a typical day."

"It has for us. Death is an everyday event in this household." Father stepped back to allow Mother and me out of the study first and into the dining room.

Arthur settled my parents in their usual seats, but I looked after myself, pulling out my chair and dropping into it with a sigh. I shouldn't have been surprised my parents were so cold about Molly, but I had hoped they'd feel a touch of sadness.

Arthur served the evening meal. He was always the member of staff who remained late when my parents returned at an unexpected hour. He set a tomato and basil soup in front of us and then left the room.

"Elbows off the table," Mother said. "And stop pouting. What's the matter with you?"

"I'm sad about Molly," I mumbled.

"Her death is unfortunate," Father said. "She served this household to an acceptable standard."

I nodded. At last, they were paying attention. "It was such a shock, finding her in the yard."

"You were the first to find her?" Mother said.

"No, that was Lucy. But I'd been with her just before she was killed."

"The Magic Council has informed us of the details," Father said. "They're dealing with things."

Mother set down her spoon. "We'll find her a place in one of our cemeteries. It's only right. Her family is of limited means, so they'll appreciate the financial burden being taken off their hands."

"I have no problem with that. And Molly will be no trouble. She had no excess of magic or spirit to cause her to rise," Father said.

"Molly would like that," I said.

"That settles the matter." Father nodded at me. "No more of this misery."

I bit my tongue as the usual silence descended over our late supper. Of course, my parents had a detached relationship to death. When you're around something all the time, no matter how distressing, the sharp edges fade. I'd been foolish to think they'd have any sadness over Molly's death.

I abandoned my pretense of eating. "I've been wondering who did it."

"Did what?" Mother said.

"Killed Molly! Who strangled her?"

"That's not our concern," Father said.

"It happened in our home. Shouldn't we be worried about safety?"

Mother sipped her soup. "We have plenty of protection."

"The detective who contacted us is following several leads," Father said. "He's bringing in the criminal types in this area to see what he can find out."

"He has a lead?" I said.

Father set down his spoon and pushed his bowl away. "It's not our place to interfere in the investigation."

"Don't you want to know who killed Molly?"

"You need to focus on your cemetery guardian practical examination," Mother said. "Don't become distracted by something you have no control over. You must ensure you're top of the class, or people will talk."

"Yes, you must study," Father said. "That young Brightlingsea girl almost beat you in the last practical."

"I was clear of her by two points. And I don't need to study. Knowing how to deal with the dead runs through me as hot and sure as my blood."

"There's no need to become complacent. Your father and I practice every day. Never take it for granted that you'll always have such firm control over the dead."

"I wish it would go away," I muttered under my breath.

"What was that?" Father said.

The door to the dining room opened, and Arthur came in. He cleared our soup and brought in a beef wellington with honey glazed vegetables.

Mother pushed the food around her plate and took a couple of bites. "I've been thinking about the female corpse downstairs. I sensed darkness in her essence. Cleansing grave dirt would be in order."

"I agree. She incited anger in the others. We'll set up a new coffin with fresh grave dirt and lay her in it for seventy-two hours. That should remove any excess urges," Father said.

I sat in silence, forcing down my food even though my stomach churned. My parents had done what they considered necessary to fulfil their obligation to Molly, and the matter was closed. They weren't even bothered someone snuck into our yard and strangled her.

As they continued discussing their new corpses, their faces grew animated. For them, being around the dead was thrilling. When they spent time with the living, their daughter included, it was a strain, and they never hid the fact they only had me to carry on the family legacy. Their marriage wasn't based on intimacy and affection. It was based on mutual respect for power.

I stabbed a spear of asparagus. I could never marry someone because we were a power match. I was glad I had Emory. He wasn't a powerful magic user, but I had enough for both of us. I'd have a love-filled, equal marriage. It would be the thing I clung to when life got hard or the corpses too demanding.

Mother pushed her plate away, most of the food untouched. "We should get to work."

"Wait! Cook made a Pavlova," I said.

"Why would she go to such extravagance on a weekday?" Mother said. "We have no guests."

"I thought you'd like it. After everything that happened here with Molly, you deserved something nice."

"Forget Molly. She is not your concern," Mother said. "There's no need to discuss it any further. Arthur will contact Molly's family and let them know where her body will be laid to rest. But that's it."

"I was thinking a visit to Wildwood is in order." My father stood, pulled back my mother's chair, and they left the room without saying another word to me.

My head lowered, and my heart sank. I should give up on them. They'd always been coldly indifferent toward me and were only ever interested in my grades and making sure I didn't let down the family name. It had been a waste of time having a nice dinner prepared for them.

Arthur entered the room and gently cleared his throat. "Shall we undertake our usual outing? There is plenty of food, and Cook made an extra batch of soup."

"That's a wonderful idea. And after that, we need to make a detour." I'd salvage something positive from this unpleasant evening.

With the rest of the neglected dinner packaged, and Cook's excellent tomato and basil soup in an urn, I took the carriage and left the house with

Arthur. It was almost three in the morning, but it wasn't unusual for me to be out so late. Corpses rose at all hours.

I always hated to see food go to waste, and my parents ate like anorexic sparrows, no matter how incredible the meal was. Their minds were always occupied by the dead.

But there were always empty bellies at the local poor shelter. It was open all night, and they were never surprised to see me show up in the early hours with gifts.

The carriage pulled up outside a large red brick building. The lower floor was open plan and mainly contained rows of single beds available to those who had no home or whose work paid so little they couldn't afford rent.

It was easy to assume, because everyone had magic, life was easy. But as with all societies, there was a power imbalance, and that was often exploited. The underdogs suffered.

Arthur carried the food to the kitchen, while I lingered in the main corridor.

"Miss Digby! I thought that was you." Evanore Wyrm strode out of her office. "This is late, even for you." She ran the shelter and was a champion for those in need.

"It's been a long, unhappy day," I said. "I wanted to end it by doing something positive."

Her eyes widened. "Of course. I heard about Molly. So sad."

"You knew Molly?"

"Just to say hello when passing on the streets. A terrible business. Any idea who did it?"

I fell into step with Evanore, having to hurry to keep up with her long strides. "There's someone from the Magic Council investigating. According to my parents, he's bringing in local criminals to question, but I'm not sure that'll be effective."

"Some guy from the Magic Council with a serious face and a notepad dropped by and asked if anyone had heard anything. Of course, it's always going to be someone from here, isn't it?" Evanore rolled her eyes. "You don't get the high and mighty strangling each other. Sorry, I don't mean to sound bitter, but we just got rid of some snooping official who said our regulations are out of date. They'll cost me an arm and a leg to sort, all so he can tick a few boxes on his form."

"I'll help with that. Whatever you need." I went to open my purse.

She stopped me and patted my arm. "That's good of you. Another time, though. And from the delicious smells coming from the kitchen, we're already in for a treat."

"It's nothing. Soup, bread, and some beef wellington. I should have brought more."

"You bring plenty. And your kindness is the most welcome thing, and that costs nothing." Evanore stopped by the door leading into the dormitory. "I expect you'll be too busy for us soon. It's almost time to take on your own cemetery, isn't it?"

I wrinkled my nose. "As my parents keep reminding me. I'll still have time to visit."

The door to the dormitory banged open, and a young man with a bright red face strode out.

"Jack! Mind your manners," Evanore said. "You almost hit me."

"I caught some jerk looking through my bag." Jack's hand was clenched in a fist. "He's lucky I didn't thump him."

"You know you need to keep your things with you at all times. There are desperate people in there," Evanore said. Her sharp expression softened. "He didn't take anything, did he?"

"No, and I threatened to break his head if he tried it again," Jack said.

"You need to go to the Marriage household and ask for your job back," Evanore said. "Then you'll have enough money so you won't need a bed here."

"You're Jack Solstice?" I said. "You dated Molly Tomkins."

Jack stared at me, and recognition hit his face. "Who told you that?"

"Molly."

"Huh! She talked about me with you?"

"Yes. Have you got a moment to talk?"

He adjusted the bag on his shoulder. "Why?"

"Jack, be polite. Miss Digby is an important shelter patron. She looks after the likes of you when no one else will. Show her some respect."

He sniffed. "You should make a rule about not allowing thieves in. I'd respect that."

"If we did, the place would be almost empty," Evanore said. "You can spend a moment with Miss Digby. It's not as if you've got anywhere else to go."

He scowled at her and then glanced at me. "Sure. I've got a minute."

"You can use my office if you want to talk," Evanore said. "I was about to do a quick walk around the dormitory."

"Thanks. We won't be long." I led the way back to Evanore's office and pushed open the door, glancing back at Jack to ensure he followed. The place was piled with papers and books, but it was clean.

I took a seat, and after a second of hesitation by the door, Jack did the same.

"I'm so sorry for your loss," I said.

"Thanks." He dumped his bag down. "Molly was a good girl."

"Had you been dating long?"

"Six months."

"And I heard you were talking about getting married."

"Molly told you that?"

"The subject came up in conversation." Jack didn't need to know the conversation hadn't been with Molly. "Had you set a date?"

He shuffled about in his seat. "We were just talking."

"Molly had agreed to marry you, though?"

"Why wouldn't she?"

"I'm not sure. She enjoyed her work. Perhaps she was worried she might have to leave."

"I had no problem with her working."

"Did you have a problem about anything else?"

Jack kicked his bag. "You ask a lot of questions. Why the interest?"

"I was fond of Molly. She was my dresser, and we'd often confide in each other. I was considering offering her a job in my own household once I was married." I swallowed to ease the ache in my throat. "It was a shock to learn what happened to her."

"Yeah, I suppose."

"So, everything was good between you?"

"Sure."

"No recent arguments?"

Jack's eyes narrowed. "Who have you been talking to? Her sister, I suppose. Jealous, spiteful creature."

"No, I haven't been talking to anyone. I just want to find out what happened to Molly."

"You sound like you're from the Magic Council. They've already been poking around and asking me questions. They're trying to set me up for this."

"They wouldn't do that. They do want to catch the guilty person, though. They must have hoped you knew who wanted Molly dead," I said.

"It wasn't me." Jack shrugged and tucked his hands under his armpits. "Maybe we had a fight or two, but Molly was coming around to marriage. She wouldn't get a better offer."

"You've just lost your job," I said. "Why was that?"

"None of your business. And I'll soon have another one. I'd have provided for Molly."

"I'm sure you'd have taken care of her. We both wanted the best for Molly." I sat up straight. "And I will make sure whoever hurt her pays for their crime."

He stood from his seat and loomed over me. "You think that person was me? You think I'd hurt the girl I loved?"

I refused to shrink away and stared up at him. "I sincerely hope you didn't."

He glowered at me but took a step back. "Her death won't get pinned on me. I've got an alibi. I was with my friend Devin. I've already told the Magic Council. Now, I'm done being questioned." He grabbed his bag and stalked out of the room.

I turned in my seat to find Arthur in the doorway. His expression was blank, but a small muscle twitching by his right eye showed he was worried about me.

"Miss Digby, is your continued investigation into what happened to Molly wise?"

I stood from my seat and smoothed my skirts. "I can't sit around and do nothing."

"The Magic Council will solve this crime. You've already heard they're investigating."

"I don't trust the detective who came to the house. And Molly deserves a restful death. She was murdered, so her corpse will be in torment. You know how troubled the murdered become. Their corpses are confused, and their world is one of confusion and pain. Her life was ripped from her with no warning."

"The Magic Council has years of experience dealing with unfortunate deaths," Arthur said. "Molly will be looked after."

"She'd better be, or I'll be having strong words with Detective Noir." I fixed Arthur with a stern look. "Not a word to my parents about this. As far as I'm concerned, Jack is a suspect until I've checked his alibi."

"Very good, Miss Digby. You're going to keep investigating?"

I pulled back my shoulders and nodded. "You can guarantee I am."

Chapter 8

Tap, tap, tap.

I rolled over in bed, disturbed from my deep, dreamless sleep.

Tap, tap, tap.

"Come in," I mumbled into my pillow.

The bedroom door remained closed.

I lifted my head, blinking the sleep out of my eyes. "I said, enter." And there had better be hot tea and warm breakfast crumpets on a tray to make up for waking me so early.

The door didn't budge.

Tap, tap, tap.

With my senses less muddled, I realized the noise wasn't coming from my bedroom door. It sounded like someone was at my window.

I slid out of bed and padded barefoot to the window. I inched aside the curtain, and my mouth dropped open. Molly stood on the small balconette, clutching the black railing.

"Oh, you poor girl." I gestured for her to step back so I could open the window.

She shuffled her gray, slightly bloated legs back, her eyes bloodshot and milky.

I opened the window and caught hold of her arm, afraid she may slip and plummet to the ground. Dead or not, corpses still sustained injuries. Her chilled, clammy skin stuck to me, but I didn't let her go.

"Come inside. You must be frozen. How did you get up here? Have you been trying to get in for long? You should have alerted Arthur. Oh! No, he would have put you in the cellar and informed my parents. You did the right thing by coming up to my room. But how did you do it?"

Molly simply grumbled a noise in response to my babble of questions.

I assisted her to climb over the window ledge. Once she was inside, I peered over the edge of the balconette. She must have climbed up the rose trellis to get to me. Such a clever corpse.

I hurried back inside and closed the window. I pulled open the curtains and turned to face Molly.

She stared at me and blinked once. Purple veins speckled her hands, which were clasped in front of her as she shuffled her bare feet.

"Grave dirt! You need grave dirt. Stay here. Don't move." I pushed a command into my words. My power meant I had complete control over corpses should I desire it. And I desired Molly to stay in my bedroom.

I dashed out of my room, tiptoed down the stairs, and hurried to the cellar door. I only had to open it and grab a pot off the top shelf. If either of my parents were down there tending to their new arrivals, they wouldn't notice me.

I tucked the pot under my arm and fled back up the stairs. Once I was in my bedroom, I opened the urn and poured a handful of grave dirt into my palm. I rubbed my hands together and smoothed them from the top of Molly's head, down to her feet. I completed the movement several times, and each time I did, her energy calmed.

"That's it. There's nothing to fear by being here. You're with a friend."

She opened her mouth to speak, but only a garbled noise came out.

"Try not to force your voice. You're a fresh corpse, so you won't have the power of speech for many months, if ever." I kept stroking and petting, letting Molly know she was in a safe haven. Unfortunately, speech required higher brain function, and most of the corpses never developed that level of ability after they rose. Only the extremely powerful and dangerous corpses spoke, and what came out of their mouths was rarely pleasant.

She garbled more noise, and her milky eyes filmed over, suggesting she wanted to cry.

"Molly, you can understand me, so at least we can communicate." I took one of her hands, my fingers dirty and caked in mud. "Did you come back because the Magic Council wasn't looking after you properly?"

She shook her head.

"Did they leave you unattended? I knew not to trust them to be responsible with you. Detective Noir is too young to know what he's supposed to do with a murder victim. He probably hasn't had his full training, and I'm certain he knows nothing about the care and management of corpses. Foolish man."

She shook her head again and gently jiggled my arm to get my attention.

"Sorry, I don't like to complain, but I'm so angry about what happened to you. And the detective investigating dismissed my help. He thinks I'm of no value to the investigation." I smiled at her. "I've been looking into what happened, though, and I have ideas. Come, take a seat, and I'll tell you everything." I led her to one of two chairs set by the window looking out on the rose garden.

Molly followed willingly enough, although seemed reluctant to dirty my cream flowered high-backed chair.

"Sit. You need to be comfortable." I gently eased her into a seat. "We can figure this out between us. I'll make sure whoever did this to you is put away for the rest of their life."

Molly kept hold of my hand, and the coldness from her skin seeped up my arm, but I didn't let go. Most corpses repulsed me, but I remembered the vibrant, young, laughing Molly who'd been in this bedroom recently. I kept that memory in my head, so the slight smell of decay didn't turn my stomach.

"Has Detective Noir arrested anyone for your murder?" I said.

Molly shook her head.

"I know he's questioning suspects, so he is doing something. He needs to work harder. Molly, I visited the poor shelter last night. I met Jack Solstice."

She tensed and groaned.

"You recently broke off your relationship with him, didn't you?"

Molly tilted her head from side to side, a bone cracking. Or it could have been a tendon snapping.

"If you hadn't broken things off, you were fighting, is that right?"

Molly nodded and tightened her grip on my hand.

"Was it Jack who strangled you?"

She gestured for me to stand then walked behind me and put her hands around my neck.

"Oh, you didn't see who did it. They got you from behind?"

She returned to her seat and nodded.

I settled back in my chair, eager to scrub my neck clean but not wanting to offend my dearest servant. "Do you have any idea how tall they were? Did they speak? Could you identify them if you heard their voice?"

She shrugged and shook her head.

"Do you think Jack could have done this to you?"

Molly shrugged again.

"He told me he had an alibi. A friend called Devin. Do you know who that is? I plan on speaking to him to make sure Jack isn't lying."

She nodded, and the film in her eyes faded.

"If your relationship with Jack was troubled, he may have thought he was losing you. Men can be violent when they don't get their own way. Some of the damage we see to the corpses coming through this house is enough to give you sleepless nights. Well, of course, you know all about that."

Molly made a little moan of agreement.

"My parents will find you a nice resting place when the time comes. And your family won't have to worry about paying."

Molly smiled, causing the skin on her lips to crack.

I smoothed grave dirt over her mouth to heal the wounds. "I promise I'll visit regularly. And I know your favorite flowers are yellow roses. I'll bring you some, and we can catch up on the household gossip. You won't miss out. Death doesn't mean the end. Not when a cemetery guardian protects you."

She tried for another smile, but it faded quickly.

My heart ached for her obvious despair. "I understand why you're sad, but I'm not giving up on you. I will make things right, and then you can rest easy."

Molly gently tugged me to my feet and wrapped me in a hug.

I hugged her back, not focusing on the cold skin pressed against me or the stench of decay filling my nose and mouth. She'd been my friend. She'd been killed in my home. Those were the important things. I owed Molly this debt.

A knock on my bedroom door made me jump. Molly cringed away and stared at me with big, filmy eyes.

"Who is it?" I said.

"Miss Digby, there's a visitor to see you. It's Detective Tristan Noir. He says it's urgent," Arthur said.

I looked at Molly and grimaced. "He must have noticed you left. It took him long enough."

"Should I say you're not available?" Arthur said.

"I'm very available. I insist on speaking to him. I'll be down straightaway." I grabbed my robe and tugged it over my pink silk nightgown. "Detective Noir is about to get a piece of my mind. He must have looked after you terribly to enable you to leave and get all the way here without being stopped. And your feet are bare! You're not in pain, are you?"

Molly shook her head, a guilty look on her face at the small specks of blackish blood she'd trailed across my carpet.

"Detective Noir will feel pain after I've dealt with him. Come on. We're doing this together." I marched to my door and flung it open.

Arthur was still outside. He took a step back, his face remaining impassive when he saw Molly. Ever the professional. "Welcome home, Miss Molly. It's good to have you back with us."

She gave him a toothy grin.

"Where is Detective Noir?" I said.

"In the front parlor. Do you need me in attendance?" Arthur's gaze ran over my nightwear.

"No, but a strong coffee would be wonderful. Thank you." I hurried down the stairs, still holding Molly's hand. I dashed to the parlor and pushed open the door. "Is this who you came for?" I presented Molly to Detective Noir.

His eyebrows flashed up. "I thought Molly might have come back here. How long have you been concealing her?"

"Concealing her! She's just arrived. The poor lamb must have been wandering the streets for hours." I gripped Molly's hand to reassure her that her sudden appearance hadn't caused my anger.

"Fresh corpses get easily disoriented. What were you thinking, leaving her unguarded? Do you know nothing about the newly dead?"

"Molly was looked after with respect," Detective Noir said.

"She must have been left on her own if she could escape your care so easily," I said. "How long has she been risen?"

Detective Noir adjusted his cuffs. "We were unaware she had risen. There'd been an initial examination of her injuries, and we were about to begin an autopsy. That was when we discovered her gone."

"You must have offended her or stirred her remaining magic to life and caused her to flee. Perhaps she saw you weren't doing your jobs properly when finding her killer. Molly knew she'd get help if she came here."

"We have every intention of learning who strangled Molly," Detective Noir said. "I must insist you give her the command to remain with us. She is of no use to you."

"I'll command her to do no such thing. She doesn't want to be with you. She wants to be with her friends. The people she can rely upon." I kept Molly close, aware of her trembling. It was hardly a surprise with this incompetent man demanding control of her.

"Miss Digby, this is not up for debate. We can't have corpses wandering the streets."

"Molly wouldn't have wandered anywhere if you knew how to do your job."

We glared at each other in silence for several seconds. The tension was interspersed with small groans of distress from Molly.

Detective Noir finally broke eye contact. "Where are your parents? They'll understand this is the logical thing to do."

"Leave them out of this. Molly stays with me. They won't command her to go with you."

"We'll see about that." Detective Noir stamped off along the hallway, opening doors and looking into the rooms. He had no respect for a person's private dwelling.

I patted Molly's arm. "If we ignore him, he'll get the hint and leave us alone." I glanced along the hallway. It was odd my parents hadn't emerged to see why there was an argument in their front parlor. The corpses in the cellar must be particularly taxing.

Molly's mouth turned down at the corners, and her hands trembled. She pointed at the front door.

"You're safe. No one will hurt you. I've always looked after you, haven't I? I let you have extra time off, gave you nice things, and always made sure there was plenty of food in the kitchen. My care for you won't change because you're no longer breathing."

Molly wrapped me in another shudder inducing hug.

I patted her on the back. "Everything will be well, providing we can get an alternative detective to look into your murder. This one isn't up to the job."

"They're gone!" Detective Noir strode toward me with a piece of paper in his hand.

"What do you mean?"

"Arthur gave me this." He thrust the paper at me.

The note was brief and written in my father's scrawling hand.

We received a summons regarding an outbreak of corpse pox. You're in charge of the household, with guidance from Arthur.

We have mollified the corpses in the cellar, so they'll be no trouble. Although don't go down there unless you have an urgent matter to deal with that requires supplies.

Arthur has access to any resources, should you require them.

I read the note several times. They'd gone again. Molly's murder needed investigating, but they'd abandoned their family and servants because of the corpses they were so obsessed with.

I lifted my chin and directed my frustration at Detective Noir. "It appears you have no choice but to deal with me, since I'm in charge of this household once again. Molly stays with me."

Rather than returning my anger, his gaze softened. "You didn't know they'd gone? They didn't even say goodbye?"

I stepped back. "It's not an unusual occurrence."

"This happens often?"

"As often as it needs to. Being a cemetery guardian isn't a nine-to-five job. It takes over your life." I had to pause because annoying tears were threatening, and I refused to cry in front of this man.

Detective Noir was quiet for a moment. "I see now why you would prefer to be a dancer. It must be hard, going to sleep every night and not being certain if your parents will be there when you wake."

"If I was a child, perhaps it would be hard, but I don't need your pity. This was the life I was born into. It's what I expect."

"That doesn't mean you have to like it."

"None of this prying is helping Molly." I'd had enough of his unwanted questions and comments. "I demand to speak to your superior. And I insist on seeing the preparations you had in place to care for Molly."

"We did everything by the book." The softness in his gaze vanished, and I was glad to have the sharp-eyed, suspicious Detective Noir back. He was easier to deal with.

There was a knock on the front door, and Arthur hurried along the hallway to open it. He stepped back, and Emory walked in. He was resplendent in a soft gray top hat, matching three-piece suit that I'd bought him, and a gaily colored cravat in purple and green.

"Silvaria! What are you doing in your nightwear? And who is this gentleman?" Emory took in the scene with wide eyes and disapproval on his face. "Is that corpse Molly?"

I hurried over to him. "I'm glad you're here. Molly came back. The Magic Council hasn't been looking after her."

Detective Noir stepped forward. "I'm the lead investigator in Molly's murder. Detective Tristan Noir." He held out a hand.

Emory didn't shake it. "Don't they teach you it's unacceptable to question a lady of status while she's barely clothed?" He took off his suit jacket and passed it to me. "Cover yourself."

I grabbed it and placed it around my shoulders. I'd been so surprised by seeing Molly and then incensed by Detective Noir's arrival that I'd given no thought to propriety.

Detective Noir lowered his hand. "My only interest is in retrieving Molly and continuing the investigation into what happened to her. I'm not in control of Miss Digby's attire."

"If you were a man of decent morals, you'd have waited for Silvaria to dress before questioning her." Emory caught hold of my arm. "Go into the parlor."

"I still have questions for Detective Noir," I said.

Emory handled me roughly as he tugged me into the parlor and closed the door before Molly could join us. "This is a worrying situation I find you in. An unmarried woman discussing matters of an inappropriate nature with a strange man. People will talk."

"You have nothing to worry about. Arthur was hovering in the kitchen, as I'm sure all the servants were. I wasn't alone with Detective Noir. And I'm only in my nightwear because Molly startled me when she climbed to my window. I was getting her settled when the detective arrived. I was so annoyed that I confronted him. I didn't think..." I looked at my nightgown. It had been impetuous to attack Detective Noir while still in my sleepwear.

There was a scratching on the door and a low groan from Molly. I went to open it, but Emory blocked my path.

"You know how to behave in company. Why do you always make such a drama out of every situation?"

"Molly's murder isn't an insignificant situation. And Detective Noir had some explaining to do."

Emory shook his head. "You have no experience in solving a crime. You can't be involved with this."

"I am involved. I care very much for Molly. Now move aside, so I can let her in. She's distressed."

He caught hold of me by the tops of my arms. "Silvaria, listen to reason. I don't want to exclude you from this because I'm cruel, but you're too close to the situation. You had an excess of affection for the serving girl, and you're unable to keep a level head. Look at your dress! Is that the action of someone sensible?"

I glared at him. "What do you suggest I do?"

"Nothing! Oh, you sweet girl, that's what I'm here for. Allow me to deal with this matter. In your current emotional turmoil, you'll miss important details, and that could harm the investigation. Surely, you don't want that, do you?"

"Well, of course not. I want the killer captured as soon as possible."

"Good. You're seeing sense. Now, take a step back. If you had a better control of your emotions, you wouldn't find yourself with a strange man in the hallway while wearing your nightgown and clutching a corpse's hand." Emory smoothed a hand down my hair. "If you'd been thinking logically, none of this would have happened, and you wouldn't have put yourself in this inappropriate situation."

Embarrassment replaced my anger. "I didn't mean to make you disappointed in me. I was so surprised by seeing Molly, and then the unannounced visit from the detective…"

He gave me a brief hug. "I'll deal with everything. You remain here while I talk to the detective. Don't come out of this room while you're not properly dressed. Do you understand?"

I frowned at him but nodded. "At least let Molly in."

"Very well. Your corpse may keep you company." Emory opened the door to discover Molly and Detective Noir standing outside. Arthur hovered in the background.

Molly dashed in and clung to me. Emory stepped out into the hallway, though I made sure to catch the door so it didn't fully shut, so I could hear what they said.

I was grateful Emory was looking after things. That irritating detective would get what was coming to him. When Emory wanted something, he always got it. He had a way of convincing people to do anything for him.

"You're here for the corpse?" Emory said to Detective Noir.

I'd prefer it if he didn't call Molly a corpse. She was barely dead, and there was only the faintest smell of decay and bloating about her, but he was often abrupt when angry.

"That's right. We searched for some time when Molly disappeared. When we didn't find her at her family home, we concluded she'd returned to somewhere she liked," Detective Noir said. "Miss

Digby was fond of Molly, so this seemed a logical place to search."

"Yes, yes. These corpses can be troublesome. Why have you not taken her away?"

"Because Miss Digby refused to give the command. Molly will remain with her until she gives the order."

I pressed my lips together. Detective Noir made me sound like a misbehaving school girl.

Emory sighed. "I understand. The next time you visit my fiancée, send a formal request first. Your manner of approach isn't appropriate for this household. Miss Digby and her family have high standards. Society holds them in great esteem, but that comes with scrutiny. My bride-to-be cannot be at risk of tarnish to her excellent reputation."

"I understand, but these were extreme circumstances. It's important to get evidence swiftly in a murder investigation. Leads go cold quickly, and I don't want Molly's killer getting away."

"There is always a place for politeness. Remember that the next time, no matter how urgent you believe the case to be." He turned to the door. "I know you're listening, Silvaria. You must hand Molly over and then make yourself presentable."

"I can't leave Molly with him," I said through the crack in the door.

"You must. She's an important piece of evidence in this investigation."

Detective Noir nodded. "We need to complete our investigation into her injuries. It's important Molly cooperates, or we'll have to close the case."

Emory moved to the gap I peeked through. "Darling, I came here today with a surprise for you. And an important proposal. I've booked a table at your favorite restaurant for brunch. Now, it's all been spoiled. Don't be difficult. Things can still be salvaged, but only if you cooperate."

"I'm not being difficult. And I want to be helpful." I glanced at Molly. "I'd love to come to brunch with you, but..."

"There's nothing you can do for your former servant. Hand her over to the Magic Council." Emory turned to Detective Noir and nodded. "This matter can be forgotten, but you must cooperate. It's best for you, the Magic Council, and your corpse. And it's best for us. We have a future together, and we can't live that if you're wrapped up in solving something you have no business being involved with."

I pushed open the door and looked at Detective Noir. His expression was strained, and he was glaring at Emory. I turned to Molly. "Perhaps you should go with Detective Noir."

"I'll do my best for Molly," he said. "Miss Digby, we want the same outcome, but I need Molly in my care to ensure that happens."

I took hold of Molly's hands. Her life was over, but mine was just beginning. I still didn't want to let her go.

Emory leaned closer. "You can't let the disaffected dead interfere with our joy. And don't forget I have a surprise for you. You'll love it."

Molly groaned softly and nodded at me, a sad look in her cloudy eyes.

I felt terrible about what I was about to do, but it was for the best. "Molly, listen to my command. Go with Detective Tristan Noir and remain with him. He'll find out what happened to you. The Magic Council will take the greatest of care of you. And if they don't, they'll have me to answer to." My gaze cut to Detective Noir, a clear warning in my eyes.

He simply nodded. "Come with me now, Molly."

With much reluctance, she shuffled away from me, now under the command of Detective Noir. He paused by the front door, and his gaze went from Emory to me. It appeared he wanted to say something but simply shook his head.

Irritating man. I cared nothing for his thoughts, only for his care of Molly.

With one last pointed look in my direction, Detective Noir left.

Was I doing the right thing? I wanted to chase after Molly and protect her, but what good could I do? I had no idea how to find a criminal and get a confession. If I stayed involved, I'd only make things worse for Molly.

Emory interrupted my thoughts by lightly squeezing my elbow. "Now the corpse has gone, make yourself presentable. Then it's time for your surprise."

I forced a smile, but my heart was aching.

Chapter 9

"I should contact the Magic Council." I went to stand, but Emory shook his head, so I remained in my seat at the table in Rolin Mogue. "I need them to give me regular updates about Molly."

Emory sighed as the waiter placed a crisp white linen napkin in his lap. "There's nothing you can do. Forget about her."

"That's impossible. And I was making progress. I'd found a suspect."

"Silvaria! Keep your voice down." Emory cast his gaze around the rest of the diners. "That's not your business. You can't poke around in some shabby murder. Focus on our future."

I had to fight to stop my jaw from wobbling. "I can't. Not while justice for Molly hangs in the balance."

"You're being dramatic. My dear, I've already told you I'll keep an eye on the situation. Later today, I'll contact Detective Noir's superior. If anything important arises, I'll let you know." Emory studied the wine menu, even though he knew I wasn't a day drinker. "You shouldn't be so obsessed with your serving girl."

I gritted my teeth and focused on the menu. Emory didn't understand how important Molly had been to me. I had friends, but I'd been able to be myself with Molly. All my other friends were society ladies, and while there was always a place to talk about balls, dresses, and relationships, my conversation had felt easier with Molly.

Emory caught hold of my hand. "Focus on us, not the corpse. Molly's your past. You've done what you can for her. She'll be thankful for that."

"It doesn't feel like I've done enough, though."

"You don't even like your cemetery guardian power, but if you keep this corpse in your life, you'll have to use it. And, if I'm being honest, your morbid fascination with Molly's death isn't attractive." He let go of my hand and eased back in his seat.

"I'm sorry my power repulses you." I wished Emory understood, but he didn't come from a family of guardians. A risen corpse was more than a vessel for a deceased person and their power to live in. There was still a sort of life there, even after death. But I didn't want to make things awkward by explaining that to him.

"You don't repulse me, but you often say how much you hate your ability."

That was true. Although when I'd helped Molly, I hadn't shied from my ability. I'd been grateful I could calm Molly and help her understand. That had felt natural and the right thing to do.

I tried a smile on Emory. "If you don't want me to use my natural ability, you'd be happy if I was a dancer instead?"

"Dancer! You'll be my wife. Isn't that enough? Our social calendar will be full for the first year, and after that, motherhood will occupy you. I hear children are a full-time job, although I struggle to see how."

I chewed on my bottom lip. I wasn't sure marriage and children would be enough. I loved Emory and adored the idea of being married to him, but I wanted more than that. I wanted to shine on stage.

Emory placed down the menu. "It's the stress of what happened to your serving girl that's making you quarrelsome. It's unsettled you. You need to calm your mind and focus on our wedding. How did the cake testing go?"

"It was put off. That was the day we found Molly, so I didn't feel like eating."

"We won't have a wedding cake? My parents will be so disappointed."

"There'll be cake. But Molly's death was more important to me than which type of cream frosting to have."

"My love, you're worrying me. You're usually so content. You're not having second thoughts about our marriage, are you?"

"No! I want that more than anything."

"It doesn't seem like it. Our relationship used to be your top priority, but something's changed." Emory sipped from his water glass. "I'm not sure I like it."

"Nothing has changed about me. I still want our future together. I want you to be successful with your property development and for me to dance. And I will tell my parents my plans, so long as I have your support." I kept my voice low so the other diners couldn't hear our small disagreement. "But corpses will always be their priority, so it'll be a struggle to get them to understand why they're not for me."

"It seems they are your priority. You claim you don't want your cemetery guardian power, but you're still obsessing over Molly. Let this go. You must to ensure we have a happy future."

I lowered my gaze. I hated arguing with Emory. "I'm trying."

He shooed away the waiter who'd come to take our order. "You think I don't understand what you're going through because I have no great power of my own. You don't think I'm enough for you?"

"This isn't about us or you. It's true, our abilities differ, but that doesn't mean either of us is more or less. We can be different and happy."

"Your behavior suggests otherwise. Because I'm unable to command the dead, you look down on me." He sighed and shifted in his seat. "I always wondered when you'd realize I wasn't enough for you. I'm trying to build my business empire so you're proud of me, but it takes time."

"You are enough, and you do make me proud. I can't wait until we're married. If that annoying detective had shown up at our door once we were man and wife, you'd have seen him off, and I wouldn't have been troubled. You'd have looked after me, like you always promise you will."

"And what about Molly?"

"What about her? You've made it clear you don't want me to keep talking about her."

"What if she'd arrived at our marital home? You know my thoughts about keeping corpses around the house. If you're giving up your guardian role, there'll be no walking cadavers in the house or in the grounds. Not even ones you have an association with."

"I'll do my best to make sure that doesn't happen. But it can be—"

"No! They must be banned from coming near you. You can command that. Your parents have always said you have a remarkable control over the dead, despite your lack of practice. Command them to stay away from us."

"What about when my parents pass? I'd want them close."

"You may visit them at their graves." Emory touched the engagement ring on my finger. "Our marriage will involve compromise, but no corpses around the house is something I'll insist upon."

That didn't sound like much of a compromise to me. I held in a sigh and looked at my menu, not seeing the words. Should I ignore my power entirely? I didn't want to serve the corpses, but commanding them was as simple as breathing. But my love of dance and Emory were my only two passions. Corpses weren't on the list.

"Let's move on, shall we?" Emory said after several minutes of stilted silence. "I hate it when we argue. We're normally so happy."

We'd resolved nothing, but he was right. Usually, our relationship was idyllic, and I wouldn't let this hiccup derail us. "Tell me about your surprise. You said you'd brought me here to make a proposal.

You've already asked me to marry you, so it can't be that."

He grinned, his gaze shifting over my shoulder. "Your first surprise has arrived, right on cue."

I turned in my seat and gasped. My estranged cousin, Rupert Whitehall walked over. I hadn't seen him in over two years.

I jumped from my seat. "What are you doing here?"

Emory stood and shook Rupert's hand. "Do you like your surprise, my love?"

I kept staring at Rupert. "Of course. But I don't understand. Why are you here?"

He kissed my cheek before settling into a chair brought over by the waiter. "It's good to see you, Silvaria. You're looking well."

"As are you." I was desperate to move past the pleasantries and learn why he'd decided to meet me after such a long period of silence. Silence he'd instigated.

Rupert smiled. "I've been talking to Emory for months, and he made me see sense. I hated the way we parted on bad terms, and I was happy to hear you'd found a man to take care of you. When he proposed a meeting, I felt it was the right time."

"You're not still angry with me, are you?" Rupert and I had been childhood friends as well as cousins and had played together most days. I'd considered him the brother I'd never had. But then, when he'd turned twenty-one, things changed.

"I'm not. And I'll be the first to admit I was the one who behaved inappropriately. I was jealous of your power, and when your parents rejected my request to train under them, I blamed you. I thought you told them I wasn't good enough."

I was shaking my head as he finished speaking. "I begged them to train you. I thought it was the perfect solution. With your parents gone in such tragic circumstances, you had no one to guide you."

"It's been almost six years since they lost their lives in the black magic corpse uprising. Sometimes, it only feels like yesterday." Rupert cast his gaze downward. "Your parents were right to turn me away. I was in the wrong headspace to complete any training under their care. I needed time to come to terms with my situation and loss, and I needed space to figure out my future."

"I was heartbroken when you left," I said. "I reached out to you, but you never replied to my letters. I thought I'd lost you for good."

"Because I was angry with you, and that was wrong. I looked for someone to blame, and there you were. You've always been the golden girl in our world."

"No, not me. And it's not what I want."

A flicker of interest crossed Rupert's face. "So Emory's been telling me. I grew intrigued when I learned you were considering stepping away from your duties. How do your parents feel about that?"

My mouth twisted to the side. "I'm sure they'll be disappointed. I'm still working up the courage to tell them."

"Oh! That'll be tricky." Rupert glanced at Emory, and they nodded as if they had a silent understanding. "Silvaria, I hope you forgive me for the way I treated you. I can only apologize and let you know I wasn't in my right mind. I was eaten up with grief, bitterness, and jealousy. Every time I looked at you, I saw the future I'd never have."

"I'm sorry, too. I should have kept reaching out to you. When you moved away and didn't leave a forwarding address, I assumed you wanted nothing more to do with me."

"And I didn't, not for a long time. But the years away have matured me, and I've accepted the role of cemetery guardian isn't for me. I only have a quarter of your ability, so it would always be a struggle to control the corpses."

"You've given up entirely? I could always put in a word with my parents now you're back. I'm sure they'll see the sense in supporting you, especially with me stepping aside," I said. "And it could be perfect for both of us. They need someone to train and take over when they slow down."

"I'm done with all that. That life isn't for me. And since I've made such an excellent connection with Emory, I don't want corpses and grave dirt in my life."

"A connection? I'm not sure I understand," I said.

"This is part of my surprise," Emory said. "When Rupert expressed an interest in reconciling, I encouraged it. I knew you were lonely, and I've heard so many stories about you and Rupert when you were children. I wanted to bring that joy back into your life."

I kissed him on the cheek, our previous argument forgotten. "You are a wonderful man."

Emory chuckled. "I'd do anything to make you happy. You are pleased Rupert is here, aren't you?"

"More than anything." I clasped Rupert's hand. "I'm thrilled to have you back in my life. And we have so much to catch up on. I've missed you."

"And I've missed you. I've been really lonely without you," Rupert said. "Although, I suppose the days of playing in the cemeteries are over. We have to pretend to be adults now."

I giggled. "I'm sure we can find fun things to do, even though we're grown up and sensible. Now you're here, you can help me with a puzzle, just like we did when we were younger."

"Intriguing. Fun already. What do you have in mind?"

"Has Emory told you one of my servants was recently murdered?"

"Silvaria, let's not go over that now," Emory said.

Rupert's eyebrows rose. "He mentioned it. It sounds like a terrible business."

"Oh, it's the worst. I've been looking into what happened, but I keep getting blocked by the Magic Council. I need supporters, preferably male, since the stuffy council doesn't think a young lady is capable of puzzling out a crime. Emory has been marvelous with them, but they'll listen to you, too. You always had incredible luck convincing people to help you."

"I'm not sure what I can do to make a difference, although I'm happy to listen to any theories you have."

"Silvaria, we agreed to move on from that," Emory said, the smile on his face fading.

"And we will in a moment. Rupert understands my situation, though."

"My dear cousin, that's kind of you to say, but if you want to figure out how this unfortunate servant died, I'm not sure I can be of service," Rupert said.

A little of my joy faded. I wanted back the closeness I had with Rupert, but perhaps it was gone for good. We used to have such fun solving puzzles, but if he'd lost interest, maybe we didn't have much in common.

"Silvaria, don't look so pensive. I'm here, and I'll support you in any way I can," Rupert said. "If you want to talk about the ghastly business of murder, then I'll be here for you. We'll figure things out. Just like we used to."

"Providing your sleuthing doesn't get in the way of my second surprise, I don't see it being an issue. Now, my proposal," Emory said, "and it involves both of you."

"What proposal are you talking about?" I was smiling at Rupert, still so shocked to see him. Everything felt like it was coming together.

"As Rupert mentioned, we connected several months ago, and it wasn't so we could figure out a way to get you two talking. Rupert has a head for business, and after some negotiation, we agreed to be partners in my new development project."

"That's wonderful news. I'm happy for both of you. It'll mean I get to see even more of you, Rupert."

"That's the plan," Emory said. "And I told you I want us to be equal in all aspects of our relationship. So, Silvaria Digby, how would you like to go into business with me and your cousin?"

Chapter 10

My feet felt like they were several inches off the cobblestones as I walked back home after the most wonderful brunch with my adorable fiancé and clever cousin. I'd been so thrilled they wanted me to join them in their new business venture, I'd barely been able to speak.

But I'd absorbed everything they'd said about their plans for the business. It sounded exciting, although complicated. They'd figure things out. They were already looking at various development sites, building materials, hiring crews to do the laboring, and submitting plans. It was so thrilling. And I'd be in the heart of it with two people I loved dearly.

I'd had so much fun talking about our wonderful future together, I'd barely given Molly a second thought.

As I got home, a little of that joy crumbled in on itself like a mummified hand. This was the scene of a terrible crime. Detective Noir had better be looking after Molly. I'd write him a stern note as soon as I was settled to make sure he didn't forget his duties.

Arthur opened the front door and ushered me in. Uncharacteristically for him, he appeared a little rumpled, and there was a light sheen of sweat on his forehead.

"Is anything the matter?" I handed him my jacket and purse. It took a lot to perturb Arthur.

"Your aunt Ruby is here," he whispered.

I tensed, and a small squeak popped out. "Were we expecting her? I haven't forgotten an invitation from her, have I?"

"She arrived unannounced half an hour ago. I informed her you had a brunch appointment with your fiancé, but she insisted she wait for your return. She has been a little... difficult, Miss Digby."

"Typical Aunt Ruby." Her unexpected presence wouldn't dampen my mood, though. "I'll take a moment to freshen up and then join her. Does she have tea and cake?"

"Yes, I found her something she deemed acceptable. It vexed her no one was home to provide a suitable greeting."

With my parents away, something they wouldn't have informed her about, and me off on a fun adventure with Rupert, it was no wonder she was in such a bad mood. Aunt Ruby insisted on being kept informed of all family activities. This oversight would not be easily forgiven.

"Hold the fort, and I'll be as quick as I can." I dashed to my room, freshened my hair, and dashed on a little sweet perfume, and then hurried down the stairs and into the back parlor, which was reserved for exclusive guests. And Aunt Ruby was one of the most exclusive members of society to come through the front door.

"Aunt Ruby, this is an unexpected delight." I hurried to her seat, and we engaged in brief air kissing.

"I wish I could say the same. I've been waiting for almost an hour. Where have you been?"

I settled in the seat opposite her and waited for Arthur to freshen Aunt Ruby's cup and place one out for me. I hoped the brew was strong. From the tart expression on my aunt's face, I'd need it. "I've been having a wonderful time."

"Arthur mentioned something about your young gentleman friend taking you out. I hope you had a chaperone."

"Aunt Ruby! This is the modern age. And I am engaged to Emory, so a chaperone wasn't required. I'm a respectable lady, and he's a gentleman, and we were in a restaurant in broad daylight."

She inspected the contents of her cup. "Even so, we have standards."

"And I kept to those standards." I decided not to mention my very un-standard like behavior this morning involving my nightgown, Molly, and Detective Noir. It would scandalize Aunt Ruby. She lived in a bygone era, when men were dangerous and women prey.

If any man was foolish enough to predate me, I'd set an army of corpses on him. He wouldn't stand a chance. Of course, Aunt Ruby wouldn't approve of that behavior. There was little she approved of.

She turned her head to inspect the family portraits, revealing her displeasure at the situation she found herself in. Aunt Ruby always looked to our ancestors when she was vexed by the present.

"You won't believe who came to brunch with us," I said.

"I can't imagine they'll interest me."

"I'm happy to correct you. It was Rupert Whitehall."

A rare flash of surprise appeared on Aunt Ruby's face. "My nephew?"

"Yes! I was as surprised as you to see him."

"I haven't seen the boy for two years." She waved a hand in the air. "He only comes around when he wants something."

"He wanted something from me, too, and something I'm happy about. We've reconciled. He apologized for his behavior and said he was jealous of my powers."

"Is that so?" Aunt Ruby regarded me coolly. "And you were content to accept his apology?"

"Why wouldn't I be? Rupert was my best friend growing up. I missed him so much when he moved away. I thought I'd lost him forever."

"Why pick now to become civil with you?"

"I have my wonderful fiancé to thank for that. Emory convinced Rupert now was the right time to rejoin the family. I expect he'll be in touch with you any day."

Aunt Ruby inspected the chair arm, looking for dust. It wasn't there. Arthur made sure of that. "I was never sure of the boy."

"Did Rupert do something wrong? He could be cheeky, but it was only childish play."

"He has a shifty look about him."

"He looks like Father! Do you think he's shifty looking?" It was meant as a gentle tease, but I should have known better. Aunt Ruby had buried her humor six feet under.

"Your father is different. Rupert's side of the family has always had dubious connections."

"They're connected to us, and we couldn't be any less dubious. We follow the social rules and make sure our name is never tarnished."

"Which assists them by association. But the marriage was a bad one, and Rupert didn't benefit from being raised in such company."

I wasn't sure what to say. Aunt Ruby had never spoken so plainly about her dislike of that side of the family. I'd liked Rupert's parents, and his mother had always snuck me cookies when I'd visited.

"I'm glad to have him back in my life," I said. "And Emory gave me another surprise. He's going into business with Rupert, and I'll be joining them."

"Joining them how?"

"As an equal partner in Emory's development business."

"How does that fit with your cemetery guardian duties? You see how tirelessly your parents work. They have no time for hobbies or fun."

"Or family," I muttered under my breath.

"We all sacrifice to protect the vulnerable."

"Of course. My apologies."

"Well? How will you do what your parents have never achieved?"

I resisted the desire to chew my bottom lip. "We haven't figured out the fine details, but they want me actively involved. It sounds so exciting."

"It sounds complicated and inappropriate. How will you be an equal partner while travelling to deal with cemetery issues?"

Aunt Ruby wasn't putting a dampener on my good mood, so I kept a smile on my face and settled my hands in my lap. "We'll figure it out."

She raised a thin eyebrow. "As if I don't have enough to concern myself with."

"Is something the matter?"

"I have heard upsetting rumors."

"I'm sorry to hear that. Who do they involve?"

She drew herself up to her full height. "You. You're considering a different career path."

"That's right! With Rupert and Emory. And I promise, it won't affect my family responsibilities."

"Not that. I'm sure your cousin and fiancé's ideas seem fascinating to you, but until they begin any developments, I won't believe a word of it."

"Aunt Ruby, what are you saying?"

"Despite your cousin's voluntary removal from our family, I made it my business to keep watch over him. The boy never settles on anything. He gets interested for a few months and then sees something sparkly and moves on to that."

"You've been spying on Rupert?"

"I've been ensuring his foolish activities don't haunt us. It's simple common sense."

Unease trickled down my spine. "Do you watch me, too?"

Aunt Ruby sipped her tea.

"Rupert has grown up. He's different from the excitable boy I played with, and I saw nothing about him to make me doubt his word." I smoothed my dress over my knees. "Besides, Emory would never associate with anyone who wasn't responsible. You should trust him."

"I trust nobody. And neither should you."

"I trust my family and my fiancé. They all care for me."

"They care for what you can give them. You're no different from me. I know people spend time with me and are polite because they know about the enormous fortune I'll bestow once I am dead."

"Don't talk like that. You've got at least two hundred years left in you."

Her thin lips pursed. It was the closest she ever got to a smile. "My plan is to outlive you all."

"There you go. There's no point in any of us pretending to be kind to you in the hope of getting your fortune." Aunt Ruby was so sharp when considering people's motives, and she could be a querulous old lady but was in excellent health. Cemetery guardians were long-lived if they didn't get caught in a corpse skirmish and smashed to pieces.

We sipped our tea in silence. I'd hoped my news of forming a happy alliance with Emory and Rupert would have pleased Aunt Ruby. I should have known better.

Aunt Ruby had been married five times. Her first husband, who was rumored to be the love of her life, died during an issue involving tainted grave dirt and a voodoo cursed corpse. Unsurprisingly, that loss and her subsequent failed marriages had soured her mood, and no amount of good news would make her smile.

But I wasn't letting that concern me. Aunt Ruby had lived a long life, and if she chose to see out her final two centuries in misery, I wasn't joining her. I had a full, happy life ahead of me with Emory and now Rupert, and I intended to live it.

"Returning to my concerns about your unsanctioned endeavors," Aunt Ruby said. "I had word you were seen entering an establishment associated with dance tuition."

My cup shook in my hand, making it rattle against the saucer. "Who told you that?"

"That is not important. What were you doing?"

The milk in the tea curdled in my stomach. "Perhaps I was having lessons."

"I am not an idiot. I remember your love of music and movement when you were a child. You were never still. Always bobbing and twirling. It gave me a headache."

I took a few seconds to settle my cup on the table. I hated lying, but I hadn't prepared for this meeting. "I was there because of my wedding. I must ensure I perfect my first dance with Emory. It's important the day goes perfectly."

Her narrow-eyed gaze drifted over me. "That seems old-fashioned, dancing at your wedding."

"You said yourself, I've always loved moving. We're having an evening of live music, and I'll expect everyone to dance, even you."

She gave a delicate snort. "I shall not be dancing."

"Aunt Ruby, it's my wedding day, and I'm your favorite niece. It's my only request of you."

"You're my only niece."

"Which, by default, makes me your favorite." I smiled at her until she gave a small nod of acknowledgement. "I can't embarrass the family by tripping over my feet while in Emory's arms."

"Then don't dance at your wedding."

"I must. And it's my special day. Please, indulge me."

She grumbled and stared at the portraits again. "I shall expect to be provided with ear defenders."

I giggled. "I'll have some made to match the flowers."

"Foolish girl."

"Wonderful aunt." I wanted to kiss her, but she'd only complain. "Although, I must admit, I'm not comfortable with you having me followed to my dance lessons. I feel like a criminal."

"I never said I had you followed."

That was hardly a denial. Aunt Ruby had to ensure everyone behaved, and she'd already admitted she kept tabs on Rupert. Although, I wasn't sure how reliable her source of information was in that respect. I saw only good in my cousin.

"Don't let your dancing interfere with your studies. When is your next practical exam?" Aunt Ruby said.

"In a week. And I'm prepared. I know what to do. And Molly's unfortunate death means I've been getting impromptu practice on my doorstep."

"Keep at it. Death before dance."

"Of course, Aunt Ruby." I looked around the parlor, at a loss for what to say. As much as I adored my aunt, she was difficult. "Oh! I have the perfect idea. I know what I can do to help Emory's business."

Aunt Ruby didn't reply. She simply waited for me to continue.

"I'll decorate the offices. I'll make sure Emory and Rupert have an impressive environment that showcases their developments. Of course, it'll be tasteful and masculine, and I could create color palates for the show homes, too."

"Aren't there tradespeople who do that? Why not hire them?"

"Well, we will. And I won't do the actual painting, but that's how I can add value to the business. Maybe I could design the company logo."

"Now you're a designer and a painter. My niece is a genius."

"Thank you." I was so pleased with myself that her sarcasm trickled away like raindrops on a marble headstone.

She harrumphed. "What will this company be called?"

"We haven't decided. Would it be appropriate to use our surname?"

"No! Digby's are known for their cemetery guardian work, not building little brick boxes for people. The only boxes we're interested in come in mahogany, pine, or oak."

"Aunt Ruby, don't tease."

"You know me well enough to understand I'd never tease. Our name will not be associated with this business."

"You're right. After all, it was Emory's idea. We could use our first names: Emory, Rupert, and Silvaria Construction. Or ERS Construction."

"It sounds common." Aunt Ruby set down her cup with a clatter. "I rarely give my opinion unless it is asked for, but I must in this matter."

I gently bit the inside of my cheek. Aunt Ruby always gave her opinion and loudly enough for anyone within earshot to hear.

"Silvaria, you're a sweet girl. Often annoying, but you're the least troublesome of my family, so I wish to give you advice." She settled her stern gaze on me. "You're too trusting, and people take advantage of you."

"That's not true. And why shouldn't I trust people?"

"Because they're not as kindhearted as you. Just the other week, I saw one of your servants wandering the stores as if she had all the time in the world. When I questioned her, she informed me you'd given her the afternoon off."

"You must mean Amanda. I remember her asking for a few hours to attend to personal matters."

"And you didn't think to question her? The girl was looking at hat ribbons and gloves. Those are hardly personal matters. You must pay more attention to those who will exploit you."

"Maybe she got her personal matters dealt with faster than expected, so she used the time to run errands." Aunt Ruby was making a burial mound out of a mole hill.

"No good will come of this soft heart. You must toughen up."

"Why? I have everything I've ever wanted, and I'm happy. The people who love me and those I care about the most will always protect me."

"If that's true, where are your parents? Why aren't they with you after that girl was strangled in the yard? Do they not fear for your safety?"

I cast my gaze down. "They've been called away on urgent business. Their work in the cemeteries always comes first. We both know that."

"And what about this wonderful fiancé of yours or my idiot nephew? I expect they've gone off drinking to celebrate this ridiculous business proposal. They should be with you, making sure you're safe after a girl was murdered not far from our feet."

"They would be here if I asked them. I... I didn't think. Do you think this house isn't safe?"

"You're missing my point. You feel too much, and that's your weakness. All this heart led nonsense will only end in that weak heart of yours getting broken. You'll be robbed blind, conned out of everything, or double-crossed by someone who is supposed to be your ally."

I took a deep breath, my emotions frazzled by her blunt beliefs. "Aunt Ruby, this is too much."

"Finding an unexpected body in your own home is unsettling. Don't deny it."

"We have bodies in the house all the time. There are several them in the cellar as we speak."

"Those were invited in. Your serving girl was killed." Aunt Ruby seemed determined to tear down my happy house brick by brick. "Where are all these people who are supposed to protect you and look out for your best interests?"

"You're here."

She didn't respond. I should keep defending my family and my fiancé, but Aunt Ruby had a point. Although corpses were part of my every day, finding Molly had been shocking. I'd have appreciated more support, but when I'd talked to my parents, they'd dismissed it as unimportant. So had Emory.

"I know what people think of me," Aunt Ruby said. "I'm bitter, mean-spirited, and want to stop everyone from having fun. But I've lived a long life and experienced unpleasant things. Other people and their ill intent has always caused those things."

"I'm sorry you've experienced that."

"As my least annoying relative, I don't want you to go through the same thing."

"Neither do I."

"While you engage in society, you're vulnerable."

"Then what should I do?"

"Stop being so gullible and question everything. And be watchful. People never do something for nothing. This world can be as cold as a grave. There will always be someone wanting something you have and not caring how they get it off you."

Aunt Ruby rarely talked about her past. If it had been so full of treachery and unkindness, I could understand why she was so suspicious and blunt. But just because bad things happened to her didn't mean they would to me.

There was a quiet knock on the front door, and footsteps hurried along the hallway.

"I've said my piece," Aunt Ruby said. "The rest is up to you."

Her words worried me, but I saw this as a test. I'd show Aunt Ruby and everybody else I was capable. I wasn't a gullible fool. I'd know if someone was deceiving me or being unkind. Maybe I was lenient with the servants, but I treated them well, and they respected the household. It was commonsense to do them a kindness now and again.

There was a knock on the parlor door.

"Come in," Aunt Ruby said, even though it wasn't her home.

Arthur opened the door. "Detective Tristan Noir has returned."

I grimaced. I wanted nothing more to do with that man.

"He said it was a matter of urgency. He has requested he speak with you, Miss Digby," Arthur said.

"Very well. Send him in," I said.

Arthur stepped out of the way, and Detective Noir walked into the room. His hair was disheveled. He had a red mark on one cheek and a small rip in his shirt. "Miss Digby, I need your help."

Chapter 11

I was so startled by Detective Noir's unkempt appearance, I simply stared at him.

Aunt Ruby rose from her seat in a cloud of stately entitlement. "Since my niece has lost the power of speech, I'll make my own introduction."

I lurched from my seat. "Sorry, Aunt. Detective Noir, this is my Aunt Ruby."

He made an attempt to smooth his hair before giving a small bow. "It's a pleasure to meet you. And my apologies for showing up unannounced, but I have a situation with Molly."

"I shall take my leave. All this talking has drained me." Aunt Ruby gave me a pointed look. "Consider what we've discussed."

"Of course." I walked with her to the door and, after a brief goodbye, dashed back to the parlor. "What's the matter with Molly?"

"As you can tell by my appearance, she's not herself."

"She escaped again? Not possible. She wouldn't disobey my order to remain with you."

"Molly has become aggressive. She attacked two of my men and fought me when I questioned her."

My hand went to my chest. "She hasn't become rogue, has she?"

He adjusted his tie. "I'm not an expert on restless corpses, so I can't be certain darkness hasn't inflicted her. I've only encountered half a dozen rogue corpses during my career."

"I knew it! I knew you didn't have the experience to look after Molly. You must have done something to make her react so strongly."

"If I did, I don't know what it was. I followed the protocols in our manual. To begin with, she was calm, but she was anxious about being in a cell."

"You put Molly in a cell as if she were a criminal?" I felt too hot and longed to loosen the strings of my corset.

"It's what we do with corpses. The cells are warm, safe, and secure, and by keeping them there, we can separate them from anyone else in case they become aggressive."

"No, no, no! Molly was the victim. She was strangled and her body left in my yard." I threw up my hands. "It's no wonder she's panicking if you locked her up. A newly risen corpse doesn't have higher brain function. She's more like a three-year-old child than an adult."

"I thought she would remain calm, since you had control of her."

"Not total control of her every action." I grabbed my cup and drained it. "Molly is reacting to the way you've treated her. And your treatment suggests she's done something wrong. She won't understand. That's why she's fighting. And I'm glad she is. It's no less than you and your idiot colleagues deserve. Who wrote this manual for handling corpses? I have things to say to them."

Rather than arguing the point, Detective Noir let out a sigh. "I suggested to my superior a cell wasn't the best environment for Molly, but the interview rooms were being used. He insisted we put her somewhere secure."

"Then your superior is more of a fool than you." I marched past him. "Take me to her. I insist on seeing Molly."

"I'm glad you said that. Molly needs a calming influence." Detective Noir hurried after me along the hallway.

"Arthur, I'm leaving. Fetch my purse and jacket. The pale blue one with the embroidered flowers. Molly likes that."

Arthur materialized a few seconds later with everything I required. "Will you be needing a carriage?"

"Mine is outside," Detective Noir said.

"Then let's go."

Arthur opened the door, and although his expression looked impassive to those who didn't know him well, there was a hint of concern in his eyes.

"I'll be fine. Molly needs my help. I won't be back late," I whispered. He worried about me more than my parents.

"Very good, Miss Digby."

I dashed to the plain black carriage waiting outside. I pulled open the door and hopped in, ignoring Detective Noir's outstretched hand.

He climbed in after me and settled on the seat opposite before rapping his knuckles against the roof as a signal to depart.

The seat in the carriage was uncomfortably thin, and several springs pressed into the back of my legs. There was also a faint smell of mold. My gaze went around the carriage before Detective Noir caught my eye. There was a hint of amusement on his face.

"Not what you're accustomed to?"

"It serves its purpose." I ignored the unpleasant smell and glared at him. "Have you caught Molly's killer yet?"

"No, and I've made little progress. With Molly being so aggressive and unhelpful—"

"Which was your fault."

"Perhaps it was, but I haven't been able to question her effectively. And since she's not talking—"

"Which she won't be able to for several months, if at all. You should know this, or has your manual failed you again?" I was happy to direct my anger at this infuriating man.

The whites of his knuckles showed as he gripped his hands together. "What I meant was, because she can only answer simple questions, it makes it hard to discover who may have wanted her dead."

"I have someone you must speak to. The gentleman she was involved with, Jack Solstice. I met him and believe all was not well between them."

Detective Noir's eyebrows flashed up. "You've been questioning murder suspects on your own?"

"Not intentionally. I took food to the poor shelter the night Molly was killed. Jack was staying there. Or rather, he was storming out because someone tried to steal something from his bag. I discovered he'd recently lost his job. When I asked him about Molly, he said they'd been fighting. That gives him a motive."

"Miss Digby, that was risky behavior. Jack Solstice is known for starting fights with anyone who angers him. What if he'd attacked you?"

"I may look unimpressive, but I have backup whenever I need it." I wriggled my fingers and a wisp of magic drifted from my palms. "If Jack had been foolish enough to harm me, he'd have regretted it."

"Miss Digby, you're the opposite of unimpressive."

My cheeks heated, and I was uncertain if I'd just been complimented.

"You can't always rely on your reputation to keep you safe. What if Jack hadn't known who you were?"

I huffed out a breath. "Unfortunately, everyone knows me and my family. Jack knew me, and he was aware of my ability. I was at no risk. Well, minimal risk, but no worse than I am when walking a cemetery at midnight on a full moon."

"I'm not sure how dangerous that is."

"Try it sometime and let me know if you survive." I arched a brow.

"It was still a reckless move." Detective Noir looked out of the carriage window. "Sorry, this case has me troubled, and I feel like I've hit a brick wall. I don't mean to take my frustrations out on you. And you're correct in your belief that Jack is an obvious suspect in Molly's murder."

I'd have loved to say I told him so but settled for a smug smile and shifted back on the uncomfortable seat. "You've questioned him?"

"Yes. Given his well-known hothead, he was the first person I visited. Jack was cagey at first and denied any problems between him and Molly, but he soon gave in and admitted there'd been trouble."

"So he strangled Molly?"

Detective Noir shook his head. "He didn't. He has an alibi, and it checks out."

"His friend, Devin?"

"You have been doing your research. Yes, an old school friend of his. Apparently, Devin must have needed a specific tool for a job and asked Jack to bring it to him. They were together when Molly was strangled."

I slapped my hands against the tops of my thighs. "That's bad news. This information takes us back to the start."

"It takes me back to the start," Detective Noir said. "While I appreciate your efforts to help Molly, you can't keep investigating her death."

"It sounds as if I need to. Do you have any more suspects?"

"Hopefully, providing you can calm Molly so we can communicate with her."

"You mean so I can communicate with her?"

"Touche, Miss Digby."

We arrived at the Magic Council office a few moments later. There were branch offices found in most towns, so residents had a reassuring Magic

Council presence close by. Well, reassuring for most.

I allowed Detective Noir to assist me out of the carriage, glad to be off the uncomfortable seat. Rather than going through the main door, he led me around the side and in through the staff entrance.

We went to the cells, and I pushed past him when I discovered Molly pacing inside one. "Get this door open immediately."

"She's not safe. I can't have her attacking anyone else."

"I'm here. She won't attack anyone. Get the door open." I reached through the bars and caught hold of Molly's hand.

She turned and snarled, her eyes black. The blackness vanished, and the old Molly was back. She sank to her knees and bowed her head.

"Oh, Molly. I'm so sorry this was done to you." I glared at Detective Noir, and he had the decency to look embarrassed as he unlocked the door. "Out you come. We'll get this sorted and find you a nice, safe room where there are no bars or locks, and you're free to come and go as you like."

"I didn't agree to do that," Detective Noir said.

"You're agreeing to it now." I went into the cell with Molly and endured several minutes of her hugging me. She trembled from head to toe and kept huffing fetid, stale breath in my ear as if she was trying to tell me something, but the words wouldn't come out.

I patted her back and stroked her hair. "I'm here now and will make things right."

Detective Noir waited outside the cell while I calmed Molly with a mixture of soothing words and gentle magic. I barely had to think about using my power to pacify this unfortunate girl.

I allowed the chilly magic to wrap around us, and Molly's panicked trembling slowed and her tight grip eased.

"That's better. Well done, Molly. Now, Detective Noir has something to say to you." I kept hold of her hand as I released myself from her hug.

He looked at me with confusion in his eyes. "Is there some formal greeting I've missed?"

I tilted my head and arched my eyebrows. "An apology."

"To you?"

"Molly!"

He looked like he'd stepped on something sharp as he shuffled about, unable to stand comfortably. "Of course. Molly, we made a mistake. You've done nothing wrong, and we should never have put you in a cell. I'll make sure it doesn't happen again. You have my word."

"Do you accept the detective's apology?" I said to Molly. "And his word? Should we consider this man honorable?"

She nodded, a tiny smile on her puffy lips.

"And do you feel up to communicating with us? It's important we find out who hurt you."

After hesitating, she nodded again.

"Brave girl. Detective Noir, we need a quiet room, a strong mug of tea for me, and no disturbances. Can you arrange that?"

A muscle flexed in his jaw. "Follow me. There'll be an empty interview room by now. We won't be disturbed in there."

After waiting a moment with Molly while Detective Noir found us a suitable room, one without bars, we entered a small, plain featureless room containing a table and chairs.

I sat beside Molly, and Detective Noir sat opposite us. I kept hold of Molly's hand and continued pulsing my calming cemetery guardian magic into her, but she was much more settled, and I had no reason to believe she'd attack the detective or anyone else.

Detective Noir cleared his throat. "My apologies again, Molly. I didn't understand how you should be treated."

"Treating her like a person with feelings would have been the best way. But you know now, and I'm sure you won't do it again," I said.

"Consider myself properly reprimanded," he said. "Molly, I need to ask you questions about what happened."

Molly looked at me, and I gave her an encouraging nod.

She copied my nod, her anxious gaze shifting to Detective Noir.

"Despite his earlier actions, he's helping," I said. "And I'm here if you need me. You may proceed, Detcctive."

He pursed his lips and took a few seconds to check through the notes on his pad. "Molly, the initial examination of your injuries suggests you were strangled from behind. Did you see your attacker at any point?"

She shook her head.

"Any sounds or smells that could connect to the person who killed you?"

He got the same response from Molly.

"You were in a relationship with Jack Solstice. I've already spoken to Jack, but could you confirm the status of your relationship? Were you both happy?"

Molly hesitated then shook her head again.

"I'm not sure they were together," I said. "Having spoken to my other servants, it was revealed Jack was pressuring Molly into marriage, and she didn't feel ready."

Molly nudged me and widened her eyes.

I lifted a hand. "I wasn't gossiping about you. I was looking for useful information about what happened. The detective and I consider Jack a prime suspect."

"Not necessarily," Detective Noir said hastily, "but we always look at those closest to the victim first. It's unusual for a murder victim to have no connection to their attacker. Molly, do you think Jack could have done this?"

She hesitated, her head wobbling slightly, before she gave a small shrug.

"Has he been violent toward you before?" I said.

Molly gave another nod.

"Then you were right to get rid of him. Dreadful man."

"Molly, did Jack threaten you when you left him?" Detective Noir said.

Molly stood and waved her arms around, opening and closing her mouth and looking angry.

"You argued?" I said.

She nodded.

Detective Noir's expression grew pensive, his forehead wrinkling and his eyebrows lowering. "Jack is a person of interest, but he has an alibi for the time you were strangled. He was with his friend, Devin Mustof."

"Could they have done it together?" I leaned forward.

Detective Noir sighed. "Miss Digby, you're here to support Molly, not ask questions."

"I'll ask as many questions as I like if you're not asking the right ones," I said.

He glowered at me.

Molly wrapped her arms around herself and swayed and moaned, misery stretching her mouth into a frown.

"You don't like us arguing?" I said.

She pointed at Detective Noir.

"You don't like him?"

"Devin? You have an issue with Devin?" Detective Noir said.

Her nose wrinkled, and she poked out a graying tongue.

"Could Devin have lied to protect Jack?" I said.

Detective Noir tossed down his notepad. "Why don't you lead on this investigation, since you're enjoying jumping to conclusions so much?"

"I'm simply getting to the truth." I wished I could use my guardian magic to settle Detective Noir. He was such an infuriating man. "If Jack and Devin are close, what's to say they're not covering for each other? You always want to protect your friends. I do a lot for my best friend and am hosting a birthday party for her soon. Hundreds of guests, flowers, food and drink, and entertainment."

"Sounds like hard work. Can't your friend organize her own party?"

"That's not the point. Jack could have persuaded Devin to give him an alibi. You should look into Jack's alibi again."

"And now you're telling me how to do my job."

I fixed a serene smile on my face. "Isn't it the logical next step?"

Detective Noir grumbled under his breath. "I'll take another look, check them out."

And so would I if I didn't get satisfactory answers from Detective Noir in the near future.

"Molly, this won't be an easy question for you to hear, but can you think of anyone else who wanted you dead?" Detective Noir said.

She pointed at his notepad.

"Can corpses write?" he asked.

"Sometimes, and Molly always had excellent handwriting. It was neat and perfect. I got her to address my letters because I smudge the ink." I yanked the notepad away and held my hand out for a pen.

Detective Noir handed it over without protest, and I passed the pad and pen to Molly.

She scribbled for a few seconds and then handed the pad back to me. Although the letters were twisted around and back to front, it was easy to read the word sister.

"You think Hettie killed you?" I showed the writing to Detective Noir.

"Hettie? Molly's sister?"

"Yes, her older sister. I've only met her twice, but she had an accident a few years ago and has been unable to work since. Now I think about it, Molly said Hettie was jealous because she had so much freedom. She was always complaining Molly didn't know how lucky she was."

Detective Noir's eyebrows rose. "I've been to speak to her. Do you think she'd be jealous enough to kill?"

I looked at Molly, and she nodded.

"Let's find out," I said.

Once I'd settled Molly in the interview room with explicit instructions for her not to be disturbed, we'd left the building and were approaching Molly's home in Detective Noir's carriage.

"I'm still not sure it's a good idea you being here," he said. "I didn't miss the disapproving look from your aunt when I visited."

"Aunt Ruby disapproves if the birds sing too loudly, the tea is too hot, or the post is late by more than a minute. It's how she is." Once again, I was on the seat with the uncomfortable springs. "You have nothing to worry about. And it won't look odd I'm visiting Molly's family to pay my condolences. She was an excellent employee."

"I was thinking of us being together when you visit."

"We're being efficient, traveling at the same time. If Hettie questions us, I'll simply say my carriage was out of commission."

"Which one?"

"You sound jealous of my transport options, Detective Noir. Although you desperately need these seats re-sprung. I'll have bruises on my legs after this adventure."

"The next time, I'll make sure we have satin cushions for you to sit your delicate derriere on."

"I'd appreciate it." I ignored his sarcasm and looked out the window. We were heading away from the affluent part of town and into a rural area. The houses were smaller and built for farmers and staff working in the larger households.

It had been a long time since I'd been out this way. In fact, it had been a long time since I'd done anything other than be surrounded by the demands of my family and friends. It was easy to forget there was another world out there, one not obsessed with corpses, society balls, or who was getting married.

"When we arrive, I intend to offer compensation to Molly's family for their loss. With Molly's income gone and Hettie out of work, I imagine they'll struggle financially," I said.

"That's good of you. Have the sisters always lived with their uncle?" Detective Noir said.

"Perhaps. I know nothing about their parents, but I assumed they were dead or unable to look after the girls. Molly only spoke of her uncle a few times, but I sensed they had a difficult relationship."

"Why was it difficult?"

"Most likely because she was a headstrong young lady testing her boundaries."

"Like you, you mean?"

"I'm not headstrong. I behave impeccably."

He chuckled. "Which is why you're in a Magic Council carriage about to question a potential murder suspect."

"These are extreme circumstances. And wouldn't you do something like this for someone you truly cared about?"

Detective Noir was quiet for several seconds. "You really were fond of Molly, weren't you?"

"I still am. Just because she's a corpse doesn't mean she doesn't deserve love."

"It's unusual to find such a relationship between an employer and those who work in the household."

"It's not unusual for me. I'm closer to the staff than I am my parents." I pressed my lips together. I shouldn't reveal so much to a stranger, but Detective Noir was curious, and it was rare anyone asked me a question or my opinion on anything.

"I'm sorry to hear that," he said.

"Why are you sorry?"

"Because you don't have a good relationship with your parents. I lost my mother when I was six, but I had an amazing relationship with my father."

"You had? He's no longer with us?"

"He died a year ago. For a long time, it was just me and him against the world. I could tell him everything, and he always had sensible advice. I miss him."

"That's natural. I hope you still talk to him when you visit his grave. Even the corpses who don't rise appreciate a conversation with someone they were close to, even if it is one-sided."

Detective Noir grimaced. "You're making me feel bad. I haven't been to his graveside in over a month. This job keeps me busy."

"Make time for the dead, or they'll come creeping out to visit when you least expect it."

He smiled. "More good advice."

"Perhaps you should listen to some of it."

Detective Noir went quiet again. "You have other people to look out for you, don't you?"

"Stop with the sympathy act. You keep trying that on me, and it only makes me angry."

He looked startled. "It's not an act. If you don't mind me saying, you seem lonely."

"I do. And I'm not. I'm about to marry a wonderful man, and my cousin has just come back into my life. I'm surrounded by friends, and even if my parents are absent a lot of the time, I understand their responsibilities. We're a respected and noble family, and our reputation is important. It's the most important thing."

"Of course. How could I understand when we're from such different backgrounds?"

I was too annoyed to make a pleasant comment or tell him that didn't matter, so I returned my attention to the outside.

We completed the rest of the journey in uncomfortable silence. Detective Noir was right. We had so little in common. Our paths would never have crossed if it weren't for Molly being murdered.

The carriage stopped outside a row of small pale stone terraced houses.

We left the carriage, and Detective Noir checked his notes and then led me to number ten. He knocked, and we waited a moment.

"Hold on. I'll be with you soon," a high, thin female voice said from inside the house.

There was a scraping noise that grew closer to the door. The door was opened by a tall, thinner version of Molly. She held herself up with crutches. "Detective Noir? Were we expecting you?"

"No, but I have some more questions. Have you met Miss Digby?"

"Hettie, you may not remember me. I'm Silvaria Digby. Molly worked in our household," I said.

Her eyes widened, and she shuffled back. "I remember you. You had that enormous food hamper sent over last Christmas. Molly wouldn't stop going on about how generous you were, although she didn't share any of the chocolate with me."

"That's right, I did. It was a little gift for the servants." I smiled at her. "We're here to talk about what happened to your sister. I'm so sorry for your loss."

Hettie blinked rapidly. "Thank you. You'd better come in. Sorry the place is a mess. I'd have tidied if I'd known we were having visitors."

"Please, don't concern yourself with that." I stepped straight into a small living room and could see a tiny kitchen at the back of the house. Most of these terraces were basic, with two rooms downstairs and two small bedrooms upstairs with the bathroom. Perhaps Molly and Hettie had shared a room.

Hettie gestured to a drab brown couch in the corner.

I headed over to it and settled next to Detective Noir.

"Would you like tea?" Hettie balanced on her crutches by the door.

"No, don't trouble yourself," I said. "We won't take up much of your time."

Hettie heaved herself into a chair opposite us and set her crutches to one side.

"Do you mind me asking what happened to you?" I said.

A sharp look crossed Hettie's face. "I fell. I was messing around in that abandoned house on Willow Lane. Molly and her idiot friends dared me to go in. We took it in turns to look for the ghost. I went to the top floor and stepped on something rotten. The next thing I remember was waking by the front door."

"That must have been terrifying."

"It was. It changed my life. I lost my job, my friends abandoned me, and I never even got a sorry."

I glanced at Detective Noir. "From Molly?"

"Of course. It was my sister who kept daring me to do it. She said my injuries were my own fault because I didn't look where I was going." Hettie shook her head. "Now, I barely leave the house because it's too painful to walk."

"That sounds difficult to live with," I said.

Hettie glowered at her crutches as if they'd whispered something offensive to her. "It is. Anyway, what can I do for you?"

"When I informed you about Molly's death, I said there was evidence pointing toward strangulation." Detective Noir adjusted his position. "She was definitely murdered."

Hettie simply nodded.

"And since Molly's corpse has risen, we've been able to ask her questions about what happened."

"She's not coming back here, is she? I know you came by looking for her. Uncle said she'd run off." Hettie's panicked gaze landed on me. "Miss Digby, your family knows about corpses. We don't want her here. Keep her away."

"Molly's shown no desire to return to the family home," I said. "She came to my room after she'd risen."

"Oh! Well, that makes sense. She spent more time with you than me." Hettie visibly relaxed. "She never could wait to get out of here in the mornings."

Given the unkind way Hettie spoke about her sister, that was no surprise.

"Has Molly told you who did it?" Hettie said.

"She didn't see her attacker," Detective Noir said. "She was strangled from behind."

Hettie let out a sigh, and I couldn't tell if it was one of relief or annoyance. "That's a pity. Then this would all be over."

My gaze went to Hettie's hand. "Oh, you have the ring."

She looked at the small silver ring on her right index finger. "This? Molly gave it to me. She said it wasn't her style. But I know the truth. It was a guilt gift."

"A guilt gift?" I said.

"Because of my fall. Molly was to blame, so she was always giving me things to make up for it." Hettie said it so matter of factly, I almost believed her. "Was she with you when she bought this?"

"Something like that." I glanced at Detective Noir again. He looked at me curiously but didn't pursue questions about the ring. They'd come later if he was a decent investigator.

"We're still looking at leads into who killed Molly," Detective Noir said.

Hettie lifted her chin. "You won't find any here. I've already told you I was at home with my uncle."

"I don't consider either of you suspects, but have you thought about who may have wanted Molly dead?"

Detective Noir's comment didn't surprise me, not after seeing Hettie's physical limitations. She didn't even have the strength to walk to the kitchen and brew tea for her guests.

"I have. I always thought she was making this up, but several times, Molly talked about this creepy guy who kept following her," Hettie said.

"She had a stalker?" I said.

"So she claimed, but Molly loved to exaggerate to get people's attention. She said he followed her home sometimes, but when our uncle went to chase him off, there was never anyone there. It was obvious she was doing it so people would worry about her."

"You're certain he wasn't real?" I said. "Maybe this stalker came after her. Did he know where she worked?"

"Maybe. Molly said he'd watch her when she was at work. If that was true, why didn't anyone else see him?"

"Did Molly tell you what he looked like?" Detective Noir's tone was swift and direct. He realized we were on to a new lead.

"Not that I remember, but I never paid attention when she went off on one of her stories. Molly's life was one long exaggeration after another. That's something I don't miss."

I doubted Hettie missed anything about her sister. It was sad. I'd longed for a brother or sister to keep me company when I was younger.

Detective Noir looked at me and nodded, a shine of excitement in his eyes.

Despite my misgivings about his competence, I felt the same and was happy to share the thrill with him.

We had a new lead, and it was time to pursue it.

Chapter 12

After spending a few more minutes talking with Hettie and learning nothing useful about Molly's stalker, it was time to leave.

Hettie tried to convince us he was a fabrication, but I wasn't so sure and was eager to learn more about him.

We left the terraced house and headed back to town in the carriage.

"I noticed you didn't pursue the possibility Hettie strangled Molly," I said to Detective Noir.

"There was a good reason for that. Why do you think I didn't ask about her obvious dislike of her sister?"

"The poor girl could barely walk, and she has an alibi."

"Should I have pressed her more? After all, it was clear she thought little of Molly."

"True, there were no tears shed, but you were right to move the conversation along." I tried to find a comfortable spot on the seat. "It's sad they didn't have a close relationship. Hettie blamed Molly for her trouble walking."

"I pulled the file on that incident after visiting Hettie to inform her of Molly's murder," Detective Noir said.

"There was an investigation?"

"Of course. A young girl was injured after trespassing in an abandoned house."

"Was Molly to blame?"

"It was no one's fault. There'd been high winds the night before the accident, and the fencing surrounding the house had blown over. Teenagers, being teenagers, saw an opportunity and took it. It was one of those tragic things. Hettie was unlucky enough to step on a rotten floorboard, and it didn't take her weight. She's fortunate to be alive."

"But is clearly unhappy and wants someone to blame other than bad luck," I said. "She's so full of anger and frustration, and she directed it at Molly."

"We always hurt the people we're closest to."

"That's a ridiculous statement. You should love them, not hurt them. Whoever said that was a fool."

Detective Noir simply smiled.

"It must have been a difficult home to live in," I said. "I didn't realize how bad things were for Molly."

"I think she'd have had a good life with you once you were married and set up in your own household."

I blinked my eyes several times. "I'd like to think so. I always treat the servants fairly."

"More than fairly if you're giving them expensive jewelry."

"I thought you'd have questions about the ring." I shook my head. "It's puzzling, though. Molly said she needed to get it resized because it didn't fit. She said nothing about giving it to her sister."

"Perhaps Hettie guilted her into handing it over," Detective Noir said. "If she told Molly she blamed her for her injuries, it would have made the doubt creep in, even after the investigation ruled Hettie's injuries no one's fault. Molly was trying to win back Hettie's favor by giving her that ring."

"She should have told me she'd done that. I'd have understood."

"As much as you care for Molly, she was still your servant. They know not to cross lines."

"Oh, I suppose so." I hoped Molly considered me a friend and not just someone she had to be nice to because my parents paid her wages.

"We can rule Hettie out of this investigation," Detective Noir said. "Don't you agree?"

I was enjoying this conversation. It was different to how Emory and my parents spoke to me. Detective Noir was asking questions and seeking my opinion, and he hadn't once belittled me. It had been a long time since anyone had taken me seriously. It felt good.

"Could Hettie be lying about how bad her injuries are?" I said. "If she wanted Molly to feel guilty about what happened, she could be faking her mobility issues."

"I haven't checked her doctor's records, but it's a thought. If she was planning on killing Molly to get revenge for the accident, her disability would give her an excellent cover story."

"Although her injuries should have been healed with magic if they weren't too severe, so perhaps she is telling the truth."

"If it was only broken bones, that wouldn't have been a problem. I'll look into her medical records, just to be on the safe side." Detective Noir made a note on his pad.

"If we're ruling out Hettie, I'm interested in this mysterious stalker," I said. "He must have been worrying Molly, but she never mentioned him to me."

"Was Molly always truthful with you?"

"I thought so, but I was surprised she hadn't mentioned giving the ring to her sister. Perhaps she hid other things, too. Or she didn't want me to worry about her being followed, in case it put her job at risk."

"Or she could have been making it up, just like Hettie said," Detective Noir said.

"Why do that? Her life was complicated enough with a difficult gentleman friend to manage and trouble at home."

"It could have been an escape for Molly. People imagine things that aren't really there to give them something else to focus on. A portal into another world, so they forget their troubles for a short time."

"Creating a fake stalker is a way to relax? How strange," I said. "Why not imagine something nice, rather than a terrifying stranger skulking after you?"

"Sometimes, people do strange things," Detective Noir said. "I suppose that's why I went into this business. I want to figure out what makes people tick."

"You do that, and I'll watch for this stalker. If he was following Molly, I'm certain he'd have known where she worked."

"No, thank you, but you've done enough for this investigation."

"It's no trouble. I can sit at a window and watch the grounds."

"I'll take you home. You have other things to focus on."

"No! We're not done yet, Detective. Please, let me speak to Molly, and we can ask her about this stalker. This could be the clue we need to find her killer." I leaned forward. "And you need me. Molly is still nervous around you."

He massaged his forehead with his fingers. "Very well. But that's it. Then you go home and forget about this."

"Once we've found the stalker and arrested him."

"No! You talk to Molly, and then that's the end of your involvement."

"We'll see." I grinned at him, and after a second of glowering, he returned my smile, even though there was concern in his eyes.

We were soon back at the Magic Council office, my posterior bruised from the uncomfortable seat. After accepting an unpleasantly weak cup of tea from Detective Noir, we met with Molly again in the interview room.

I gave her an update about our conversation with Hettie. Molly wasn't happy but accepted the information.

"One thing that came up in our conversation was that you had a stalker," I said.

Molly leaped from her seat, her eyes growing wide.

"Please be calm. We just need to find out more about this person. Why haven't you mentioned him?" A wave of fear slammed into me as it plumed out of Molly. I curled back in my seat, my heart racing and my mouth going dry.

"Miss Digby, what's wrong?" Detective Noir said.

"Molly's panicking," I gasped out. "Give me a moment with her."

"Should I get help?"

"Stay in your seat and don't move." I drew in a deep breath and forced down the panic threatening to overwhelm me. It wasn't coming from me, but it was undulating out of Molly and threatening to consume me.

I stood from my seat and faced Molly. "All is well. No harm will come to you here. Be at peace." I curled my cemetery guardian power around Molly.

She snarled, snapped the magic, and lunged at Detective Noir.

He yelped as she hit him in the chest and sent him flying off his seat.

I threw out a burst of cemetery guardian power and jumped on Molly's back, squashing her on top of Detective Noir. I wrapped my arm around her torso and held on tight. "Molly, be at peace. No one will hurt you. You have nothing to be afraid of. We're here to help. Rest, Molly. I'm your guardian. Hear my commands."

The fight drained out of Molly, and she slumped down. I kept hold of her, murmuring comforting words until her panicked rasps eased.

"Miss Digby, if you don't mind moving. I'm not comfortable." Detective Noir's face was bright red as he lay beneath us.

"I'm sorry, Detective, but you'll need to remain where you are for a few more minutes. Molly's condition is in a delicate balance. One wrong move, and our bond will snap again."

"She has her knee in my groin," he wheezed out. "It's a very hard knee in a very delicate place."

My cheeks grew warm. "Endure the pain. If I move her too soon, she'll go rogue again."

He shut his eyes. "What happened to her?"

"Sometimes, when new corpses get flooded with a particular emotion, it destabilizes them. They lose themselves in the feeling."

"And in Molly's case, she was angry?"

"More like terrified. Her fight-or-flight response activated, and she chose to fight."

"Why attack me?"

"She'd hardly attack me, would she? We're friends. Besides, you were the only male in the room. Maybe you look like her stalker."

"We don't even know if her stalker is real."

Molly growled.

"Don't say such foolish things, unless you want a corpse bite inflicted somewhere soft and delicate," I said. "Pay no attention to him, Molly. We believe you had a stalker, and he frightened you."

"We don't even know the stalker was male," Detective Noir said.

"Since she lunged at you and not me, it's safe to assume he was." I uncurled my arm from around

Molly's torso and gently stroked her hair. "Do you feel ready to communicate?"

She gave a small nod. I carefully eased off her back and assisted her to stand. I left Detective Noir to tend to his own injuries and get back on his feet.

Once we were settled around the table again, I caught hold of Molly's hand. "Are you at peace?"

She nodded, a sorrowful look on her face.

"You have nothing to be ashamed of. You're learning how to be something different, and that will always mean hiccups along the way. But we need to find out about this stalker. Was it a man?"

She grimaced but nodded.

"Does he look like Detective Noir?"

Molly pointed at his hair and eyes and nodded.

"Excellent. So your stalker has dark hair and dark eyes."

"What about his height?" Detective Noir said. "Taller than me?"

She nodded and patted her stomach.

"And fatter?" I said.

That got me another nod.

"Older than Detective Noir?"

She lifted a hand and moved it from side to side.

"About the same age?" I said.

Molly nodded.

"Did you see him on the day you were killed?"

She shook her head.

"But you have seen him recently?"

Molly nodded again.

"Any other distinguishing features?" Detective Noir said. "Scars, tattoos, beard, anything that could help us narrow down our search for this man?"

Molly pressed a hand against her forehead and groaned.

"That's enough questioning," I said. "Despite giving Molly direct commands, I'm using a lot of magic to keep her stable."

"That's not enough information. It could be one of a thousand people, and that's assuming he's local."

"We can make this work. We already have a plan of how to find him," I said.

Detective Noir stared at me. "We do?"

"Yes. Now, leave me to settle Molly. I'll talk to you in a moment and explain everything." I nodded at the door.

Detective Noir didn't look happy about being dismissed, but when Molly growled again, he took the hint and disappeared.

It took me twenty minutes to make sure Molly was calm enough to be left alone. I was worried about my fragile corpse. She was so bewildered and miserable about her new existence. It made me even more determined to figure out who killed her and make sure she would have a permanent, peaceful rest.

I eased the door shut and discovered Detective Noir standing outside. "Don't be angry with me. You know my plan to find this stalker. I watch to see if he visits my home, then I talk to him."

"That's a plan I haven't agreed to. And you'd be wasting your time. If this stalker murdered Molly, he'll have vanished."

"And if he didn't kill her, he could still be lurking around. He may even have seen something useful."

"Such as?"

"Someone creeping into the yard and murdering Molly."

Detective Noir huffed out a breath. "If this mystery man knows anything, I'll get it out of him."

"Or we could do it together. If he doesn't know Molly is dead, he'll still be watching my house."

He tipped back his head. "You just said he killed her."

"Where's your open mind, Detective? We explore all possibilities until only one remains."

"No, it's too risky for you to remain involved."

I glowered at him. "So, what do you propose we do?"

"If you'll allow someone in the grounds and house so we can observe, that would be appreciated."

"I could do that. I—"

A door slammed open, and Emory rushed toward me, his hat clasped in his hands. "Silvaria! You're okay."

"Of course. What are you doing here?"

He scooped me into his arms. "I've been so worried. I thought something terrible had happened to you."

I gasped at how tightly he held me. "I'm fine."

His gaze cut to Detective Noir. "You again. Are you leading my fiancée astray?"

"No! Emory, there's no need for you to be here. Detective Noir is being helpful."

"What are you doing here if you aren't in trouble?" The anger pulsing out of Emory made me uneasy.

I stepped out of his embrace, aware of Detective Noir's scrutiny. "If you must know, I'm about to solve Molly's murder."

Chapter 13

Emory stared at me and then burst into laughter. "I've always adored your humor."

"I'm being serious," I said. "And I'm being useful to Detective Noir. I found suspects, and we have a new lead."

"That's enough, Silvaria." Emory's laughter died. "I understand you've been upset over what happened to Mary—"

"Her name is Molly." I rarely spoke over anyone, but Emory was being unkind. "And Detective Noir needed my help."

"I'm sure he made you think he did." Emory's gaze hardened as it settled on the detective. "Next time you set your sights on a lady, you'd be wise to choose one who isn't engaged to be married."

Detective Noir pulled back his shoulders. "My interest in Miss Digby is professional. I called on her expertise regarding Molly."

Emory snorted. "Expertise? You're agreeing with her?"

"Why wouldn't he? Molly was troubled and needed calming," I said.

"Hush. You're getting overexcited. Stop wasting the Magic Council's time." Emory placed a hand on my elbow and attempted to guide me to the door.

I refused to move. "I can't leave. We have a new lead. I've been able to communicate with Molly, and we learned about her stalker."

"Very good. You're so clever, but let's leave the detecting work to the experts." Emory leaned toward Detective Noir. "I shall speak to your superior. It's inappropriate to involve civilians in criminal investigations, especially someone as young and inexperienced as Silvaria."

Detective Noir didn't flinch. "Actually, it's not. The Magic Council often calls on specialists in difficult cases. We needed the expertise of a cemetery guardian, and Miss Digby was happy to assist."

"You should have gone to her parents. Silvaria isn't trained. You could have put her at risk."

"I was never at risk from Molly." Was that why Emory was behaving so mulishly? He was worried I might have been hurt?

"You don't know that, my love. You haven't taken all your practical exams to show you're competent in your abilities," Emory said.

"If you ever watched me with a corpse, you'd know I'm more than capable. There's no need for me to study or practice. If I wanted to, I could walk out of here and control every corpse within a five-mile radius."

Emory shuddered. "There's no need to show off your ghoulish talent."

"I'm telling the truth. And ghoul magic is a different area of specialism. I don't manufacture anything ghoulish."

Emory tugged on the bottom of his waistcoat. He let out a sigh. "Detective Noir, my apologies if Silvaria wasted your time. I'll take her home and make sure she settles into a less vexing occupation. You won't be bothered again."

Detective Noir's gaze slid to me. "I found Miss Digby helpful in this investigation. She discovered several useful clues and ensured Molly didn't go rogue. I wouldn't have made any progress if it weren't for her."

I was so surprised by his compliments, I didn't know what to say.

Emory stepped closer to Detective Noir and lowered his voice but not low enough I couldn't hear. "I appreciate you saying those kind words, but there's no need. Silvaria is bored and looking for a distraction. You know how women get so close to marriage. They become skittish and foolish. I assure you, she won't be a problem once we're married."

I clenched my hands and glared at his back. Emory may be my fiancé, but he had no right to dictate what I did with my life.

Detective Noir nodded, his expression blank. "I wish you every joy in your upcoming marriage. Thank you, Miss Digby, for the time you've given me. It's been appreciated. As has your company."

"Silvaria, we're leaving." Emory caught hold of my arm and propelled me to the door.

"What about Molly? And our lead?" I resisted him, but he was much stronger than me.

"The detective has everything in hand. There's nothing to worry about." He glared at me. "Don't cause a scene."

"I must say goodbye to Molly. She'll wonder what happened if I vanish."

He leaned down so his mouth was close to my ear. "You don't want your parents to learn about this, do you?"

"They'd support me. I'm helping a corpse." They wouldn't. They'd already told me to forget Molly and focus on my studies. They'd be appalled if they learned what I was doing.

Emory's expression softened. "Please, darling. We have so much to do for the wedding. I understand this is an anxious time for you, and there'll be lots of change, but we must face it together. These petty distractions aren't helping us get our happily ever after."

"This has nothing to do with our marriage. I'm not anxious about that. I'm looking forward to it." At least, I was. Would this be what married life would be like? Emory would contradict me and ensure I knew my proper place?

He stroked a finger down my cheek. "I'm nervous, too, but we'll both have to make compromises once we're married."

"Really? What compromises will you make?"

"Silvaria! I'm doing this for you. I don't want your reputation to suffer. A lady of your status shouldn't wander around Magic Council offices solving crimes. You'll soon be a leader in the cemetery guardian community. Everyone will judge what you do."

I glanced along the corridor to see Detective Noir watching. "Please let Molly know I'm fine. If you have any problems with her, get in touch."

He simply nodded. His attention was on Emory, a frown on his face.

I didn't want him to see us fighting. It was too humiliating that my perfect man was behaving badly.

Detective Noir eventually turned slowly and walked away, pausing by the door and looking back a final time.

"Finally, you're seeing sense." Emory escorted me outside to the waiting carriage.

"I'm leaving to save face." I stomped to the carriage.

"I'm not saying any of this to be cruel, but your path is unusual, and our life together will be different, too. People will always be watching and expecting us to behave a certain way. Detective Noir misled you. This is his fault."

"This has nothing to do with him." I settled into the plush, soft seat of the carriage, and Emory sat opposite me. "What if I don't want to behave in that certain way? What if I wish to behave differently?"

"You won't feel like that when you're my wife. You must remember to show decorum at all times."

I stared at him, my mouth slightly open. "That's all I do."

"Your recent actions have shown that not to be true," Emory said. "Just this morning, I heard two ladies gossiping about you. The things they said weren't kind."

"I don't care about idle gossip. I care about making sure my dear servant gets the justice she deserves."

"At the cost of your reputation and your parents' legacy? At the cost of our happy marriage? You know if they were here, they wouldn't allow this behavior." He tried to catch hold of my hands, but I tucked them under my armpits.

I was shocked and angry. Emory was supposed to be on my side but was acting more like my draconian aunt.

He sat back in his seat, and neither of us spoke for several minutes as the carriage trundled away from the Magic Council office.

I'd always been happy with Emory, ever since that day he'd chosen me over all the eligible ladies. I'd felt privileged to be with him. He was usually sweet and charming and would tease me about my love of dance. But recently, as our marriage had grown nearer, the teasing had become less kind, and his obsession with propriety had taken over. Maybe Aunt Ruby had been tutoring him.

"I'm sorry," he said quietly. "I was heavy-handed back there, but I was so scared when I went to your house and Arthur said you'd gone with that detective. I thought you were in trouble or witness to a crime. You were vulnerable. You've experienced so little of the world that you're open to being mistreated."

"Or rather, you thought it would smudge my reputation and make you look bad." My heart raced so fast it made me dizzy. "Emory, you do love me, don't you?"

"Silvaria, I'm saddened you ask that question. I tell you enough."

"You do, and you're always giving me gifts and taking me for nice dinners, but isn't love more than that?"

"It is. It's why I want you as a partner in my business with Rupert." Emory leaned forward and gently touched one of my knees. "Forgive me. I'm bad with this sort of thing. When I get scared I may lose something, I become angry. I didn't mean to take that anger out on you."

I arched an eyebrow. "Perhaps you're bad at this with me, but you are extremely good at charming ladies, so you get what you want."

He looked shocked. "You make me out to be a smooth talking charlatan."

I closed my eyes for a second. "Why did you pick me? You were the most handsome man at that ball, and you had dozens of ladies to choose from, yet you came to me."

"Because I admired you. You have all the qualities I want in a wife."

"Which are?"

"You're talented, committed to doing right by others, and you have a good heart. Rupert was saying that just the other day. He said it was one of the things he most missed about you."

"You really think that about me? There are ladies out there who are much prettier and more fun. My magic will always leave a dark cast over our joy."

"You're pretty and fun, too, and your power is something to be admired."

"I deal with corpses. It's not something to laugh about. And you've seen how my parents are. What if I can't get out of being a cemetery guardian? That will be our life."

"No, because we'll set boundaries and have balance. You don't have to accept your power. We've already talked about this."

"I talk about it, but I'm never sure you take me seriously. And... in the Magic Council office, I was helping Molly, and I wanted to help her." Tears brewed, and I took a moment to compose myself. "Emory, I feel drawn to the corpses, even though I don't want to take on my duties."

He succeeded in taking hold of one of my hands. "It's another reason I picked you. You have a strong and noble heritage, yet you want to forge your own path and make your power something unique. And I'll be by your side to ensure that happens."

"Even if I want to be a dancer?"

He indulged me with a smile. "Even that. And I know what you've been doing to get a step closer to your ambition."

My eyes widened. "You do?"

"The dance lessons. I encountered your aunt, and she revealed she'd seen you going to private lessons. Of course, I supported you when she expressed her concern. It'll be wonderful to show your family and friends your passion, and I'll be your dance partner and your husband."

"You really don't mind? I wanted it to be a surprise on our wedding day."

"It's a charming surprise. We'll have a wonderful wedding and an incredible reception, and then we can go on our honeymoon and figure out our future. If you want to dance, help with the business, and do your guardian duties part time, we'll figure it out. Anything is possible when we're together."

A faint flicker of hope lit inside me. Emory understood. He could see my struggles and was prepared to stand with me. "I'd love that, but it won't be easy. Are you willing to stand against Aunt Ruby and my parents?"

"It'll be easier if we're together. And that's all I want." Emory kissed the back of my hand. "I'm sorry if you thought I spoke down about you. You're capable of anything. You're an incredible woman, and I'm privileged you allowed me into your life."

The flicker of hope grew bigger. "I'm glad I found you, too. But I can look after myself. You didn't have to race to the Magic Council and rescue me."

"That's what I'm here for. Why look after yourself when you have me?" He shifted seats, so he was settled next to me and wrapped an arm around my shoulders. "You're my partner. I adore you. And I'll do anything to make you happy."

I finally softened and leaned against him. The old Emory was back. I loved his sweet side but still wasn't certain about our future. His over protectiveness was stifling, but there was no point in telling him. Emory would always watch out for me and want to keep me safe.

And I'd let him. But I wasn't giving up on Molly.

As soon as I could, I'd contact Detective Noir and then set myself up as a lookout for the stalker.

After dining with Emory at my house, he left me to rest for the evening. The servants had also gone home since there was little to do with my parents gone, and only Arthur remained.

I sat up late reading, but really, I was waiting for Arthur to retire to his room.

Once I'd heard his door gently closing, I left it another twenty minutes before tip-toeing downstairs and settling into the large window seat in the study. It had the best view of the grounds and was a perfect location to see anyone lurking and watching for Molly.

If this stalker was any good, and he hadn't killed her, he'd know what was going on, so this could be a waste of time. After all, with Molly dead, he'd have no reason to watch the house. But I needed to be certain.

I curled up in the seat and propped my chin on my hand. I had a lot to think about. Although Emory's words had settled me, I was concerned about our future. I wanted us happy and helping each other, but what if his sharp, sarcastic side kept showing up? Would I be content to live with that?

I shook my head. This was pre-wedding nerves. Everyone had them.

If my mother was here, I could ask her if she'd felt the same before marrying my father. But their marriage wasn't built on a foundation of love and affection. They'd joined to strengthen their power. I had no need for such a union.

Perhaps it would have been simpler if I had. I'd have chosen the most powerful male cemetery guardian who was roughly my age and not unpleasant to be around, and we'd have had a formal union.

My heart didn't like that idea one bit. I was glad I'd found Emory and fallen in love. It was such a heady, complicated experience, but I embraced it. We would find true happiness together. And he was right. All relationships involved compromise. We'd find that balance, so long as we were open and honest with each other.

I ignored my mild guilt. After all, he'd told me to leave this case alone, and here I was, on a secret stakeout, waiting for the stalker to appear.

Half an hour passed, and there was no sign of anyone in the grounds. I snuck to the kitchen, took out two slices of treacle tart, made a pot of tea, and returned to my seat.

I shouldn't overindulge. I'd worked hard to ensure I'd fit perfectly into my stunning white wedding dress, but I deserved a treat. Solving crime was exhausting.

I'd sent a message to Detective Noir to let him know I'd take the first watch this evening, but I hadn't heard back from him. Did that mean he no longer considered me relevant to this investigation and wasn't intending to respond? Or was he keeping a low profile because Emory warned him off?

While contemplating a third slice of treacle tart, a movement outside made me freeze. I abandoned my tea and snuck to the back door. I inched it open and peeked out.

There was a quiet moan in the air, and I sighed. I grabbed a coat and stepped outside.

Two wobbly corpses ambled toward me.

There would always be some old bones lurking around this house. With all the cemetery guardian power within these walls, it was no surprise there wasn't a row of them lined up outside the door every morning.

"What are you two doing out here?" I whispered. "Not causing trouble, I hope."

They drew close, the fetid smell of decay rich in the air.

"Go back to your graves. Be at peace."

They shuddered as I commanded them then turned and wandered away.

Wretched things. I wish I didn't have this power. Life would be so much simpler. My gaze followed the corpses. Although it would also be a little boring. My power was shockingly strong, yet I'd barely explored how far it would take me.

Something metallic crashed to the ground, and a second later, a dark man-sized shape streaked out of the shadows.

A cry of surprise shot from my lips. It was the stalker!

Without pausing to think, I raced after him.

Chapter 14

Red velvet, soft-soled shoes weren't suitable for running, but I had no appropriate shoes for giving chase to a stranger who'd been lurking outside my house.

He was getting away, darting ahead of me, and pumping his arms.

"Stop! Who are you?" I yelled.

He didn't answer or obey, only sped up.

"You're trespassing. I can have you arrested for that." I was gasping and had a stitch in my side. I'd never been a fan of exercise, and it showed as the stalker kept gaining ground.

I yelped as my foot hit something hard and I landed in the dirt.

I was grabbed on either side, and after a brief struggle, I realized the corpses I'd sent away were helping me.

"Thank you. That's so kind." Their cold, clammy fingers barely repulsed me as I got to my feet.

The corpses stepped back and waited, as if expecting something from me.

I bit my bottom lip. Neither of them looked long dead. They had all their limbs and most of their fingers. A swift plan formed. "Forget my last command to return to your graves. I need you to capture that person for me." I pointed at the stalker. "Run like the wind and don't stop until you've captured him. Do you understand me?"

They nodded, turned, and raced away.

I blinked several times. Corpses were usually slow, but my magic had sparked something in them, and they'd shot off like Olympic sprinters.

I had no hope of keeping up but maintained a fast stride as I kept watch over my corpses. They were impressive. They dashed along, racing after the mysterious shadow person like their lives depended on it. Well, they had no choice since I'd commanded them, but a willing corpse always worked better than one forced to do something they didn't want to do.

The stalker turned, stumbled over his feet when he saw he was being pursued by the living dead, and yelled. Then he was off again.

I silently willed more guardian power into the corpses. My magic was young, and everyone told me it would take years to finesse the energy to control the corpses, but I knew different. My power was ready. It simmered beneath the surface, waiting to explode. I'd held it in check for a long time, but it felt good to allow it to blast out of me.

I broke into a gentle jog as the corpses neared the stalker. If they were hungry, they may take a nibble out of this stranger before I could stop them.

One corpse lunged and jumped nimbly on the stalker's back. He yelped and crashed to the ground.

The second corpse joined in, and between them, they pinned him down, his face in the dirt.

"Well done. You're such clever corpses." I was surprised by how well that had gone. I'd never thought about utilizing my corpses to do good. I'd always considered them troublesome and an obligation to undertake. But working together had been invigorating.

"Get them off me!" the stalker shrieked. "They stink, and one of them is drooling in my ear."

"They're staying where they are. You have some explaining to do." I took a moment to catch my breath, content the corpses would control the stalker while I regained my composure and dabbed the sweat on my top lip.

"You're crazy, lady. I've done nothing wrong. Why did you set your attack corpses on me?"

"They're not attack corpses. They were simply out for a late night stroll. You, on the other hand, were up to no good. Explain yourself. What were you doing lurking around my roses?"

He heaved out a breath but said nothing.

"And don't lie to me. I already know who you are. You're Molly's stalker."

He tried to twist his head, but the larger of the two corpses growled, and he froze. "What are you talking about?"

"Get him on his feet," I said. "I need to see this cowardly individual, so I know who I'm dealing with."

The corpses did as I commanded, and I came face-to-face with a dark-haired man with several days scruff on his chin and narrow dark eyes.

"You're just as Molly described," I said.

His eyes kept darting from me to the corpses. "Molly who?"

"You can't fool me. She saw you watching her, and you scared her. Who are you?"

"No one. Just out for a walk."

"You were lurking! Your name, or do you want my attack corpses to bite it out of you?"

"Tom! Tom Mathison."

"And you live around here, Tom?"

"I live anywhere I can find a bed and work. I got a couple of months' work at a farm nearby and hoped they'd keep me on, but things didn't work out. Since then, I've been taking whatever jobs I can and using the local shelter."

"The shelter? I know the place." Tom's clothing was shabby, and he reeked of alcohol. "Tell me what you did to Molly."

"Nothing. Please, get these corpses off me. I don't want trouble."

"It's too late for that. Trouble has found you, and it wants to take a bite."

The larger corpse lifted Tom's arm to his mouth and bared his teeth.

Tom trembled and closed his eyes, muttering under his breath.

"Wait a moment," I commanded the drooling corpse. "We need to keep him alive for a short time. I must hear his confession."

"Don't feed me to these corpses," Tom whispered. "I don't deserve that."

"Just like Molly didn't deserve to die."

"No, she didn't."

My breath caught. "Was that a confession?"

Tom tugged his arm away from the corpse's mouth, but my magnificent corpse was strong and had no intention of letting go.

"Answer me. You'll survive this questioning, providing you respond truthfully," I said.

"You won't kill me. You'd get in trouble for feeding me to a corpse."

"That's quite possible, but the Magic Council would need evidence to show that was what happened to you." I repressed a smile, feeling deliciously scandalous. "You've most likely never seen a corpse eat. Nothing is left. They're more efficient than pigs for waste disposal."

"You're joking, right?" His panicked gaze shifted from one corpse to the other.

"I never joke when it comes to my corpses. And I've been around them all my life, so I know what they're capable of." I stepped closer, attempting to look intimidating. "I also know what *I'm* capable of. One of my dearest friends was brutally murdered, and I want to know if you killed Molly."

Tom gulped. "I didn't kill her."

"But you have been watching her?"

"Sometimes. It was no big deal."

"It was a big deal to Molly. She was frightened of you. So scared that when I asked her about you, her corpse turned rogue."

His mouth dropped open. "Her corpse? You mean..."

"Molly has arisen. She won't be at peace until her killer is found."

Tom shuffled his feet and stared at the dirt. "I didn't want it to be true. When I heard people talking about someone called Molly getting strangled, I didn't believe it was her. I had to find out for myself."

I narrowed my eyes. "You must have seen what happened if you watched her all the time. It happened at this house. In the yard."

"I didn't watch her all the time. I sometimes get odd jobs to earn money. The day it happened, I wasn't here, so I didn't hear about her death until two days later."

"Where were you?"

"I'd been working on clearing an old yard. After I was done and got paid, I went straight to the bar. I drank myself almost senseless and then staggered to the shelter. I didn't leave for two days. I'd snuck some drink in, too. You're not supposed to, but I was discreet, so I got away with it. No one saw me."

"Which bar did you visit?"

"The Stag and Wand. It's my local."

I'd not heard of it, but I intended to visit and establish if Tom's alibi was true. I'd also visit the shelter manager and see if she remembered seeing Tom.

"And how did you come to know Molly?" I said.

"From the shelter. I saw her a few times, bringing packages of food and bedding. She was really kind and always laughing. She had time to stop and chat, too."

Guilt gently nudged me. "I sent her with those parcels. I wasn't always able to get to the shelter."

"I'm glad she came. I liked her, and she liked me, too. I asked her out for a drink, but she said she was seeing someone. I asked if it was serious, and Molly just laughed at me."

"You didn't want to take no for an answer?"

His cheeks flushed. "Molly led me on. She was always so nice and obliging."

"That wasn't her leading you on. That was simply Molly's nature. Even though she's a corpse, she still has kindness within her."

"It was more than that. She said I was handsome and a catch for the right woman. If that were true, why wouldn't she date me?"

"Because she was in a relationship. What did you do after she refused you?"

Tom looked at the ground again. "Nothing."

I glowered at him, and the corpses growled.

He raised his head. "Fine. I followed her one evening after she'd been to the shelter. She went to this little house in the country."

"You've been watching Molly here and at her home?"

Tom shrugged. "It was only once or twice to begin with. I thought if I got to know her better and showed her I was good enough, she'd ditch her guy and we'd get together."

"Did you ask her out again?"

"Several times. Each time, Molly gave me a gentle brush off. I said I could have a word with the guy she was seeing and let him know she wasn't interested in him."

"Let me guess, Molly laughed?"

"She was always laughing. I got angry. Why was she being so sweet if she didn't want something more from me?"

"We've already established Molly was a good human being. You're the one at fault. You misinterpreted her kindness as something else."

"I didn't. I could see there was more between us than friendship. She was being shy."

I pressed a hand against my stomach, certain I was only seconds away from hearing his confession. "Did you act on your anger?"

"I kept watching her. I just liked to be close to her. When the job ended at the farm and I had more free time, I could see her most days. But I couldn't survive on handouts and charity for long, so I took the barn clearing job on the day it happened." Tom shook his head and sniffed. "When I first heard the rumors, I didn't believe them. I even punched one guy when he said it was Molly who'd been strangled. Still, I had to know."

"What did you do to find out the truth?"

"I went to her house and waited close by for a whole day and night. Molly didn't come back."

"So you started watching here?"

"I thought you'd given her a room to lodge in. But she'd have come out sometime to get food or visit her family. The longer I waited, the more fearful I became. Molly had gone. She really was dead." He sniffed again.

"I have every reason to believe she is dead because of you," I said. "You had an unhealthy obsession with her."

"No! I already told you I was out drinking and then passed out drunk in a cot at the shelter."

"The Magic Council already knows about you. They're looking for you. Why haven't you come forward if you have nothing to hide?"

"Because I look guilty. I can see in your eyes you think I'm guilty." His head lowered. "And I have a record."

"You've killed before?"

"I haven't killed, but I've stolen. I got caught. But I promise I cared for Molly, and I'd have made her happy. She didn't understand how serious I was about her."

I didn't believe him, but I needed more proof to be certain he'd killed Molly. "What time did you finish work in the yard?"

"Around noon. I got my money and went to the Stag and Wand."

"The landlord will confirm this? He saw you?"

"It's a she, and yeah, she was there. Oh, wait. I got food from a cart in the square. I ate that and walked around and then got to the bar around two. I remember now."

"Are you sure? Molly died during those hours. Perhaps you walked to my house and confronted her."

"I didn't. I'm not certain about the time, since I wasn't keeping an eye on it. It wasn't like I had anywhere to be. It could have been later or earlier. The landlady will know. She'll show you I'm innocent."

I didn't trust this man. He was a drunk, a thief, had violent tendencies, and had intimidated Molly.

She'd turned him down one too many times, so he got his revenge. Perhaps in Tom's twisted little drunken world, he decided if he couldn't have Molly, no one would. He'd finished his work, crept over here and strangled her, and then drank away his guilt.

"The Magic Council will need to talk to you," I said.

Tom struggled in the corpses' grip. "I've done nothing wrong. Let me go. I've told you everything."

"Oh, no. We're just getting started." This man was guilty of murder. I just knew it.

"Silvaria!"

I twisted around and discovered an angry looking Detective Noir running toward me. "What are you doing here?"

I grinned at him. "Your job. And you're too late, Detective. I've just solved the case for you. Here's Molly's stalker. And your killer."

Chapter 15

I felt wonderfully pleased with myself the next morning, and a pot of Earl Grey tea and some tiny macaroons Cook was so clever at making were the perfect treat to celebrate finding Molly's killer.

Detective Noir had been so shocked by my discovery last night that he'd barely been able to speak. His cheeks had been bright pink with embarrassment, and he'd kept muttering to himself as he'd taken Tom away for questioning.

I selected my second macaroon and took a tiny bite. I sighed and kicked my feet back and forth on the baby blue chaise lounge. Mr. Idiot Detective was only angry and jealous because I'd beaten him. And I was completely untrained in the art of detection.

I was so proud of myself, even if he pretended not to be impressed by my cunning and intellect.

Detective Noir was probably worried about how he'd explain himself to his superior. Why hadn't he taken the stalker suspect as seriously as I had? It had been left to a single, untrained person to solve this crime. If it weren't for me, Tom would have left town and never been seen again. Then justice would never have been done.

As I pondered the successful capture of Molly's killer, I couldn't help but think how strange it was that Tom was still hanging around. I'd have liked the opportunity to question him more, with no interruptions from the Magic Council. If he'd strangled Molly, he should have fled.

I gave a little shrug. Tom was a drunk and not to be trusted. He'd admitted he'd spent most of the afternoon, after strangling Molly, drinking away his earnings. He must have done it to blot out the guilt. And he'd kept drinking, so he didn't have to face what he'd done. Perhaps the alcohol had damaged his short-term memory, and when he came around from his drinking session, he couldn't believe what he'd done and thought he'd dreamed his horrible actions.

It was sad to see a person so lost, with nothing to live for but violence toward others. It was no matter. The man was guilty. I was certain of it, and there were only simple formalities to complete until he was charged. Tom would be off the streets and wouldn't harm anyone else.

I was excited to visit Molly and tell her the excellent news. And then, once my parents were home, we'd find her a lovely, peaceful spot in a cemetery. She'd like to be laid to rest close to a tree. She enjoyed nature and would often go on long walks. Yes, that would be a fitting end to this whole tragedy.

There was an Arthur-like knock on the parlor door.

"Come in," I said.

He appeared. "Mr. Farr is here to see you."

I swiftly tucked the macaroons out of sight. Emory had made a point of mentioning how important it was I looked perfect for our big day. If he saw me snacking on treats, he wouldn't be impressed. "Thank you. Send him in."

Emory strode in and kissed my cheek before settling in a seat next to me. "How was your evening?"

"Oh, nothing exciting happened. I mostly stayed in." I longed to tell him about last night's adventure, but he wouldn't understand. He'd made his thoughts on my association with Detective Noir and solving Molly's murder clear. And what he didn't know wouldn't hurt him.

"I'm glad you had a pleasant evening. I've been up most of the night working on the final documents for our business." He patted his jacket pocket, which bulged with papers.

"How wonderful. You and Rupert must be excited."

"You should be, too. After all, we're equal partners in this venture."

"We are, and I am. Even though I'll admit I know nothing about buildings."

"You don't have to, but you'll learn the important things. And with all your other duties once we're married, I don't expect you to come to the office."

"I'd like to be there sometimes. At least two or three days a week."

"Will you be able to manage that? After all, you'll have our household to look after, and it won't be long before we start our own family." Emory took my hand. "I'm so looking forward to being a father. And then, you have to arrange what you're doing with your cemetery duties. And your dancing."

I let out a sigh. There was a lot to juggle. Being a responsible adult was exhausting. I almost wished I could stay here, eating macaroons, letting my parents handle the grisly corpse business, and enjoying my time with Emory. Once I was married, things wouldn't be so carefree. And if I had a household, children, the property development business, dancing, and possibly even cemetery duties, how would I manage it all?

"There's nothing to worry about. We're in this together." Emory kissed the back of my hand.

I smiled at him. This was what happened when you matured, and I was happy to take on the challenges, especially with Emory by my side.

"I've been working with Rupert on the business financing," Emory said. "I won't bore you with too many details, but we need capital up front for materials and buying plots of land."

"Of course."

"We've arranged loan financing but need to contribute funds ourselves. I have some money, and so has Rupert, but would you be able to contribute a small amount, too? Not a lot, just a demonstration of your commitment."

"I'd expect nothing less. This is a business we're equally involved in."

"We'll have our funds repaid as soon as the business turns a profit, but we need to show the finance company we're trustworthy and have our own resources."

"That makes sense. Do you know when we'd get the money back?"

"Within five years. Possibly less. It depends how quickly we can get the developments up and running. That won't be a problem, will it?"

"No, you know I have my own funds. I'm happy to use them for our business."

"And of course, we can draw salaries, too."

I smiled and nodded as Emory outlined the finances and investments he was planning. Financial matters weren't my strong suit. My parents paid for everything and gave me an allowance that I could use for whatever I wished. I'd never had to think about money. And I came into my trust fund a year ago, so I had a comfortable cushion if I needed money for exciting events such as this.

"I've got papers for you to sign," Emory said. "They're a formality to make you an official partner."

I clasped my hands together, joy bubbling inside me. "I never thought I'd part own a business at such a young age. Or any age."

"It's exciting for us all."

There was another knock on the parlor door, and Arthur entered. "Miss Digby, Detective Noir is here to see you."

I glanced at Emory and bit my lip. "Ask him to make an appointment for another time if he must see me."

"What's he doing here?" Emory said. "He's no longer welcome. Is he still bothering you? You have made it clear you're unavailable, haven't you?"

"Of course. And Detective Noir has no romantic interest in me. Arthur, tell him to leave." I gripped the arm of the chaise lounge.

"Miss Digby, I must insist on seeing you." Detective Noir barged into the room.

I stood and glared at him. "As you can see, I'm otherwise occupied by important business matters with my fiancé. Please, leave."

"My apologies, but I need to talk to you about Tom Mathison. Or have you lost interest in what happened to Molly?"

"Of course not." I spoke sharply. If I didn't get rid of him this instant, he would reveal my secret late night escapades to Emory.

"Do not speak to Silvaria like that," Emory said. "The lady has asked you to go. I suggest you do just that."

"I won't take up much of your time." Detective Noir refused to budge. "But I have questions about last night."

"Leave, this instant." I burned with curiosity to find out if Tom had confessed, but if I asked, everything would be revealed to Emory.

"I will. Soon," Detective Noir said.

"What's going on? What happened last night?" Emory stood, his unhappy gaze shifting from me to Detective Noir.

I glanced at Arthur, my top lip growing damp with sweat. If I insisted, Arthur would physically remove

Detective Noir from the house, but that would only make matters worse.

Detective Noir sensed he was on dangerous ground because he strode closer, out of Arthur's immediate reach. "Miss Digby, what did Tom say to convince you he'd murdered Molly?"

"This is inappropriate." Emory clutched the paperwork in his hands. "We were about to complete a momentous moment in our lives, and you blundering in and blathering on about that dead servant is spoiling everything. And who is Tom?"

I glared at Detective Noir, sending him a silent warning to remain mute. Sadly, he wasn't one of my corpses I could command.

"Miss Digby accosted a suspect in Molly's murder last night in the grounds of this house," Detective Noir said.

"That's enough!" I turned to Emory. "I was going to tell you, but I didn't want to spoil your good mood."

"Tell me what?" he said. "You're done with all that investigating nonsense, aren't you?"

"Not quite," Detective Noir said. "Miss Digby confronted the suspect and is convinced he confessed to her. But there's a problem. Which is why I'm here."

"Is it Molly?" My anger morphed into concern.

"Molly is well," Detective Noir said.

"I'd say there's a problem." Emory's face turned puce. "Silvaria, you're putting everything in jeopardy. I came here so you could sign these papers, which will take us to the next phase of our lives, but you're still running around playing at catching criminals. What's the matter with you? Don't you want our future together?"

I bristled at his rudeness. "Nothing is the matter with me. But someone was stalking Molly, and he was lurking around this house. I spoke to him to see what he knew about her murder."

"You spoke to him alone?" Emory couldn't look more scandalized.

I looked down at my hands. "Two corpses helped. I was perfectly safe."

"And I was there, too. I'd set up a night watch so we could observe the house to see if Tom made an appearance," Detective Noir said. "Miss Digby was never in any real danger."

It surprised me to hear this. Detective Noir had shown initiative and hadn't ignored my message after all.

Emory grimaced. "I don't know what to say. I'm so disappointed in you, Silvaria."

"I'm sorry if this has caused a problem," Detective Noir said to me. "Miss Digby, why are you so certain Tom murdered Molly?"

Emory spluttered a few words, but I placed a hand on his arm, hoping to placate him. I'd have to deal with this mess after Detective Noir left, and he was going nowhere until I'd answered his questions.

"Tom had been following Molly. He'd watched her here and at her home. He believed she loved him and got angry when she rejected him. He must have decided if he couldn't have Molly, then no one else would," I said.

Detective Noir's forehead wrinkled. "He confessed he killed her?"

"Not in so many words, but it was easy to read between the lines. Tom made up a feeble excuse about working and then going to the Stag and Wand for most of the afternoon. When I challenged him on the times, he became confused. He said he hadn't gone straight to the bar but had bought food and walked around. Maybe he walked right to the yard and accosted Molly then went drinking to blot out the memory."

"Silvaria, your imaginative ramblings are ridiculous. Forget about this," Emory said.

"I can't! Tom murdered Molly. He can't be allowed to get away with it."

Emory turned to Detective Noir. "You have the man in question?"

"We're holding him."

"Then it's under control." Emory faced me. "I must get your signature on these papers and lodged with the solicitor before the close of the day. All the financing is at risk if I fail."

"I'll sign the papers in a moment. Detective Noir, it sounds like you don't believe me about Tom."

"Silvaria, I must insist," Emory said.

"Emory, we have time," I snapped. "Detective Noir, I solved this murder for you. It was Tom. Perhaps your questioning hasn't been thorough enough, which is why you still haven't gotten a confession. Do you want me to assist?"

"I know how to question a suspect. And Tom gave me the same alibi as you," Detective Noir said. "I went to the Stag and Wand this morning, and the landlady confirms the time Tom arrived and left. It would have been impossible for him to have murdered Molly."

I drew in a deep breath. This was terrible news. "Are you sure?"

"I spoke to the landlady herself and two other customers who confirmed seeing Tom at the time Molly was killed. He's not her killer."

I glowered at him. I didn't trust this detective. What if he'd gotten things wrong? I should doublecheck Tom's alibi.

I sank onto the chaise lounge, my energy seeping from me like a weakened corpse standing on a tainted mound of grave dirt. If three people alibied Tom's whereabouts, had I made a mistake? Last night, I'd been certain Tom had killed Molly. And her reaction when I mentioned him was extreme. She was terrified of Tom. But she hadn't seen her killer, so maybe the terror came from her fear of being watched by him.

Emory sat and took hold of my hand again. "Silvaria, I know how much your serving girl meant to you, but you must forget this. Let the Magic Council figure it out."

"I haven't done enough," I whispered. "I was certain I was right."

"This detective has just shown you that you haven't got a clue what you're doing." Emory shook his head. "You just tried to have an innocent man charged with murder."

Tears filled my eyes. "I... I was so sure. The way Tom behaved last night. And he was stalking Molly. Surely, that's a crime." I looked up at Detective Noir.

He shrugged. "It is, but with Molly gone—"

I sat up straight. "In case it slipped your mind, she's very much still with us. And I hope you're treating her kindly."

"Of course, my apologies. Molly is being treated with respect." Detective Noir rocked back on his heels. "We may charge Tom with harassment but not with Molly's murder. Her killer is still on the loose."

"You must give up on this foolishness." Emory handed me a pen. "Sign these papers and focus on our future."

I looked at the three sheets of paper. I couldn't focus on the words. "I need some time."

"To do what? If you don't sign these, you can't join the business with me and Rupert. I thought that was what you wanted."

"It is. But this is all so much. If Tom didn't murder Molly, then who did?"

"Have you heard nothing I said?" Emory said. "It's not your job to solve this crime. This detective will eventually figure things out, won't you?"

Detective Noir was looking increasingly unhappy. "Of course."

"Who else are you investigating?" I said to him. "If Tom didn't do it, and Jack didn't do it, and we know Hettie wasn't capable—"

"Silvaria, this is unacceptable." Emory guided my hand to the papers. "I have an appointment with my lawyer in an hour. I can't be late."

"It would be sensible to have those papers checked by an expert," Detective Noir said.

I looked at him with surprise. "You don't think I know what I'm doing with this, either?"

He lifted a hand. "It's not my business, but you should always know what you're signing."

"I don't need your interference in this matter," Emory said. "You've already filled Silvaria's head with nonsense. And seeing you again has reminded me to have a serious conversation with your boss. It's clear you've had no training in how to conduct interviews, question people, or handle society members who are your superiors."

Detective Noir's eyes narrowed, but he said nothing more.

Emory returned his attention to me. "Silvaria, do you trust me? I want the best for both of us."

"Yes, of course I trust you."

"Then sign the papers. Unless you don't want to be involved in this business with me and your cousin. Are you picking crime solving over us?"

"No! And I do want to be involved in the business. Absolutely." I glanced at Detective Noir. He looked like he wanted to say something but then turned his head away.

I took a breath, carefully signed each document, and handed them to Emory. This was a signal I was ready to move on. I was done with this childish investigating and thinking I knew how to do the right thing for other people. I had to look toward my future with Emory.

Emory kissed my cheek and hopped up. "I must go. I can't keep the lawyer waiting." He dashed out of the door after giving Detective Noir a stern look.

I settled my hands in my lap and focused on the detective. "You appear to have something on your mind."

"I've already been told to hold my tongue once."

"Not by me. What is your concern?"

He hesitated. "Only this. You need to stop putting yourself in danger."

"I've already decided not to keep interfering with Molly's murder investigation."

"Not that kind of danger. Not everyone is as good as you."

"Meaning?" He sounded like my aunt Ruby.

"Meaning... it's not my place. I should leave."

With that elusive comment, Detective Noir turned and walked out of the room.

He left me alone with a pot of stewed tea, my macaroons, and a head full of questions.

Chapter 16

I was up so early the next morning, I even beat the servants' arrival. I'd dressed myself and made the best of my hair, the curls refusing to behave. I missed Molly's tender attentions when it came to dressing. Amanda did her best, but she was so rough, I'd rather look a little disheveled than have her dress me regularly.

While I'd been badly lacing my corset, I'd briefly considered finding a replacement for Molly, but it was too soon. No one else would take her place.

I crept down into the quiet kitchen and was looking for a cup when Arthur came in.

"Miss Digby, couldn't you sleep?"

"Not really. I had a lot to think about," I said. "I... I feel stupid after yesterday. I was certain I'd figured out who killed Molly. But now, we're back at the beginning. I've annoyed Emory, and I'm certain Detective Noir will never speak to me again." That last belief bothered me more than it should have.

Arthur bustled around, boiling water, stoking the fire, and setting out breakfast things for me.

"I'll eat in here. The dining room feels lonely when I eat on my own."

"Of course." He laid the kitchen table for me. "If I may be so bold, we all know how fond you were of Molly, and she cared very much for you, too."

"We still are fond of each other."

He bowed his head. "Of course. And it's natural you want to do the best for her."

"I do, but I've only made things harder for Detective Noir. I thought I was helping, but I made a horrible mistake by accusing someone who had nothing to do with her murder." I swallowed, hoping the lump of self-pity in my chest would shift. "I should do what Emory tells me. I need to prepare for being a good wife and helping in the business."

A rare flash of annoyance crossed Arthur's face. It was there for such a short time, I wasn't certain I'd seen it. "Miss Digby, you are meant for astonishing things. I have served this family a long time, and I've never met a cemetery guardian with such an extraordinary ability."

"It's not that special."

"I understand you don't enjoy your power and are considering alternatives, but if you can embrace your magic, you'll be an astounding guardian. Possibly the most influential and powerful this world has seen."

I blushed under his praise. "You're kind. I wish I could feel the same about my power."

He quietly poured the tea and set a rack of toast in front of me with a variety of different preserves. "Did your mother ever tell you she wanted to be a dressmaker?"

I stared at him with my mouth open, despite knowing how ridiculous it made me look. "You must be teasing me."

"I was only an assistant butler at the time. She had such a way of creating beautiful clothes. She designed her own gowns when she was younger and was never happier than when she was creating something. Your mother loved to show them off at the balls."

When Arthur paused, I was so enthralled by the story, I gestured for him to continue.

He smiled. "But then, when your grandparents died in such tragic circumstances, she put away that dream. The desire is still there, though. It's just buried under layers of obligation."

"Or grave dirt. Mother has never spoken of this to me." I reached for a slice of toast. "Do you think she'd be supportive of my desire to do something different?"

His smile faded, and the usual impassive neutrality was back in place. "The family legacy is everything."

I wrinkled my nose. "Something I'm well aware of."

"And sometimes, you must look at the bigger picture," Arthur said. "Cemetery guardians are rare and important. You keep the rest of us safe. If there were groups of rogue, powerful corpses roaming out of control, the world would be a different place."

I sighed. "I know. That doesn't mean I have to love what I was born into."

He was quiet as he freshened my tea. "Find a balance so you can be happy. Your parents are alive, so you have them to share the burden. Commit to embracing your power and your passions."

"Must I do both? Surely, there have been cemetery guardians who've decided not to follow this path."

"You are free to do as you wish. Of course, your parents will work hard to persuade you otherwise, but you can walk away from it all. That is your choice."

"Do you think it's the wrong choice? It's selfish."

"Not selfish, but I don't think you'd be happy."

"I'd feel guilty, but I am considering doing it."

"Perhaps a role in law enforcement at the Magic Council would be more suitable for your talents." Arthur's face remained impassive, but I sensed he was concealing a smile.

"Thank you, Arthur. I appreciate your words." I picked at my toast. "I need to close the door on my sleuthing. I just want to do one final thing before I finish this matter for good."

"May I be of service with that?"

"No. I'm going to visit Molly's family and settle compensation on them. I forgot to mention it on my previous visit, and my parents would do it if they were around. It's only right I give Molly's family something to help in their time of grief."

"They'll appreciate that." Arthur patted my shoulder. "Now, what shall I tell Cook to make you for lunch?"

As I left the house, I was in a contemplative mood. My conversation with Arthur had illuminated things for me. He was a man who rarely gave his opinion, so I always listened when he did. I could find a way to be happy with the different roles in my life. It would take trial and error, but I'd find a way.

I alighted from my carriage outside Molly's home and knocked on the door.

A short, plump man with a dark receding hairline and a double chin opened it. "Miss Digby! This is a pleasant surprise. I'm not sure you remember me, though. We've only met briefly a few times."

"Of course, Mr. Tomkins. I hope you don't mind me dropping by unannounced."

"Of course not. It's an honor to have you here. Come in." He stepped out of the way, and I entered the small living room. "Hettie mentioned you'd dropped by to pass on your condolences. I was sorry to have missed you."

"I did. I wanted to make sure you both knew I was thinking of Molly. She was such a kindhearted girl."

"She was a lot more than that." A tall, thin man with white hair down to his shoulders appeared in the kitchen doorway. He nodded at me. "Miss Digby. I'm Samuel Featherstone."

"Samuel is a friend of mine," Mr. Tomkins said. "We were just discussing some business."

I didn't like the way Samuel's gaze kept tripping up and down my body. "It's a pleasure to meet you, Mr. Featherstone. Is Hettie here? This also concerns her." I felt the need for female company under such intense scrutiny.

"She's out the back. She'll be in shortly," Mr. Tomkins said. "Would you like some refreshments?"

"No, that's kind of you, but my visit will be short." I tilted my head as a clunking sound reached my ears.

"Here she is." Samuel stepped out of the way as Hettie shuffled past.

She stopped when she saw me. "Miss Digby! Back again?"

"Yes, I thought it would be good to speak to both of you. I'd like to settle compensation on you for Molly's loss. I don't want to think of either of you struggling. From my understanding, she brought in a valuable income."

"That she did. And it's most appreciated, Miss Digby." Mr. Tomkins gestured to the couch. "Please, make yourself comfortable."

Samuel assisted Hettie into a high-backed chair. He took his time getting her settled, unnecessarily putting his hands on her shoulders and arms. Hettie didn't object. Perhaps there was a romantic connection between them, although he was much older than her.

When we were all seated, I began. "Mr. Tomkins, the Digby family intends to settle a year of Molly's wages on you. I hope it provides a small amount of comfort during this difficult time."

"That's incredibly generous," he said. "Since Hettie's accident, she's been unable to bring in any income, and with Molly gone, the burden falls to me. And I'm not getting any younger. My back plays me up all the time."

"It's not the poor girl's fault she can't work." Samuel patted Hettie's knee. "She's a good girl. Never any trouble."

Mr. Tomkins nodded. "She is. I'm glad to have Hettie living with me, even though she can't contribute. Her sweet nature more than makes up for that."

I glanced at Hettie. When we'd met, I hadn't thought her sweet. "I'm glad to hear that."

"At least we know Hettie won't end up like Molly," Samuel said. "I always knew something bad would happen to that girl."

"What do you mean?" I said.

His lecherous gaze ran over me again. "She wasn't settled swiftly enough. She was a wild one who needed taming."

Mr. Tomkins nodded along sagely as his friend spoke. "I tried to get her settled several times, but she always refused."

"Even I wasn't a good enough catch for her," Samuel said.

I tried to maintain a neutral expression, but I was horrified. Samuel was in his mid-fifties, and Molly was only slightly older than me. She wouldn't have wanted anything to do with such an old man.

"You made a proposal of marriage to Molly?" I said as serenely as I could.

"Several times. Each time, she turned me down." Samuel tugged on his frayed jacket. "I'm a respectable businessman, and I make a good living from the slaughterhouses, but it wasn't good enough for her. And when Molly started running around with those feckless young men with no sense, who whispered dreams in her ears, I knew how she'd end up."

"So did I," Mr. Tomkins said. "I begged her to accept your proposal, but she wouldn't take it seriously. I despaired about what to do with her."

"I don't like to say this, but it's been on my mind, so don't take offense," Samuel said. "What happened was probably a kindness to Molly. Her reputation was already tarnished. Soon, no one would have married her."

"Her being murdered was a kindness?" I couldn't hold my tongue.

"She'd have gotten herself in trouble. Molly would have ended up an unmarried single parent, and no one would have wanted her," Samuel said. "Not even me, and I'm always generous and forgiving to those who make mistakes."

"Molly wasn't like that," I said. "She always behaved respectably."

"You'll forgive me for saying this, Miss Digby, but you didn't know her," Hettie said. "Molly was always causing trouble. She thought she was better than everyone else because she worked in your household. I told her I could have done that job twice as good if it weren't for my injury."

"Molly never listened to sense," Samuel said. "She made her family agonize about what to do with her. We discussed several marriage options and even a job in the countryside to avoid distractions."

As the men debated Molly as if she was cattle that needed branding and sending off to the breeding field, I studied each man. What if they'd decided Molly was too much trouble, and she was better off out of the way? And Hettie, who had no love for her sister, would have supported that, especially now she was the center of attention.

When they paused in their discussion of Molly's deficiencies, I gently cleared my throat. "It seems like only yesterday I discovered Molly in my yard."

Mr. Tomkins gave a swift nod. "I still expect her to come through this door. Of course, I wouldn't want that to happen now. No disrespect to your business, Miss Digby, but we can't have a corpse here."

"Molly is content where she is," I said. "I mentioned to Hettie on my previous visit that my parents are locating a suitable site for Molly in one of our cemeteries. I'll take the best care of her. You won't ever have to see her again." And I had a feeling Molly would be very glad about that.

"Again, your generosity shines through," Mr. Tomkins said.

"When did you learn about what happened to Molly?" I said to Samuel.

He glanced at Mr. Tomkins. "I was here having lunch and then had some matters to discuss with Hettie." Samuel patted her knee again and gave it an overly friendly squeeze.

I hid my revulsion. He'd switched his affections from Molly to Hettie, and she didn't seem to mind one bit. If she wasn't so immobile, I'd be tempted to put her back on the suspect list.

"You were together when you got the news?" I said.

"We were all here," Hettie said swiftly.

"You didn't mention Samuel being here when I talked to you the other day."

"I forgot."

"Is that important?" Samuel said.

"No, I'm just curious. You all clearly had so much affection for Molly, so I'm glad you were here for each other during such a trying time."

"Well, it's all over now," Mr. Tomkins said. "I always knew Jack was a bad one."

"You think Jack killed Molly?" I said.

"Of course. I heard the Magic Council had him. He'll confess soon enough. He's not a bright lad. He gambles on his charm and good looks to see him through, but that won't do any good with getting off a murder charge."

"You're mistaken. Jack didn't kill Molly," I said. "He has an alibi."

"I heard he'd been arrested," Samuel said.

"Jack was taken in for questioning, but his friend, Devin, told the Magic Council they were together. It wouldn't have been possible for Jack to strangle Molly."

Hettie laughed bitterly. "Jack and Devin are as thick as thieves. They'd probably die for each other and definitely lie for each other."

My eyebrows rose. "You're suggesting Devin created a fake alibi for Jack?"

"Those two were always getting in trouble when they were younger. If ever the Magic Council came after them, they'd cover for each other. They got away with all sorts. I've heard them laughing and joking about it loads of times. Jack would tell Molly he could get away with whatever he wanted because he had Devin looking out for him."

"Have you told this to the Magic Council?" I said.

"I assumed they'd look into it," Hettie said. "From the rumors we've heard, Jack had been charged with the murder, so there was no need for us to get involved."

I stood from my seat, my pulse racing. "They must be informed. This is important news. Jack's been assumed innocent because of his alibi. From what you've just told me, it could be a lie."

"It most likely is," Hettie said. "Jack was an obsessive, stupid, hothead, and I'd seen him strike Molly. If he was already beating her, the next step would be to throttle her because she said something stupid."

"Molly never could hold her tongue," Samuel said. "I even had to speak to her sternly once or twice because she said inappropriate things."

I glowered at him. "Thank you for your time. I really must go."

"What about the settlement? When will we be paid?" Mr. Tomkins jumped to his feet.

"I'll send over the details shortly. You'll get your money." I dashed out after a brief goodbye.

I was so enraged, I didn't know what to do next. I was glad of my loose corset, which allowed me to take several deep breaths as I stood next to the carriage. My thoughts needed ordering. I'd just learned Jack had someone on his side who was happy to create a fake alibi for him.

The Magic Council still wasn't doing their job and believing feeble alibis without doublechecking them. This was unacceptable.

Despite Emory and Detective Noir's warnings, I wasn't giving up on Molly. I was seeing this through until the end.

Chapter 17

"Cook, a word." I gestured her out of the kitchen, where she was whisking a bowl of batter.

She wiped her hands on a towel and hurried over to me. "Is there something I can do for you, Miss Digby?"

"I'm looking for someone. Jack Solstice's best friend. His name is Devin Mustof. That's all I know about him. Do you know this person?"

"I'm not sure I can help. Hold on a second. Amanda, you know Jack and his friends, don't you?"

Amanda placed a tray of muffins in the oven before hurrying over. "That's right."

"Miss Digby wants to know about someone called Devin."

"Oh, Jack's best friend?"

I nodded. "I need to speak with him. It's urgent. Where can I find him?"

They exchanged a glance, but I didn't furnish them with more information. I couldn't let anyone know I was continuing to investigate what happened to Molly. I'd assured Emory I was done with this business, and Detective Noir had made it clear he didn't want me involved anymore. The fewer people who knew I was breaking those assurances, the better.

"He works at the Connell household. Lady Carolyn employs him. He does grounds work there," Amanda said.

"Will he be working today, do you know?" I was pleased to learn of Devin's location. I was on friendly terms with Lady Carolyn Connell, and we'd shared many delicious afternoon teas together over the years.

"He works full time, so he should be," Amanda said.

"What's his character like?"

"I don't know him well. He's always messing around with Jack, though, and they do everything together. Devin's been trying to get Jack a job on the estate."

"Thank you. I'll be out this afternoon. I doubt anyone will call for me, but if they do, let them know I'll be back by five if they need to see me." I didn't think anyone would visit, and Emory and Rupert would be dealing with new business matters, so I didn't expect to see them, but I had to cover my tracks as best I could.

"Of course. Are you dining in this evening?" Cook said.

"Yes. Whatever you're making smells delicious, so I won't miss it."

"Very good, Miss Digby." After casting one more curious look, Cook went back to work, and Amanda followed her.

I wrote a brief note to Lady Carolyn and gave it to Arthur. If it wasn't a matter of urgency, it could have been carried on foot, but this needed to be received immediately, so Arthur cast a spell to send it to the household.

The reply came back ten minutes later. Lady Carolyn was happy to welcome me to her home.

With no time to waste, I hurried to the carriage, climbed inside, and we headed to the Connell estate. They were an ancient family, well-known for their magical healing abilities. The grounds were something to behold, bursting with herbs, curious fungi, and huge old trees. It was a treat to visit and walk around the grounds. But this wasn't a social call.

I forced myself not to order the driver to hurry, despite impatience tying my stomach into knots. I was right this time, and Jack had lied for only one reason. All accounts of his character showed him to be an obsessive and violent individual. He'd been abusive toward Molly, and when she'd stood against his demands, he'd destroyed her.

As the carriage pulled up outside a large detached manor house with a dark gray slate roof and impressive buttresses, I was surprised to see Lady Carolyn at the open doorway. She gave a friendly wave and hurried down the steps, waiting by the carriage until I emerged.

She was a striking looking woman, pale, with long dark hair and a thin nose. She was always smiling and had a wide mouth and impressive lips.

She greeted me with two kisses before clasping my arms. "I was delighted to get your message. I was wandering around this place, wondering what to do with myself when it arrived. I can always be assured of excellent conversation when we meet."

"I'm glad my visit isn't an inconvenience."

"Not at all. And you've arrived in time for an early lunch. You will dine with me?"

"I don't want to impose. In fact, I'm here on a matter of business."

"Business with me?" Lady Carolyn stepped back, her gaze curious.

"No, but it would be wonderful to have lunch with you later, after I've completed my business."

She pursed her lips. "I was hoping we could discuss the Full Moon Ball. It's only three weeks away."

"Is it? It's escaped my notice." The ball was the highlight of the social calendar. Everyone who was anyone, and even a few who weren't, attended. Many marital matches were made at the ball.

Lady Carolyn touched my arm. "Oh, of course it has. I heard about the terrible events at your home. I'm so sorry for what happened to your servant. How shocking."

"That's appreciated. Molly was dear to me. And it's the reason I'm here. The Magic Council has been hopeless at finding Molly's killer, and I've received information that a key suspect faked an alibi."

Lady Carolyn's hand went to her bosom, which rose and fell at an alarming rate. "That sounds serious. But why are you here?"

"I'd like to speak to your grounds person, Devin Mustof. Is he available?"

"He's working on the lavender garden today. We had a bulk order for a sleeping tincture, so he's making sure the crop is ready to harvest. Follow me. I'll take you straight to him." Lady Carolyn caught hold of my elbow and led me around the side of the house. "You don't think he harmed Molly, do you?"

"No, but I think he knows who did."

The view opened to vast fields bursting with color. It was so delightful that I couldn't resist taking a moment to admire the beautiful blasts of brilliance and the vivid green of the swaying trees.

Lady Carolyn smiled warmly. "I've been here for over ten years, and I get the same look on my face every time I see the view."

"You're so lucky to have all of this."

"My magic demands it. Being surrounded by the herbs, color, and vibrancy of nature keeps my power topped up." She glanced at me. "You must be the same with the cemeteries and the bodies."

I pressed my lips together. "I feel my power surge when I'm around either of those things."

She patted my arm. "Tell me why you're so interested in speaking with Devin."

I hesitated. "I must insist on discretion if I reveal this information."

"You have it. This is only between us." Lady Carolyn leaned closer.

"His best friend, Jack Solstice, was romantically involved with Molly. The more I learn about Jack, the more concerned I am he had something to do with her murder."

"Even more shocking. Go on."

"The problem is, Jack has an alibi. Devin supplied it. But apparently, they've covered for each other before when they've been up to no good. I need to look Devin in the eye to see if he's lying about Jack."

"Oh! Then you must speak with him at once. Devin is an excellent gardener and has magical green fingers, but I've reprimanded him several times because he's been late or left early. It's always been because of Jack's influence." Lady Carolyn's sunny smile disappeared. "I've never taken to that young man. Jack's charming enough and could convince a genie to give him more than three wishes if he wanted, but there's something behind that charm that sets my teeth on edge."

"You think Jack could be a murderer?" I was thrilled to have my concerns validated.

"I'm not making any accusations, but it wouldn't surprise me. Don't worry, we'll get the truth out of Devin. This way. I see him over by my French lavender plot." Lady Carolyn marched us across the pristine lawn and over to a young man on his hands and knees, plucking out weeds. "Devin, Miss Silvaria Digby is here to see you."

Devin's head jerked up, and he stared at us. He stood and wiped the dirt off his hands. "Lady Carolyn, Miss Digby."

I nodded my thanks to Lady Carolyn. "Devin, I need to ask you some questions about your friend, Jack Solstice. I believe you provided him with an alibi for the time of Molly's murder. Is that correct?"

He tugged a dirty cloth from his pocket and gripped it between his hands. "That's right. He was with me. I needed a special tool, and he said he had the perfect one, so I invited him over. We weren't causing trouble. I was working the whole time, Lady Carolyn."

"You know you can ask for any tools for the garden," Lady Carolyn said. "There's no need to borrow them."

"I didn't want to trouble you, and I thought I'd get the job done quicker."

"What time was that?" I said. "When did Jack arrive with the tool you needed?"

Devin scratched his head. "At the time when Molly was murdered, Jack was with me."

"Devin, that's not an answer," Lady Carolyn said.

He gulped and stepped back, almost crushing a lavender bush. "I don't want to get in trouble, but I'll always support Jack."

"And that's what you're supposed to do for friends," I said. "But if your friend hurt another person, you can't stand by that. It makes you guilty by association." I wasn't sure if that was true, but I'd heard it said before, and it sounded impressive.

"He wouldn't do that. I mean, him and Molly had a few differences, but he'd never hurt her." Devin gulped again and looked around, as if assessing his escape routes.

"I've spoken to Molly's family, and they've said otherwise," I said. "Her older sister even witnessed Jack strike Molly."

Lady Carolyn gasped, and her bosom heaved some more.

Devin shook his head. "Hettie! Don't believe a word she tells you. She was so jealous of Molly, she turned green every time she saw her."

I could believe that, having experienced Hettie's bitter tongue when it came to Molly. "You're telling me Jack and Molly never had any serious troubles?"

"They argued, but all couples do." Devin gestured to the lavender. "I need to get back to work. Lady Carolyn, with your permission..."

She placed a hand on his shoulder. "Devin, you must tell the truth. If you lie, you could lose your position here. Jack won't be any use to you then, no matter how good a friend he is."

His forehead furrowed. "He's my best friend."

Lady Carolyn sighed and shot me a sympathetic look. "Perhaps he is being truthful."

I was getting nowhere using the conventional means of questioning. I stepped away and took Lady Carolyn with me. "Would you have any objection to me summoning assistance?"

"Of course not. Do you think the Magic Council could be of use?"

I gave a delicate snort. "I can guarantee they won't be helpful. I was thinking more about my special kind of assistance from beyond the grave. You wouldn't find it alarming if I summoned a corpse, would you?"

Her eyes widened, and her heaving bosom looked close to escaping its bindings. "Is that necessary?"

"I've found them effective when questioning suspects. They even helped me to apprehend a suspect who ran away."

"I won't be vulnerable to attack?"

"They won't be any trouble. The corpses listen when I issue a command."

Her tongue darted across her lips. "There's a small cemetery to the east of the estate. Could you find someone from there?"

"That's perfect. Let's give Devin one last chance before I recruit backup." I headed back to him with Lady Carolyn. "Devin, do you promise you're telling the truth about Jack?"

His anxious gaze went from me to Lady Carolyn. "I don't want trouble."

"Does that mean you lied for him?" I said.

"I need to get back to the lavender." He turned away and bent over his gardening tools.

I looked at Lady Carolyn and gave her a little shrug. I'd tried. She nodded at me.

After moving away from Devin again, I tipped back my head, closed my eyes, and unleashed the cold, crisp magic that summoned the corpses. My power felt around for a strong, capable corpse, one who'd be intimidating but not too terrifying. After a moment of searching, I discovered the perfect candidate. She was at rest but eager to find a purpose in her afterlife. I spun my power around her and felt her shift from her coffin to the fresh air.

"She's on her way," I whispered to Lady Carolyn.

"Although I'm afraid, I'm intrigued. Your abilities are remarkable."

"It's definitely an unusual ability. I'd rather have magical green fingers or the ability to heal the sick than corpse magic."

"I imagine you'll be looking after your own cemetery soon. After your marriage, of course."

"That's the plan." I decided not to mention it wasn't my plan, but my parents.

Lady Carolyn seemed to sense my evasion. She cocked her head. "And it's something you're looking forward to?"

"I'm sure everything will work itself out." My head turned as a wave of corpse power hit me. "She's here. Any second now." Despite my reluctance to deal with corpses, a rush of energy pulsed through me, filling me with a tingle of excitement.

Lady Carolyn squeaked. "You didn't... No! I didn't give you permission to do that."

I spotted the corpse approaching. "Is there a problem?"

Lady Carolyn's shaking hand pointed at the corpse marching toward us. "That's my grandmother." She wavered from side to side and fainted.

I caught her before she hit the ground and gently lowered her. What a mess. I'd aimed my power at the cemetery outside the grounds, but there must be family burial plots within the estate.

"My apologies, Lady Carolyn." I'd send her a gift basket to make up for the scare. Something with muffins and macaroons.

Once I was certain Lady Carolyn was comfortable, I stepped forward and raised my hands so the corpse would know me.

Devin had kept his head down, most likely hoping I'd leave him alone, but he glanced up and sniffed, his nose wrinkling as he smelled the new arrival. He dropped his trowel and backed away. "What have you done? What happened to Lady Carolyn? Is that... a corpse?"

"You refused to cooperate, so I recruited backup," I said. "The excitement has been too much for Lady Carolyn. She'll be fine, though."

Devin kept backing away. "You're crazy."

"I'm very sane, but I'm also very desperate. Tell the truth about Jack, and I'll send the corpse away. And I'd advise you not to run. It could trigger her hunt instinct."

"Hunt instinct!" His terrified expression froze. "Wait! Is that Duchess Cecilia?"

"I believe so. She's powerful, so be careful. Devin, please, stay where you are."

Devin turned and sprinted away.

Duchess Cecilia growled and raced after him. She shot past me and grabbed the trowel he'd abandoned.

Oh, dear. This wasn't going to plan. "Duchess Cecilia, some decorum, please."

For a corpse who looked like she'd been in the ground for at least a year, she was remarkably well-preserved and speedy. She gained on Devin as he raced through the lavender bushes, twirling the trowel around her head.

Devin turned, yelped when he saw she was in pursuit, and stumbled on.

I ran after them as fast as my soft-soled shoes allowed. "Devin, you're only making things worse."

"Worse! If she catches me, she'll kill me."

"She won't." Most likely, she wouldn't. "Duchess Cecilia, I command you to drop the trowel."

She gave an aggrieved growl but flung the trowel at Devin, missing his head by inches.

"Not like that," I muttered. I had to be more precise with my commands, or Devin would end up discovering what his afterlife was like much sooner than he imagined.

"Stop Devin," I commanded. "But don't kill him."

Duchess Cecilia increased her speed, lunged, and landed on Devin, taking him to the ground. By the time I reached them, he was eating dirt, and she was licking the back of his neck.

"Duchess, release Devin."

With a disgruntled snarl, she rolled off and stood next to him, looking ready to jump the second I gave the command.

Devin flipped onto his back, his eyes wide with panic. Wisely, he remained on the ground, a dirty, shaking mess.

I drew in a deep breath. "Duchess Cecilia doesn't want to hurt you, but Molly's murder can't go unpunished. I ask you again, were you and Jack together at the time she was killed?"

"It wasn't Jack. He loved Molly. He'd never hurt her."

"Were you together?" I said. "Don't make me order Duchess Cecilia to lick you again. If she does, she may add teeth to the mix."

Duchess Cecilia gnashed her remaining teeth.

He covered his face with his hands. "Jack was with me for some of that day, but he left for a while. Only half an hour, though. If he'd killed Molly, he'd have had to run to your house, choke her, and then run all the way back to me. It wasn't him."

"But he could have done it," I said. "And you're admitting you covered for him?"

"Because he's not the killer. Jack only told me to say we were together because he knew it would look bad for him."

"Silvaria, I must protest. This is too much." Lady Carolyn was sitting up, holding her head. "Return my grandmother to her final resting place."

"Lady Carolyn, I'm so sorry. Duchess, watch Devin. Make sure he goes nowhere." I dashed to Lady Carolyn's side and crouched beside her. "I had no idea I'd summoned your grandmother. Her energy was so robust, I couldn't resist."

"She was a headstrong woman when alive and took a long time to die. The doctor said three months, yet she lingered for eighteen. Grandmother was a stubborn creature, so I'm not surprised her corpse is as willful." Lady Carolyn accepted my arm and climbed to her feet.

"I got what I needed. I'll send her back immediately. I'm so sorry to shock you like that."

"Wait, just a second." Lady Carolyn smoothed her dress. "Grandmother died refusing to tell me where she stored her book of herbal remedies. It's an important textbook for my work."

"I'm sorry to hear that."

"She did it out of spite. Grandmother got bitter in her last few months." Lady Carolyn settled her clasped hands underneath her bosom. "Command her to tell me where the book is."

Duchess Cecilia grumbled, and more teeth gnashing occurred.

I lifted my chin. "I'll do you a deal. If you let me keep her so she can help me take Devin to the Magic Council, you'll find out where your book is."

Lady Carolyn narrowed her eyes. "I accept the terms. But she goes back in the grave the second you're done with Devin."

"Agreed."

As I issued the command to Duchess Cecilia to reveal her secret, while keeping an eye on Devin to ensure he did nothing foolish, I let out a sigh of relief.

At last, this case was solved, and Molly could finally rest in peace.

And so could I.

Chapter 18

I'd used my carriage to take me, Devin, and an enthusiastic Duchess Cecilia to the local Magic Council office, where Detective Noir worked.

My summoned corpse seemed glad to be aboveground. A quiet slumber in the dirt wasn't for everyone.

"She's looking at me funny," Devin said.

"That's because she's hungry, and you look like a tasty snack," I said.

"You can control her, can't you?" His voice wobbled, and he pressed back into his seat. "She won't eat me, will she? You hear terrible things about the walking dead."

"I'm always in control. The Digby family has been in control of corpses for centuries." I brushed a little dirt from the hem of my dress. "It's what we excel in."

He shivered and wrapped his arms around himself. "I'm glad it's not my power. I don't know how you sleep with all those decaying bodies waiting for your call."

"We all have unique talents. You nurture things and bring them to life, and so do I, in a way. It's simply that I control things that smell less fragrant than you do."

He was quiet for a moment, his gaze darting to Duchess Cecilia and then out the window. "I'm sorry I lied, but I know for certain Jack is innocent."

"That's for the Magic Council to decide. If he can't tell them where he was during that crucial half an hour, there's a good reason. You might be wise to choose a better best friend."

"He's always been there for me." Devin dug dirt out from under a fingernail. "I've not been the best behaved in the past. Jack's supported me. He even helped me with money before I got this job." His face paled. "Lady Carolyn's not going to fire me, is she?"

"So long as you cooperate with the Magic Council, you have nothing to worry about. And I'll put in a good word for you."

He nodded, his gaze lowered.

We pulled up outside the Magic Council office, and I climbed out. Duchess Cecilia stayed close to Devin as we walked in.

I stopped by the reception and was met by a startled looking man, who appeared uncertain whether to greet us or call for backup.

"I'm here to see Detective Noir. I have new evidence in a murder investigation he's leading. Tell him it's Miss Silvaria Digby, Duchess Cecilia, and Devin Mustof."

His mouth was open as he stared at the corpse.

"Hurry up. You don't want the place to smell of musty corpse." That reminded me to ask Arthur to have the inside of the carriage cleaned. Corpses left behind a less than pleasant aroma.

The man dashed away and returned a moment later with Detective Noir.

"Miss Digby! What are you doing here?" he said.

"Your job again."

He frowned at me. "I thought you'd decided to stay out of this investigation."

"I had, but then I learned worrying information about Jack Solstice's alibi. You've met Devin before."

Detective Noir nodded at Devin. "Of course. What's this all about?"

"Devin, do you want to tell the detective?" I said.

"Not really," he muttered.

"Perhaps Duchess Cecilia could persuade you otherwise."

He leaped away as Duchess Cecilia grabbed his arm. "I lied! I covered for Jack. He wasn't with me when someone strangled Molly. That doesn't mean he killed her."

Detective Noir's expression hardened. "Falsifying information in a criminal investigation is a crime. You've landed yourself in trouble."

Devin shot me a startled look. "You said I wouldn't get in trouble."

"I didn't exactly say that. I can help with your employment situation, but if the Magic Council press charges because you've impeded an investigation, there's little I can do." I glanced at Detective Noir. "Although I'm sure, since you're now fully cooperating, they'll be lenient."

Detective Noir scowled at me. "I need to re-interview you, Devin, and get a new statement."

He shrugged. "Sure."

"Not only that, but you must bring Jack in. He needs to be arrested. He lied about where he was, which makes him guilty," I said.

"Miss Digby, you need to return home." Detective Noir sounded exhausted.

"I'd like to sit in during Devin's interview. He's not forthcoming unless Duchess Cecilia is assisting with his memories."

"Come with me, Miss Digby." Detective Noir studied the corpse for a second. "I trust your accomplice will behave herself if you leave her alone?"

"She has impeccable manners. She's a duchess." I followed him into a small room at the side of the reception area. "Aren't you going to send someone to arrest Jack?"

"Miss Digby, investigations don't work like this. You can't use intimidation tactics to get information out of people."

"I haven't been."

"Summoning a corpse and threatening someone if they don't talk is exactly that." He ran a hand through his hair. "I'll be lucky if I can get any of this information included if the case goes to trial. If Devin reveals you used a corpse to force him to talk, it won't look good."

"I'd never use Duchess Cecilia to harm him. She was simply an encouraging tool."

"It was intimidation." He shook his head. "Miss Digby, go home. You can't be of any help. And take your corpse with you."

"Is this the thanks I get? I've uncovered a crucial hole in your case, and you dismiss me?"

"I'm not dismissing you." He stopped and drew in a deep breath. "But your situation is complicated. You shouldn't be spending your time investigating this murder."

"I must. You missed evidence. You were willing to accept Jack's innocence, yet it only took a small amount of digging and I discovered he'd fabricated his alibi."

"You're not as clever as you think. I was going back over the suspects and looking at all their alibis. I knew something had been missed, but I was using the proper channels. I didn't blunder in with an army of undead and terrify people into admitting things that might not be true."

"I don't blunder, and I don't terrify. Besides, my way is more efficient."

"Your way is inappropriate and causing me trouble." Detective Noir huffed out another breath. "What I'm trying to say is you don't need any more complications in your life. You're about to get married and go into business, and I expect you'll have a cemetery to look after soon. Surely, that's enough to occupy you."

"It's no concern of yours how I occupy myself." I turned to the door. "Now, if you'll excuse me."

"Wait a moment."

I turned back to him. "You'll do as I request? You're bringing in Jack and letting me sit in on Devin's interview?"

"After speaking to Devin and getting a new written statement from him, alone, I'll locate Jack and present him with this new information."

At last, Detective Noir wasn't being such an idiot. "Good. I'd appreciate an update when you've made progress. And I'd like to see Molly while I'm here."

"I'll see what I can do about an update, but Molly is resting. It's best if you don't disturb her."

"Oh, I don't like to bother her. I'll visit another day. I hope, by the time I see her again, I'll have found her the perfect resting spot, so I can give her some good news. And perhaps, by then, you'll have solved her murder."

"Perhaps." His quiet scrutiny made me uncomfortable. "You are one-of-a-kind, Miss Digby. I've never met anyone quite like you."

"You mean, a woman who speaks her mind and won't be cowed by authority?"

He arched an eyebrow. "Something like that. There's... there's something I need to tell you. It's not my place, but I'm worried."

"About what?"

Detective Noir appeared to have an internal debate for several silent seconds, before nodding. "Do you know who your fiancé does business with?"

The change in topic startled me. "Of course."

"And you have no problems with that?"

"You're referring to his new business partner, Rupert?"

He nodded. "You do know him?"

"He's my cousin. We grew up together. We lost touch years ago after a family argument, but he's recently reconnected with me. He's a decent man. I'm excited to be going into business with him."

His mouth twisted to the side. "Perhaps you should look into Rupert's activities over the last few years."

"Why? I imagine he's been getting educated so he could run a successful business."

"He's been learning some tricks but not the kind you'd want to get involved in."

I pulled myself upright. "Detective Noir, I don't like what you're suggesting. Rupert is an honorable man. There were problems when he was younger, but that's behind him. Besides, Emory would never associate with anyone who'd bring down his reputation or mine. Reputation is everything to Emory."

Annoyance flashed in his eyes. "As I've witnessed. He's always telling you to act a certain way. That doesn't bother you?"

It did, but it was no concern of his. "Emory does that because he cares. He doesn't want me to embarrass myself." I grew hot. Why was this irritating man poking around in my personal affairs? They had nothing to do with him.

"I hope you know what you're getting into, and Emory is looking out for you. I wouldn't like you to lose things you care about."

"Of course Emory will protect me. And we're going into business together because he wants us to support each other. That's what a man does when he's in love. I'm lucky to have him."

Detective Noir went quiet again. "Did you ever read those papers you signed?"

"The papers? Well, no. Emory took them before I had a chance. They had to be with the lawyer at a certain time. You were there when I signed them, so you know this."

"I know you won't appreciate my advice, but perhaps ask for a copy of the documents. Or maybe visit the lawyer and have a conversation about the business."

"There's no need. Emory told me all about it. I'm excited it's getting going so quickly."

"With your money invested?"

"We're all investing. It's important to the financiers they see we're committed by putting in our own assets. Any intelligent businessman would understand that. You have no experience in this field, so you shouldn't be giving me advice."

His cheeks reddened. "Of course. All I know is how to solve crimes, not conduct business."

"And it seems sometimes you don't do that particularly well."

Detective Noir marched to the door and opened it. "You can see yourself out. Make sure you take your corpse with you."

I glared at him for a second and then strode out. Detective Noir had an infuriating way of perplexing me. He did it every time we met. He was only behaving like this because he was annoyed I'd solved his case. I'd gotten it wrong with Tom but not this time. Jack was guilty.

"Duchess Cecilia, you're with me." I hurried out of the office without a backward glance.

We climbed into the carriage, and after I'd deposited my helpful corpse back to her resting place, I went home. I was exhausted, angry, looking forward to a hearty dinner, and not thinking about Detective Noir and his bumbling attempts to thwart my happiness.

I opened the front door, and the all-pervasive smell of grave dirt filled my nose. "Mother, Father? You're home early?" I hurried to their study, where they could usually be found. They sat around a small table, and they weren't alone. Mr. Tomkins was with them.

He stood as I entered. My parents remained in their seats, like two indifferent mannequins.

"Oh, sorry, I didn't know you had a guest. Hello, Mr. Tomkins." What was he doing here?

His expression was grim as he settled back into his seat. "I had to come as soon as I learned your parents were home. I was most concerned after your visit to our house and then you leaving in such a rush before we'd finished our conversation."

This was about the money. Greedy man. "You're not happy about the compensation? I assure you, you'll have it by the end of the week."

"Silvaria, what have you been doing in our absence?" Father said. "I've been hearing worrying tales about you gallivanting about unchaperoned. Are you really still investigating Molly's murder?"

I moistened my dry lips with my tongue. "I may have asked a few questions to ensure the truth was uncovered."

"As I mentioned, Miss Digby has been snooping. She just about came out and said I could be guilty of killing my Molly," Mr. Tomkins said. "As if I'd do such a terrible thing."

I hurried closer. "No, I didn't accuse you of that."

He turned his beady gaze on me. "I could tell you thought it."

I opened my mouth to protest, but I'd be lying.

"Go on, Mr. Tomkins," Mother said. "You were speaking before our daughter interrupted."

"Miss Digby asked where I was, and my friend, Samuel Featherstone, who is an excellent gentleman. She implied we could have been involved in Molly's murder by checking our alibis. I was so shocked after she'd left, I wasn't sure what to do. But after a conversation with Samuel, we agreed she needed to be taken into hand. Wild ways are dangerous in someone so young. Look what happened to my Molly."

"Just a moment," I said. "I'm not wild. I'm investigating a crime."

"Something you have no right to do." My father's icy tone stopped my planned argument from going any further. "If it weren't for Mr. Tomkins telling us what's been going on, you'd still be creeping around, asking inappropriate questions of innocent people."

I blinked away angry tears. "I need to find out what happened to Molly. You must understand that."

"This breaks my heart," Mr. Tomkins said. "Molly was as reckless and carefree as Miss Digby. I tried so many times to settle her with an older suitor because I knew that would help, but she wouldn't accept it. Perhaps that's what you need for your daughter."

"If you think I'm marrying you or your creepy friend, you're mistaken."

"Silvaria, that's enough," Mother said. "Mr. Tomkins wasn't suggesting that. It would be inappropriate."

Mr. Tomkins spread out his hands. "It would be an honor too great for me to handle. But a calming, older influence is what she needs. Someone settled and mature to teach her how to behave."

"I know perfectly well how to behave," I said.

"Clearly, you don't," Father said. "And perhaps Mr. Tomkins' idea isn't a bad one. Your mother and I had hoped allowing you to marry for affection would make you happy, but you've been so distracted. Not even the prospect of your upcoming wedding has calmed your nature and focused your mind on your duties."

"That's what love does to young people. It unnerves them and makes them excitable," Mr. Tomkins said.

I could barely keep a civil tongue. He was a meddling imbecile. Was Mr. Tomkins here to cause me trouble? Or perhaps I'd gotten too close to the truth, so he was trying to silence me, just like he'd done Molly.

But my parents' hard, impassive faces worried me. Surely they wouldn't deny me my marriage to Emory.

I needed to perform some swift damage control to stop things from spiraling. "Perhaps I have been too involved in the investigation. It devastated me when Molly was killed. When I'm married to Emory, I'll be more settled."

"You should consider finding her a marriage that combines two effective families rather than two foolish hearts," Mr. Tomkins said.

I jabbed a finger at him. "If you keep making such horrible suggestions, I'll set the corpses on you."

"Silvaria!" Mother stood and glowered at me. "You will not use corpses in such a way."

"You do. You use them all the time. I've seen you."

She drew herself up to her full height then turned to Mr. Tomkins. "Thank you for informing us of this troubling information. My apologies for any distress Silvaria has caused you. Arthur will show you out."

Mr. Tomkins stood, not happy at being so swiftly dismissed. "I could give you suggestions of suitable families Miss Digby could marry into. You may even find uniting with a family of humbler origins calms her even more."

Mother waved a hand, dismissing him. "Good night, Mr. Tomkins."

He scurried out under Arthur's guidance, and the door was closed.

I held my breath, waiting for my parents' cold fury to descend.

"Are you determined to ruin our reputation?" Father said.

The sensible thing to do was cower and nod, but I wasn't backing down. "What I'm doing has nothing to do with our reputation."

"You've been spending too much time with a lowly detective, grubbing around and asking questions you had no business seeking answers for. It's embarrassing. This bad behavior won't go unpunished," Father said.

"I'm doing it for Molly. For justice. That's the right thing to do. The Magic Council—"

"Magic Council employees are the experts in solving crime." Mother shook her head. "Go to your room. We need to discuss what to do with you."

I wanted to argue, but there was no point. I'd seen that look on their faces before. I'd humiliated them, and I wouldn't get away with it.

I turned and hurried away. I was halfway up the stairs, when my mother called my name.

"And just to be clear, not only aren't you a detective, but you're also not a dancer. First thing tomorrow, your cemetery guardian practical sessions formally begin. We'll be training you so we can erase this rebellion for good. Make sure you're ready."

I failed to stop the tears from falling as defeat washed over me. I fled to my room, slammed the door, hid my face in my pillow, and cried.

Chapter 19

After sobbing myself to sleep last night, I didn't look or feel my best. All I wanted was to remain in bed and feel sorry for myself, but my parents wouldn't allow that. And neither would I.

I didn't want this life my parents presented me, but it felt like I had no option but to accept. My bones ached with the sadness of my predicament. Was I doomed for a life of cold indifference, damp cemeteries, and musty corpses? There had to be an alternative, but I'd yet to discover it. And while my glum mood hung over me like a moldering shroud, I couldn't see a way out of this situation.

There was a light tap on my bedroom door.

I mustered a tiny amount of energy, but even breathing felt like an effort. "Come in."

Amanda appeared. "Would you like help to dress?"

"No, thank you, though. My plans for the day only require a simple black dress and for my hair to be tucked out of the way. I don't want an angry corpse getting hold of it and yanking it out."

Amanda's eyes widened. "That would be painful. Perhaps some nice jewelry, though?"

I couldn't be bothered with my appearance. My parents would pay little attention to what I looked like, and the corpses wouldn't care. They were like faithful dogs. Providing I offered a kind word, I could dress like a pox ridden pot washer, and they'd still love me. "No, that won't be necessary."

"Cook has made you a special breakfast. She thought you might need it, given your busy day."

I had no stomach for food, even though whatever Cook made would be magnificent. "Share it with the rest of the servants."

"You must eat," Amanda said. "Your parents have planned a full day of activity. They told Cook not to expect them back until after midnight."

"I'll eat when they do. They always take supplies."

Amanda's nose wrinkled. "They requested dried goat jerky and apricots. That's it."

"Then that's what I'll eat." It could have been cardboard, and I wouldn't have cared. My appetite for everything had been snuffed out after my world fell apart yesterday.

After a moment of hesitation, Amanda backed out of the room and closed the door.

I counted down from five then pulled myself out of bed, washed, and dressed in the plainest, drabbest outfit I could find. It matched my mood.

My parents were waiting by the front door as I came down the stairs, the door open. They barely glanced at me as they strode outside, so I trudged behind them and into the waiting carriage.

"We'll set you to work on three new corpses that arrived in Whitehaven cemetery a week ago,"

Father said. "They're restless for different reasons. You need to find out why and quieten them."

"Of course, Father," I muttered.

"Then we'll move to group control," Mother said. "Corpse uprisings are rare, but they happen. That's when lives are lost. We must always ensure we have complete control over the corpses. That'll require your concentration."

I held in a sigh. "Of course."

The rest of the journey continued in silence. I was sulking and couldn't figure out a way to shift my bad mood. My parents didn't care enough to assist me, so I was alone in working out how to extract myself from the gloominess. Perhaps this would be my life. Barely tolerated by my family, condemned to a life among the dead, and only having the briefest amounts of joy from my married life.

I clenched my hands. I was being too hard on myself and my upcoming marriage. Perhaps I would hate every second of dealing with the corpses, but I had Emory, our business, and Rupert was back in my life. And I could attend as many dances as I desired, once I was married, and have plenty of fun. The situation wasn't without hope.

As the carriage stopped outside the Whitehaven cemetery gates, that small amount of hope snuffed out. Even though we weren't even inside the damp, moss covered cemetery walls, the dead were calling me, and I sensed their restless energy.

"Let us take a moment to breathe that in." Father took my hand and then my mother's and closed his eyes. "Open your hearts to the power of the dead. This is what drives us. This is what cemetery guardians protect. This is our life and our legacy."

I mumbled the words back to him.

Mother opened the carriage door. "Let us begin."

The rest of the morning was taken up in a blur of foul decay, shambling bodies, and grave dirt. I had no trouble calming the three restless corpses presented to me. One had a request he wished to pass to a loved one. The second was unhappy with the situation of her grave, and the third simply didn't understand she was dead.

"Excellent work, Silvaria." Mother briefly squeezed my shoulder. "You're a natural."

I simply nodded. Would I ever get used to the smell of decay?

She stepped in front of me and caught hold of my other shoulder. "Why do you resist? This is what we were born to do. It should bring you joy."

"Does it bring you joy? Can you say you're content to deal with corpses every day and be around my father? You're so cold with each other."

Her expression hardened, but for once, she didn't walk away when I asked a difficult question. "I've experienced love for people and things. It didn't make me happy. It made me foolish. I made mistakes because I followed my heart rather than my head."

"Do you mean your dressmaking?"

Her eyebrows flashed up. "How do you know about that? I've never told you."

I wasn't getting Arthur in trouble by revealing my source. "I don't remember who told me. That was your passion? You wanted to do that for a living?"

"It was a fantasy I tried to live for the briefest amount of time. It got me in trouble, and there were several instances when corpses ran astray because I wasn't paying attention. My focus was on something frivolous. Lives were put at risk."

"People died?"

"Fortunately, not. But it was more because of luck than my sound judgment. When I realized how selfish I was being, I changed my ways and put aside childish fantasies. I focused on what was important for everybody else." Mother smoothed a strand of my loose hair. "We don't challenge you to be unkind, but you must accept your life isn't your own. We have an obligation to help other magic users' remains safe and an obligation to the corpses who are restless and require support. We're the last line of defense. This is what I hold close to my heart, and this is most important to me."

Above me. She didn't say it, but the understanding was there. "But your marriage. You and Father are more like business partners than husband and wife. You've never wished to fall in love and be adored?"

"I adore your father in my own way, and he does the same to me. By uniting our families, our powers increased. And our union created you." She studied my face, although I wasn't certain what she was looking for. Cowed acceptance, defeat, servitude? "Silvaria, we're aware you're hesitant about taking up the mantle of cemetery guardian, but when you embrace it, your power will blind both of us. You're unique."

"What if I don't want to be?"

"Some things we don't have a choice about. And I see how well the corpses respond to you. Your talent requires no effort."

"It leaves me dead inside. What if I want more?"

Mother shook her head and sighed. "If you turn away from your responsibilities, you must accept you're also turning away from the people who need you most. The magic users who are vulnerable to rogue corpses and the corpses themselves. Is that something you're prepared to live with?"

"Silvaria, your next challenge is ready." Father walked toward us. Trailing behind him were three corpses. They were large males in various states of decay.

"Think about what I've said," Mother said.

I didn't want to. I hadn't asked to be born into this life. Why should I give up everything I loved because of this impossible, hateful choice? I turned away and focused on my father.

"These three gentlemen have been causing a disturbance in the cemetery. For the last six months, they've refused to rest. Can you think of any reasons that may be?"

I shoved down my misery and focused on the corpses. "They're unhappy to be here?"

"They're content in this space. Their last wishes have been fulfilled, and they receive regular visitors, so loneliness isn't an issue."

I studied each corpse. The magic fizzling off them was different. It pinged against my skin and made me want to scratch. "They're dark magic users. They want to grow into that darkness."

"Very good," Father said. "What do we do with corpses tainted with dark power?"

"They're forbidden from using the power, but it must be channeled, or it'll grow unstable."

"And what do you suggest we channel it into?"

"We can use different vessels. A modified ghost jar or a stone. Something sturdy. Anything would do if it had the right magic attached to it."

"We'll leave you to make the final decision as to how to channel the dark magic. You'll not be assisted in this challenge," Father said. "We'll be back in thirty minutes. Make sure each magic user has had their darkness quenched and they're ready to return to their graves."

I got a small thrill from dealing with dark magic. It was satisfying to stop the bad guys from winning.

I watched my parents until they were out of sight then turned to the corpses and cracked my knuckles. "So, which one of you has been the most badly behaved?"

The corpses gave their own morbid versions of a smile, revealing missing teeth and decaying jaws.

There were no ghost jars to hand, so I collected three large stones and imbued them with a containment spell. I set each stone down close to the corpses and opened a channeling portal for their magic to slide along. "Gentlemen, shall we begin?"

The largest corpse on my left side lunged, his dark power crackling between his palms.

I kicked the stone, so it whacked his leg, and his power zapped from his hands and into the stone.

His expression turned puzzled, and he stopped moving.

"Got you!"

The other two corpses circled me, their smiles gone. They knew I meant business.

"We can do this the nice way. I know you're not in control of your power because darkness has taken you, but this doesn't have to be violent." I ducked and flipped into a forward roll to avoid being grabbed from behind.

The two remaining dark magic corpses flashed their power at me, while the first corpse was content to watch the tussle.

I grabbed a stone off the ground and hurled it at the nearest corpse. It smacked into his chest, and a flare of brilliant white light encased him. He groaned then stood with his arms hanging limply at his sides.

"Almost there." I scooped up the final stone and circled the last corpse. "Why don't we have fun?" I gestured the corpse closer with two fingers. "Do you dance?"

He snarled and sprang at me. As we made contact and his teeth snapped close to my neck, I smashed the stone into his back. My power flashed through him, and he shuddered in my arms. His teeth stopped snapping as I caught his hands and positioned him in a formal dance pose.

"I don't suppose you salsa, but perhaps a gentle waltz? One, two, three, one, two, three. You'll soon get the hang of it."

His gaze grew startled, but there was no malevolence in his eyes as we shuffled together. He lost a toe when I mis-stepped, though.

"My apologies. You two, provide the music. A gentle hum will keep us in time."

After a second of hesitation, the watching corpses began off-key humming.

I danced my partner around and around until I was dizzy and laughing. Then I swapped partners and danced with the other corpses. Although the smell wasn't pleasant, this was almost enjoyable. My partners weren't light on their feet, but they also weren't complaining.

Someone loudly clearing their throat close by made me stop. I'd been so caught up in the dancing, I'd lost track of time.

I jerked away from my dance partner and turned, expecting to see my parents looking on with disapproval. It was Detective Noir. "Oh! You're here. I hope you've come to thank me."

He glanced around, his expression set in the grumpiest scowl I'd ever seen on his face. "Not exactly. Are you alone?"

"Only if you discount my three wonderful dance companions."

Detective Noir's gaze flickered over the corpses. "I stopped by your house and was informed you were working with your parents."

"You were informed correctly. Just a moment." I gave the corpses a simple command to return to their resting places, and they ambled away. "Why are you here, Detective?"

"Silvaria, who is this?" Father strode over with a large pot of grave dirt in his hands, my mother beside him.

"Detective Tristan Noir, these are my parents."

He nodded. "Mr. and Mrs. Digby. I'm glad you're here, too."

"Why is that?" Mother said. "You've been leading our daughter astray as she investigated Molly's murder. You're not welcome in this cemetery."

"I'm sorry to hear that. Miss Digby was useful in helping calm Molly when she became agitated. And I thought her motives for investigating the case were innocent. I've been mistaken."

"I don't understand," I said. "Detective Noir, why are you here?"

"There's been a development in the murder investigation." He kept his scowl in place. It was almost intimidating. "Jack Solstice has been released without charge. He didn't murder Molly."

I gasped. "But he lied about his alibi."

"He may be an idiot and a liar, but he's also innocent. Jack panicked and got Devin to fake an alibi because he knew people would suspect him. He had a troubled relationship with Molly and made a mistake."

"Are you certain? How do you know he wasn't with Molly when she was killed? You can't take Devin's word for it."

"Someone else saw Jack with Devin at the time Molly was killed," Detective Noir said. "Another member of Lady Carolyn's household. It would have been impossible for Jack to have been in the yard with Molly. He's an innocent man."

My parents were uninterested in this information. My father inspected the grave dirt, while my mother looked for corpses to deal with.

"Then it was Molly's uncle. He's an unpleasant man. He showed up at our house and basically tried to get me married to someone unsuitable. He even told my parents I was wild and a difficult person. Tell him." I looked at my parents.

"Mr. Tomkins had some valid points." Father tasted the dirt on his fingers and nodded. "You're fortunate we've allowed your engagement to Emory to continue. We discussed a more suitable marriage for many hours."

I threw up my hands. "Mr. Tomkins killed Molly! She objected to being married off as if she was his property, so he silenced her to hide his failure. Mr. Tomkins even tried to get her married to one of his creepy friends. He's a wicked man. Have you looked at him again?"

Detective Noir sighed. "We've gone over all the evidence again. It left us with only one suspect."

I nodded. "Molly's uncle."

"No, some new information has emerged." Detective Noir stepped from foot to foot. "I'm sorry to have to do this, Miss Digby, but we have evidence that shows you murdered Molly."

Chapter 20

The dirt beneath my feet felt like it was giving way. It wasn't from a corpse crawling out of the ground but from Detective Noir's shocking revelation I could be a killer. Molly's killer!

"Did you just accuse our daughter of murder?" Mother said coolly.

Detective Noir nodded. "I'm here to arrest you."

I was so shocked I couldn't speak. I simply stared at him with my mouth open.

"What proof do you have?" Father was finally paying attention to the conversation. It had only taken his daughter being accused of murder to achieve such a feat.

"As suggested by Miss Digby, I reviewed the suspects and evidence in Molly's murder. It took some digging to find the connection. Everyone is so fond of Miss Digby and didn't want to say anything negative about her, but I have a statement from Molly's older sister, Hettie. She witnessed an argument between Molly and Miss Digby shortly before the murder took place."

"I've never argued with Molly. Even if we occasionally disagreed over the dress she wanted to put me in, Hettie wouldn't have seen those conversations. She's housebound because of her accident." I pressed a hand to my heart, worried it would burst out of my chest if it didn't slow.

"Hettie was clear about what she saw. She said you appeared at their door full of rage and accused Molly of stealing from you," Detective Noir said.

"What did Molly take?" Mother said.

"Nothing! Molly never stole from me."

"I have noticed some of your jewelry is missing," Mother said. "And you don't wear many of the rings or necklaces we've given you."

"Not because they've been stolen by Molly. I... I sometimes give gifts to the servants. I have so many pieces of jewelry, I'll never be able to wear them all."

"You admitted to giving Molly a ring that she passed on to Hettie," Detective Noir said.

"There you go. There's proof! I gave Molly a ring. It's not a crime. And it was mine to gift."

"Hettie believes your regular gifts gave Molly an idea. She realized you had more than you needed, so she took a few items to make extra money."

"She'd never do that. I don't know why, but Hettie is lying to you. We never argued, and I never accused Molly of stealing."

Detective Noir pulled an evidence bag from his pocket. "Do you recognize this necklace?"

I stepped forward and stared at it. "Of course. I recently gave it to Molly. It was a thank you gift because she agreed to join my household once I married Emory."

"Silvaria! That wasn't meant to be given away. It's extremely valuable and belonged to your great grandmother." Father inspected the necklace.

"Oh! I didn't know. You never told me where it came from."

"Are you sure you gave this necklace to Molly?" Detective Noir said. "It was found concealed at the bottom of her purse."

"Molly wasn't concealing it. She probably put it there after I'd given it to her. It's not the sort of thing she could wear at work, so she would have needed to keep it safe until she returned home."

"We'll have that back," Father said.

"It'll be returned once it's no longer evidence in a murder investigation." Detective Noir placed the evidence bag back in his pocket. "According to Hettie, Molly also had a small stash of jewelry hidden in her bedroom. The young ladies shared a room, so it was easy for Hettie to see what Molly was concealing."

"I don't believe it. Molly was my friend, and she wouldn't steal from me." If that was true, where had those jewelry items come from if Molly hadn't taken them? I couldn't accept she'd betray me in such a way.

"There's more," Detective Noir said. "A witness placed you in the yard with Molly moments before she died."

"Impossible! I was in my bedroom. I dealt with the coffin delivery and then returned upstairs. The delivery took longer than I'd expected, so Molly had already left. I went to the kitchen to look for her.

That was when I heard the scream and discovered what had happened. Your witness is mistaken."

"He was reluctant to tell me this information but said he had to do the right thing."

"Who is this witness?" Father said. "Do you consider him reliable?"

"I have discovered no reason for him to lie. This knowledge impacts him, too," Detective Noir said.

"Give me his name. I'll tell you if this gentleman is reliable or not," I said.

"I can't do that. But with the statement from Hettie, the discovery of your valuable necklace in Molly's purse, the stash of stolen jewelry we were shown, and the eye witness putting you at the murder scene," Detective Noir cleared his throat once again, "Miss Silvaria Digby, I'm placing you under arrest for the murder of Molly Tomkins."

I backed away, my hands raised. "I didn't do this. I love Molly."

"Don't make this difficult," Detective Noir said. "You had us all fooled. When you were so helpful with this case, I thought you wanted to help Molly. This whole time, you've been misdirecting me and implicating innocent people."

"I haven't. This is your error. Those people lied to you. You must find out why." I couldn't understand this. Why had a witness said I was in the yard? And why would Hettie lie about seeing an argument I'd had with Molly?

"You should go with Detective Noir," Mother said quietly. "We'll do what we can to help you out of this unfortunate situation."

I wanted to run as fast as I could and get away from this nightmare. I looked around for a way out, but all I saw were freshly turned graves and headstones.

"Do the sensible thing, Silvaria," Father said. "We'll speak to a lawyer and keep you safe. Just don't say or do anything else foolish."

My knees were so shaky, I doubted I could run even if I wanted to. And my parents were exchanging such worried glances, I was concerned they considered me guilty, too. What if they believed Detective Noir? Would they support me or abandon me, so I'd spend the rest of my life in jail for a murder I didn't commit?

"Let's go, Miss Digby," Detective Noir said. "I trust I won't have to put you in restraints."

I gulped back tears and shook my head. I looked at my parents. I desperately wanted a hug, but Father clutched his pot of grave dirt and Mother had her hands clasped, creating a barrier between us. I turned and walked away.

Detective Noir led me to a Magic Council carriage, and I climbed inside.

We pulled away from the cemetery, and I found myself unable to raise my head. I was stricken with horror. Could they really believe I'd kill Molly, someone I considered a dear friend?

"Does Molly know about this accusation against me?" My voice came out as a whisper.

"She has been told the new information. She's unhappy."

"Molly will know I'm innocent."

"She seemed confused, but admits she didn't see who strangled her, and because of that fact, it could have been you."

My stomach lurched. Molly was also abandoning me? "Did she also admit to stealing?"

"No, but she made little sense and retreated into herself after I informed her I'd be arresting you."

I couldn't speak for several moments and focused on stopping from bursting into tears.

"I'm sorry it has come to this," Detective Noir said, "but I have such powerful proof against you, this was my only course of action."

"Fake proof." I let out a shaky exhale. "What happens next?"

"You'll be taken to a cell, and I'll have you questioned as soon as possible."

"By you?"

"No, by a more senior employee of the Magic Council. It's believed I'm too close to this case to be impartial."

I smirked. He wasn't impartial enough to arrest me. "How long will that take? I must prove my innocence as soon as possible."

"Not long. Everyone wants this case resolved. And given your high profile and status, there is already media attention attached to this situation. The Magic Council never encourages scandalous reporting."

"You've been telling the media I'm a killer?" The news would be a terrible blow to my parents.

"No, but they always have their ears to the ground, especially when it comes to notable names who find themselves in trouble."

"I'm not in trouble. What happened to innocent until proven guilty?"

"That's a philosophy I believe in, too." Detective Noir's forehead wrinkled. "If you're innocent, I'll do everything I can to make sure you aren't charged."

"But if I'm guilty, you'll give me the harshest sentence? Do you think I've been deceiving you so I could get away with murder?"

"I'm letting the evidence speak in this case." Detective Noir clasped his hands together and dangled them between his knees. He clenched and unclenched his hands several times. "How could you?"

"Kill Molly? I didn't!"

"You were so believable. Was it all a trick? You made me grow fond of you, so I wouldn't see what you were really doing."

I stared at him with undisguised shock. "You have the strangest way of showing fondness. Every time we were around each other, you told me off or ordered me to stay out of your business."

"I didn't do that because I don't like you." He looked out the window. "You have such a strong spirit and an incredible sense of justice. I admired you. You're a striking, powerful young lady, and I wanted only the best for you. It was why I spoke up when your fiancé pressured you into signing paperwork you didn't understand. And I only told you to keep out of the investigation because I was worried about your safety. I never thought... I never thought you were deceiving me."

I was too stunned to process his words, so we continued the journey in silence.

When we arrived at the Magic Council office, Detective Noir led me to processing, took my details, and settled me in a cell.

"I'll be back soon. I expect your parents won't be far behind us," he said.

"Let Emory know I'm here, too. He'll move the moon and stars to get me out of this terrible situation."

Doubt flickered across Detective Noir's face. "Everyone who needs to know will be informed. Try to stay calm." He locked the door and left me on my own.

I paced the small, barren cell for several minutes. I settled on the cot in the corner, but then was on my feet again. This was wrong. All these lies being told about me. I'd always been kind and generous to people. I'd helped Hettie and her family, and now she was lying about me. And how did my jewelry get into Molly's possession? I'd given her a few things, but it sounded like she had a much larger stash.

It made no sense. And who was the witness who claimed to see me in the yard with Molly? All I knew was that it was a male. It wouldn't have been my father, since he was away dealing with corpses, and it wouldn't have been Arthur. Our handyman hadn't been around, so I was at a loss to figure out who it could be.

I waited for half an hour, and no one came. My despair grew. Where were my parents? Why weren't they defending me? And why wasn't Emory hammering at the door and demanding my release? These were the people who claimed to love me and wanted the best for me, but I was in serious trouble and needed help, and they were nowhere to be seen.

Another half an hour passed. Had I been abandoned? Did my parents and Emory believe the evidence the Magic Council had discovered? They'd turned their back on me for fear of family disgrace.

My parents had always been cold and reputation obsessed, but surely they'd protect their only daughter from such a tragedy of injustice.

A hardness settled around my heart as my wait continued. Aunt Ruby was right. I was too trusting. I looked for the best in people, even when they weren't kind to me and took advantage of my generous nature.

I hadn't flinched at Olivia's extravagant birthday demands. And all the times I'd supported Emory and not protested when he'd belittled my love of dance. And even though I'd told him so many times I didn't want to be a cemetery guardian, he was still pushing me into that life.

I'd even been soft-hearted with the servants, too. I'd never denied them when they'd asked for time off or an advance on their wages. I'd been happy to do it, because they were good people.

All this time, I was being taken for an idiot. Even my parents hadn't listened to my repeated protests and desire for a different life. They were focused on the family reputation and those wretched corpses.

Now a grievous mistake had happened, and I was alone.

The hardness around my heart grew into an ache in the pit of my stomach. I wasn't a defenseless, naive child. My parents said I had incredible power, so it was time I used it. If no one was fighting for me, I'd discover the truth myself. I'd unpick the evidence that proved I was Molly's killer.

I drew in several deep breaths and stilled my anger and panic. I discovered Molly instantly. She was close, but I couldn't embroil her in this. I needed corpses I had no bond with to assist me.

I passed over Molly's familiar energy and kept feeling, my magic trickling out, drifting through the magic wards around my cell and encircling the building. The cell wards drained my power, but I had so much, I could search for minutes before needing to take a break.

Finally, I found corpses strong enough to help me. I knew nothing about them, but they were close and needed a release of energy. I weaved my cemetery guardian magic through them and called them to me.

I didn't know where they were coming from or how they'd get to me, but I gave them a simple command. "Come to me. Protect me."

I dashed to the door and pressed my ear against it. I heard nothing for a few minutes, and then there was a yell and something smashed into a wall. I kept repeating my command, the cold guardian power burying into my fractured heart. "Come to me, protect me."

There were several more crashes, each time closer to the cell.

I backed away from the door and not a second too soon. It slammed open, and three enormous corpses loomed in the entrance.

I poked my head out the door. There were two unconscious guards on the floor. I didn't feel sorry for them. I had a mission to accomplish, and nothing and no one would stand in the way of proving my innocence and finding a killer.

One corpse touched me. It was a light, respectful touch, but it drew my attention to the business in hand.

I nodded at him and his companions. "Excellent work, my friends. Now, follow me. We need to get answers and clear my name of murder."

Chapter 21

The corpses had left their mark when they'd rescued me. We passed four unconscious guards, and several rooms had been barricaded by filing cabinets or tables.

I could hear voices, but no one was brave enough to step into the corridor.

There was no sign of Detective Noir, and I was glad about that. He may be incompetent and had gotten everything wrong about this case, but I still didn't want him injured or bitten by a corpse.

We dashed out of the office and raced along the street until we got to the end, and I found an alleyway. I gestured the corpses to take cover and then leaned against the wall and caught my breath.

They waited patiently for my next command.

My mind was full of questions and confusion, and it took me a moment to gather my thoughts. But I couldn't be hesitant. My freedom was on the line, and if I was charged with Molly's murder, a killer would get away with a heinous crime.

There was no point in going home. That would be the first place the Magic Council would look. And if I contacted my parents, they'd most likely tell

Detective Noir of my whereabouts. I could only rely on my corpses and myself.

"Molly's house. That's where we need to go. I must speak to Hettie and find out why she lied. And I have to see the jewelry Molly supposedly stole from me. Until I've witnessed it with my own eyes, I won't believe she was a thief." My gaze settled on the corpses. "My dear friends, you need to run fast and hard. I'm relying on you."

They nodded.

I inspected each one and selected the strongest and most well-preserved corpse. "You carry me. Keep me safe and do not drop me."

The corpse willingly held out his arms, and after sucking in a deep breath of pure air, I hopped into his arms and wrapped around him until I was secure. I gave them the address. "Let's go."

I squeaked as the corpse took off like a rocket. Despite his speed, I felt safe. I barely asked corpses to do things for me, but when I did, they never let me down.

I'd been so embroiled in disliking my power that I forgot the endless resources I had at my fingertips. Corpses were loyal, steadfast, and did as I commanded. Why hadn't I appreciated that until now?

I had to close my eyes to stop them from watering because we moved so quickly. I gave the corpse a quick pat on the shoulder. "Excellent work, my dear friend."

He grunted a response. It sounded like a happy grunt.

We sped along for twenty minutes, and I felt shaken to the bone by the time I recognized Molly's street.

"Slow down. We're almost there. You can let me down now."

The corpse carefully set me on my feet, and they stood in a line, waiting for their next command.

There was no time for tact. I had to get answers from Hettie. Perhaps she was jealous of me, too, which was why she wanted to get me in so much trouble. Hettie's injury made her bitter toward everyone, but I couldn't believe she was cruel enough to ruin my life so spectacularly by faking evidence to make me look guilty.

I tilted my head as voices drifted toward me. That sounded like Emory.

"Follow me." I gestured to the corpses as I made my way past the row of terraced houses. I paused at the last one. It was him! His voice was much clearer, and he wasn't alone. He was speaking to a woman.

I poked my head around the corner. Emory was with Hettie. Of course. He was confronting her, just as I intended to do. Emory was looking for evidence to show Hettie lied, and I was innocent.

He was a good man and a wonderful fiancé, and I felt bad about doubting him. He was getting to the bottom of this mystery and making sure I wouldn't stay in the cells.

I glanced back at the corpses, and my gaze shot over their shoulder. There was a small group heading toward us. They were dressed in black and wore wide-brimmed hats. The Magic Council was onto me already, but I needed more time.

I counted six individuals, and although I couldn't see their faces from this far away, I was certain one of them would be Detective Noir.

"My friends, I have your next command. Stop those individuals from reaching me." I pointed at the unwelcome arrivals.

One of the corpses rested his hand on my shoulder, and the word *bite* flashed into my head.

I jerked back. I had no idea corpses could communicate telepathically. "No, don't bite any of them."

They growled their unhappiness.

"You may hold them, lick them, and suck their skin. That'll give you a nice taste, but no bloodletting. They're not chasing me because they want to hurt me. Hold them off for as long as you can. Now, go."

The corpses sprinted toward the group. There were several yelled warnings for them to stay back before the magic started flying. I could only watch for a few seconds, but the corpses floored all of them in an impressively brutal display of force.

I didn't want to interrupt Emory while he got the truth out of Hettie, but I wanted to hear what they were saying, so I crept around the side of the house on my tiptoes.

Footsteps approached from inside the house, and my eyes widened as my cousin Rupert emerged. He must have learned about my arrest too and was helping Emory get the evidence to show I was innocent.

I was so glad I had them on my side. With my parents vanishing the second trouble came my way, at least I had Emory and Rupert to rely upon.

Emory stepped closer to Hettie and loomed over her. I wanted to tell him to stop because it looked so threatening, but he must be so concerned about me that he wasn't thinking straight.

Hettie cowered beneath him, grabbed the package he held out for her, and tucked it under her arm.

"You must keep quiet," Rupert said, "or you'll go the same way as your sister."

My mouth fell open. Rupert had just threatened to kill Hettie. That was going too far.

"I won't talk. You came through for me," Hettie said.

"I still don't trust her," Emory said to Rupert.

"We'll keep an eye on her, make sure she doesn't get greedy," Rupert said.

I was confused about what they were talking about. Why would Hettie be greedy?

"It's going as planned," Hettie said. "Miss Digby's been arrested."

"She hasn't been charged yet," Emory said.

"It'll be soon, once the Magic Council has all the evidence. I won't let you down."

"Silvaria! Call off your corpses," Detective Noir yelled.

I cringed against the wall, but Detective Noir's voice carried. Rupert, Hettie, and Emory looked over and saw me.

The color drained from Hettie's face, while Rupert and Emory looked stunned to see me.

A quick glance over my shoulder revealed my corpses were being restrained and Detective Noir was racing toward me. I only had a few seconds left. Would that be enough? Emory and Rupert must have found out enough from Hettie to get the wheels turning and save me from this nightmare.

I hurried toward them. "I'm so glad you're here."

"You are? I mean, I'm surprised you're here, too," Emory said. "I thought you'd been locked up. They let you go?"

"No, but I got out. I panicked when no one came to help me." I held out my hands to Emory.

He simply stared at me. "How did you get out?"

I was surprised by his tone. Emory wasn't happy I was here. It must be the shock of seeing me. "I summoned corpses, and they broke me out. I was coming to speak to Hettie, but you beat me to it. Has she told you the truth?"

"Um... we're working on it." Emory exchanged a worried glance with Rupert. "You shouldn't have escaped. It looks like you're in even more trouble than you already were."

"I can't worry about the Magic Council. How did you know where to find Hettie?" I said. "I didn't realize you knew the family."

"You must have told me where she lived. You've been so obsessed with Molly's murder, it's all you've talked about." Emory looked over as Detective Noir drew nearer. He shoved Hettie away from him. "Didn't you say you needed to be somewhere?"

"Hettie must stay and explain herself," I said. "Detective Noir will want the truth, so he can drop the charges against me."

A second later, Detective Noir arrived beside me. He was panting and his shirt torn. "Miss Digby, I'm adding your illegal use of corpses against us to your charges. Throughout this investigation, you've done nothing but create problems for me."

"Only because you've gotten things so wrong," I said. "Arresting me for Molly's murder was the unpleasant icing on the cake. Emory and Rupert will show you I'm innocent. They've been talking to Hettie."

Detective Noir stared at the two men. "Is that true?"

Rupert took a step back. "We thought we could be useful."

"I'm still so amazed you're here, Silvaria," Emory said.

"I couldn't do nothing. And although I don't approve of you threatening Hettie, Rupert, I understand you're panicked about my awful situation," I said.

He looked at his feet. "She wasn't talking."

"What did Hettie mean by the plan? She said everything was going to plan," I said.

Detective Noir caught hold of my arm. "That's enough. You can't escape and then threaten important witnesses in this case."

"I'm not threatening Hettie, but you believed her statement without question. Why did she conceal the alleged argument she saw between me and Molly the first time you questioned her?"

"Hettie said she liked you and didn't want to think the worst."

I twisted my arm out of his grip. "Detective Noir, this case has shown you that things are often not what they seem. I've learned that, too. I'll admit, I made a mistake when I thought it was Jack, then Molly's stalker, and then Mr. Tomkins. I jumped to conclusions without having the proper evidence, but I know better now. Question everything, assume people aren't always telling the truth, and dig deeper than you think you need to."

A momentary flash of surprise crossed Detective Noir's face. "That's all true, and I've also been doing that. That's what brought me to the evidence that proved you killed Molly."

"Then you're still getting it wrong. I didn't. Hettie, tell Detective Noir you lied to him. I don't care why you did it, so long as you're truthful now. You can undo this damage."

Hettie blinked rapidly but said nothing.

More heavy footsteps approached, and my corpses appeared. They looked battered by the magic but were still standing and there to protect me.

"Hold your position," I said.

They became motionless, although restrained aggression radiated off them.

Rupert and Hettie shied away from the corpses. Emory simply wrinkled his nose.

"They mean you no harm," I said, "but will do anything I command them to do. Hettie, the last thing you want is to get up close and personal with any of these gentlemen."

"Miss Digby, don't threaten people," Detective Noir said.

"It was a statement, not a threat. My corpses look after me. It's taken me time to realize they're the only people I can fully rely on."

"People! They're monsters!" Rupert said.

Emory glared at me. "Silvaria, you're talking nonsense. You have me and Rupert. We'll always take care of things for you."

"Sorry, of course I do." I wanted to hug him and get some comfort, but Emory still appeared guarded. "What has Hettie told you? And what was in that package you gave her?"

Rupert kept looking down and refused to meet my gaze. Emory seemed at a loss for what to say.

"Please! I need answers. You were here to help me, weren't you?"

"What else would we be doing?" Emory said.

I looked at Detective Noir. "Did you tell Emory and Rupert I'd been arrested?"

"I haven't been able to contact either of them to give them an update about your arrest. I tried several times while waiting for my boss to finish his meeting so he could interview you."

"How did you know what happened to me?" I said to Emory.

"Everyone's gossiping about your arrest. It's all around town."

That made sense. It was most likely why my parents had gone to ground. If they ignored my embarrassing situation for long enough, it would crumble away like an air exposed mummy.

"Who told you?" I said. "Was it Cook? Amanda?"

Emory tugged at his collar. "Yes."

"Which one?"

"Does it matter? I'm helping. Our reputations are on the line, and I'm still standing up for you." His cheeks were flushed, and he was sweating.

As much as I wanted to believe Emory, something felt wrong. Even Detective Noir sensed it, because he'd stopped reprimanding me and was staring at Emory.

My gaze went to Hettie. "Why did you lie about me?"

She pressed her lips together, and her pleading expression shifted to Emory.

"Look at me, not him. What is in the package Emory gave you?"

Hettie squeezed her arm against her side, the package tucked securely under her armpit.

"We should go," Rupert said. "We don't want to get in the way of an investigation, and we've done everything we can."

"You've proven my innocence, have you?" What was wrong with my cousin? Why wasn't he sticking up for me?

"We've done the best we could, but Hettie said she was telling the truth. Isn't that right, Emory?"

Emory simply nodded, a muscle flexing in his jaw.

I looked at the three nervous faces in front of me, and a cold worse than any grave chill sank into my bones.

The corpses growled and stepped closer, as if sensing my distress.

My throat became so tight, I could barely breathe. "Say it isn't so."

Emory glanced at Rupert again. "We're making things right."

My knees shook, but I refused to let the shock consume me. "You're not here to prove my innocence, are you? You came here because you and Rupert framed me for Molly's murder."

Chapter 22

No one spoke for what felt like minutes. My knees kept shaking, I struggled to breathe, and I felt sick and dizzy. My hope shriveled inside me as neither Emory nor Rupert denied my accusation.

"Say something! One of you, tell me this isn't true." My fingernails dug into my palms as I clenched my hands. Emory was supposed to love me. Why was he doing this?

The silence continued, interspersed now and again by the growing growls from the corpses as my anxiety filtered into them and fueled their rage.

Detective Noir squeezed my elbow and then let go. He stepped closer until he was right by my side, his warmth sinking into me. "You don't remember me, do you, Rupert?"

Rupert's gaze flicked to him. "I've had little to do with the Magic Council around here."

"True enough. But your criminal record suggests you know many of my colleagues."

My head jerked around to stare at Detective Noir. "Rupert doesn't have a criminal record. He was wild when younger, but he never broke the law."

Sympathy flickered in Detective Noir's gaze before he focused on Rupert. "Unfortunately, that's incorrect. Rupert started out with basic cons, convincing vulnerable people to part with their money or valuables. He pretended he'd invest them. They never got their investments back, did they?"

"There's never investment without risk. I always explained that," Rupert said. "It's not my fault people don't understand. And when I was learning my trade, I made a few mistakes. It happens."

"You lost people their money?" I said.

"Rupert's conned people out of millions," Detective Noir said. "He has numerous shady businesses established, and they're involved in money laundering, processing stolen goods, or setting up shell companies to take people's valuables on the pretense he'll double their money."

"You have the wrong person." My voice was a whisper. I stared at Rupert as if seeing him for the first time. This wasn't my cousin, the young, carefree boy I'd grown up with, who teased me, made mud pies with me, and chased me around the grounds. This was a stranger.

Rupert shrugged, and his expression flattened. "If you had any evidence to prove that, I wouldn't be standing here."

"After I learned of your association with Miss Digby, I reopened several unsolved cases with your name attached to them. We're reprocessing the evidence and looking for new witnesses. It won't be long before we have enough to put you behind bars."

My chest grew tight, and I rested a hand over my racing heart. "Emory, did you know about this?" He wouldn't have gone into business with my cousin if he'd known about his corruption.

Emory looked almost as blank-faced as Rupert. "As he said, sometimes things go wrong."

"Miss Digby, do you know what you've signed over to Emory and Rupert?" Detective Noir said.

"That's none of your business," Emory growled out. "Silvaria is my fiancée. We share everything."

I gulped down my panic. "I never got around to reading the paperwork, and I didn't get a copy, as you suggested. Why? What did I sign?"

"You weren't under any pressure to sign those documents," Emory said. "You willingly signed them."

"You... you put me under some pressure. I wanted to read them, but you said they were a formality so we could form the business partnership. And you said they had to be with the lawyer by a certain time. I didn't want to hold anything up and cause problems." I looked at Detective Noir. I also hadn't wanted to look like I doubted my fiancé in front of him. Had I really been such a fool?

"Emory never wanted you to read that information," Detective Noir said. "Now, I can't be certain, because I haven't seen the documents, but I suspect you've signed away more than you realized."

"I knew we wouldn't get away with this," Rupert muttered.

"Quiet!" Emory said. "Silvaria, my dearest, you're upset about nothing. The business is going perfectly. That's the last thing you need to think about."

I had so many questions and doubts, I didn't know where to start. "Are you framing me for murder?"

"No! But you're in a difficult situation, and I'm not sure how much more I can help you."

I didn't believe a word of what he'd just said. "My situation is difficult because of you and Rupert. I trusted you. I believed you were doing right by me. When I saw you confronting Hettie, I was certain you were looking for evidence to clear my name. But you weren't. Hettie, what is in that package Emory gave you?"

She visibly trembled, and her hand went to the package.

"Hettie, leave!" Emory said. "You're of no use to us."

"She's of great use to me. If I have to, I'll have the corpses restrain her and open the package. Hettie, I know you're involved in this, but if you speak up now, you may be charged with a lesser crime."

Rather than accusing me of overstepping, Detective Noir nodded. "Lying to the Magic Council is a serious offence, Hettie. If you haven't been telling the truth about Miss Digby, reveal it now. Otherwise, you'll be sending an innocent woman to jail, and your sister's murder will never be solved."

Hettie opened and closed her mouth several times. She looked at Emory and then Rupert, but neither of them came to her assistance. They were abandoning her just like they'd done to me.

"This is your final chance, or I will unleash my corpses." I gestured them forward, and they surrounded me, the tension radiating off them, making my skin tingle with power.

She slowly held out the package. "It's... it's money. They paid me. They told me to say I'd seen you fighting with Molly."

"Stop lying," Emory said. "Why would we do that?"

Hettie shook her head. "I don't know. You simply told me to reveal the argument and then put that jewelry in my bedroom."

"Don't believe her. Since her accident, she's been muddled in her thinking," Emory said.

But I did believe Hettie completely. My heart felt like it had been replaced with a heavy, ice encrusted stone as I processed this information. I should have been in tears, but none came.

There was one emotion I felt. Rage. My corpses felt it too, because their growling increased.

"No attacking," I forced out. "Not yet. We don't have all the information to show I'm innocent."

Detective Noir opened his mouth as if he was going to protest, but a glare from me silenced him. I was done with being sweet little Silvaria. I had unlimited power, and it was time to use it. If I had to use these corpses to throttle the truth out of my deceitful cousin and my lying fiancé, I would.

"We should take this back to my office," Detective Noir said. "We don't want things to get out of hand."

I did. I wanted to unleash chaos. I wanted to destroy them and laugh while it happened. It was no less than they deserved.

By some miracle, I stopped myself and simply lifted a finger. "Just a moment more. Emory, you killed Molly, didn't you?"

He didn't answer.

"Molly knew you and would have had no concerns about you being in the yard with her. When she turned her back on you, and you were certain no one was watching, you strangled her."

Emory was like a newly risen corpse and had lost the power of speech.

"You knew how to get in and out of the yard quickly because you've done it when meeting me in secret." My voice was calm, even though my pulse raced. "And you had access to my trinkets. It would have been simple to take a few without me noticing."

His gaze cut to Hettie.

"You and Rupert planned this. Neither of you loved me. You just wanted me to sign over my fortune and then get rid of me."

The men looked at each other. One of them would break. I was certain of it.

Rupert went first. "It was Emory's idea. He came to me with the plan."

"Liar! It was you. You told me how much you hated your cousin, and you were sick of her getting everything she wanted."

"I didn't know anything about her," Rupert said. "I'd left the family behind ages ago."

"You knew how rich they were and when Silvaria would come into her trust fund. You kept an eye on that."

"So did you. Why else did you target her at the ball and fake an interest?"

A tear threatened, but I banished it. These hideous creatures would never see me broken by their cruelty. That would come later, when I was alone and could fall apart without witnesses.

"When your last scheme failed, you begged me for help," Emory said. "You convinced me I didn't need to marry to get the Digby fortune. I just had to get Silvaria to sign it over to me."

"You told me she was a dumb airhead with delusions about being a dancer. You said she was so stupid it would be easy to con her out of her fortune. And you were right." Rupert was sucking in air and wildly jabbing a finger. "You made her fall for you, and she never questioned why you picked the plain corpse lover over all the pretty women with normal powers and normal lives."

"That's enough!" Detective Noir snapped. "Miss Digby does not deserve this."

Rupert wheeled around to face me. "It was all him. Emory spent most of the evening after you signed the paperwork laughing. You're a joke to him."

"You laughed, too," Emory snarled.

The blood rushed from my head, and I staggered. My corpses held me, shielding me as if I was their precious queen and needed to be protected from the stabbing words and thorny revelations.

I clutched my corpses. "Emory, did you ever care for me?"

He sneered at me. "How could I love such a broken freak?"

My ice cold heart shattered and floated around my chest, jabbing me with painful spikes of truth. "This was always about my money."

Emory's handsome face was contorted in a snarl. "Your power disgusts me, but you wouldn't let it go. I even gave you an option to destroy those awful cemeteries. A way out! Why wouldn't you agree to let me build on them?"

"Because the dead must never be disrespected and certainly not by the likes of you." I drew strength from my corpses and straightened. "You'd have destroyed thousands of peaceful resting places."

"They were dead! They wouldn't have cared."

"You fool. Dwellings built on cemeteries are always full of unstable magic seeping from the corpses beneath the foundations."

"You're obsessed with those things, even though you pretend you aren't." Emory revealed his true, ugly character. How had I ever thought him the right one for me? "I always knew you'd never pursue dancing, not that you can even dance. I've had my feet trodden on enough times to know you'd never make it."

"I'm an excellent dancer. I can be a dancer if I choose." Corpse power pressed around me, and a cold truth hit. It was a welcome truth, but one I'd shied from for too long. I belonged with the walking dead, and it had been a frivolous dream to think of escape. I didn't want that anymore. It was time I leaned into my power and embraced death.

"You were always going to choose the grave. I ignored the corpses and laid down ground rules for our marriage, but you never listened." Emory glowered at the corpses as they growled at him. "You raise the dead and use them like they're your playthings. It's creepy."

"It's my magic, my power, and it's what made me and my family so wealthy. You always knew my heritage." Finally, it was a heritage I was proud of.

"Emory was only ever interested in your financial heritage," Rupert said, a little too smugly, given I could order a corpse to tear an arm off and beat him with it. "And now you've signed nearly all of it away, so you're worthless to him."

The strength I felt faded. "You've taken it all?"

"I left a small amount. You need little. You'll always have your family home, and it's not as if you spend money on anything. You won't need expensive gowns or silks to trudge around the cemeteries." Emory's gaze turned beseeching. "This was for your own good. You have a terrible head for business."

"That was my money, and I will get it back," I said.

"It's too late," Rupert said. "Emory's transferred the funds. You'll never see it again."

My anger choked me, and it took all my restraint not to unleash my corpses on these festering excuses for men. "Rupert, you're almost as bad as Emory. You never wanted to reunite with the family, did you? You were motivated by my money, too."

He shrugged. "I was never a part of the family. I was ignored and made to feel stupid because I'd messed up a few times."

"So you wanted revenge because you got things wrong and people told you off about it?" I no longer had a cousin.

As far as I was concerned, Rupert and Emory were dead to me. Everything I'd loved and had my hopes pinned on was gone.

I turned away, not wanting them to see the distress as it hit me like a gravedigger's shovel.

Detective Noir didn't miss my anguish, though. He stepped forward, offering a shield with his back, so Rupert and Emory couldn't see me. "Hettie, will you testify against these men? If you reveal they bribed you so you'd lie about the argument, that'll provide crucial evidence to help convict them of your sister's murder."

I peered around Detective Noir and looked at Hettie. She was still shaking. Her gaze caught mine, and I was horrified to see sympathy in her eyes as she nodded. This woman, who had so little and was so bitter, felt sorry for me. It was too much to bear. I looked away again.

"I'll also get details of the paperwork you signed from the lawyer," Detective Noir said to me. "We'll trace where the money's gone."

"I'll fight you," Emory said. "Silvaria gave me her money willingly. And you won't find where it is, which means I have the resources for a court battle. I'll make the Digby name a public mockery. Everyone will learn how pathetic you were, all your stupid hopes and dreams, and how your own cousin tricked you and lied to you."

I raised my chin and glared at him. "If you do that, the public will also learn you're barely human, you have no morals, and you thrive on deceiving others. You steal, you lie, and you betray. If you ruin me, I'll take you down, too."

Emory smirked. "You don't have the stomach for it. You're too good."

"I do. And just remember, I have a power you can only dream of. You'll never have a restful night's sleep again, because you'll always be wondering if that tapping noise growing closer is my corpses exacting vengeance for me." This felt righteous. This was what I should have stood for a long time ago.

"Miss Digby, perhaps you shouldn't," Detective Noir murmured.

I raised a hand. I wasn't finished. "That's what will happen. You come after me and make this any more painful than it already is, and if you dare to destroy my family legacy, I will annihilate you. I will hunt you, terrify you until your looks are gone and your mind too, and then... then, I shall let my corpses have you. They'll eat every piece. There'll be nothing left."

All signs of smugness vanished from Emory's face, and he took a step back. "But you love me."

"I despise you. I wish I'd never met you." My mother and Aunt Ruby had been right. I should have led with my head. As my broken heart was witness, emotions led you along a dangerous, foolish path. They made you do stupid things and filled your life with regret. That would never happen again.

As I burned with rage and humiliation, Detective Noir spoke to Hettie and then had Rupert and Emory restrained by his waiting colleagues.

I didn't bother sifting through the ashes of my ruined happily ever after. It was destroyed, and I was left with nothing but the harsh taste of anger.

A familiar smell drifted up my nose. It was the musty, decaying scent of my corpses. I turned my sharp gaze to them and let out a sigh. Well, maybe I had one thing left...

Chapter 23

"You're not focusing." Father stood behind me as five angry corpses staggered toward us.

"I am. I don't fear them. When the time is right, I'll send them back."

"This is not about what you want. It's about what the corpses need."

With a sigh, I pushed my energy into the corpses and returned them to their graves with barely a thought.

"Better. But don't play with them. Remember what you're dealing with. Never forget the Great Corpse Uprising of Midwinter Mallow or the Plague Corpse War in Silver Vale." My father scattered grave dirt where the corpses had been standing.

"I can hear them, so I know what they need. They weren't seeking trouble. They were simply curious about what we were doing. They were curious about me."

His gaze shifted to me. "You hear them? That's impossible."

I shrugged. I didn't have the energy or inclination to explain anything to my father. Two weeks had passed since I'd learned the awful betrayal inflicted upon me by Emory and Rupert. Since then, I'd concentrated on one thing. My corpses. I should have embraced them a long time ago, rather than resisting my ability and thinking I could be something different.

I no longer fought my destiny. My power scoured through me like the icy hand of a winter witch, and it was a trial to keep the corpses' voices out of my head. The dead liked to chat.

Mother joined us from the other side of the cemetery, her steps purposeful and her gaze alert for signs of disturbances in the graves. "I've had a message about an incident at Danbury Cemetery. We need to leave at once."

"Silvaria's training is complete for the day," Father said. "We can be there within the hour."

Mother inspected me for a brief second. "Perhaps you would like to come with us. You've yet to visit the Danbury site. It has some of the oldest corpses on record. There's a magic user who resides there who was a shapeshifter. His corpse has never fully settled."

"No, but thank you for the invitation. I have a few things I wish to practice. I'll be fine on my own." Alone was what I needed to become used to.

Mother adjusted the collar of my plain brown dress and tucked a loose strand of hair behind my ear. "This is a positive step, seeing you engaged with the corpses. You'd begun to worry us, especially after the Emory incident."

"You have nothing to worry about. I know my place."

"And not a moment too soon," Father said. "There is unrest in many cemeteries, and we've lost several good people in the last few years. You're no longer a child. It's time you took on more responsibility. And now that marriage business has been put to one side, you'll have no distractions."

I pressed my lips together and looked at the dirt beneath my feet. I felt the opposite of a child. My bones ached, I couldn't get warm, and my heart was numb. Every time I looked in the mirror, I saw a new wrinkle, and my once beautiful hair was dry, and there were gray hints at the roots.

Had shock caused such a change in my appearance? Did a shattered heart and a brutal betrayal physically injure a person, too? I couldn't be bothered to find out, and I cared little about my appearance anymore. The corpses weren't worried if my dress was stained and I hadn't washed my hair for a week.

"We've been discussing a future cemetery for you." Mother gathered up three empty pots of grave dirt.

Of course. They always talked about me and never to me. "Where will you send me?"

"We wondered about Witch Haven. It's a powerful place. A lot of magic users go there to find peace, particularly if they struggle with their powers. The dead laid to rest in that village are always active."

"That would keep me busy." I'd heard of Witch Haven many times. I'd even visited once. It was a quaint place, but its quiet appearance and cute homes were deceiving. Some of the world's most powerful users of magic owned houses there, and it was often the target of dark magic users, determined to get that power and absorb the ancient well of energy that crisscrossed beneath the village along ley lines.

"You're not ready. Perhaps in a few decades, Witch Haven will be suitable for you," Father said, after giving me a considered inspection. "We have several smaller cemeteries that would be more appropriate, where you can hone your ability and embrace your role."

"I can take on Witch Haven now. I'm ready."

"There's already a guardian in place at that site, although she has mentioned retirement. The place wants her to stay, though," Mother said. "Your time in Witch Haven will come." Her gaze shifted over my shoulder, and her eyes narrowed.

I turned to discover Detective Noir walking toward us. His eyebrows rose as he took in my appearance, but he said nothing to me and instead greeted my parents.

"Your butler informed me I'd find you here," he said. "I have an update on Molly's case. I thought you might be interested."

"Hasn't that been closed by now?" Father said.

"Almost. Just a few loose ends to tie up."

"Then we don't require the details, unless they concern us." Father turned away.

"I'd like to hear them," I said, "with your permission, Father."

His expression sharpened. "Five minutes. We'll gather fresh grave dirt and meet you at the carriage. Don't keep us waiting."

I watched until my parents were out of sight and turned to Detective Noir. He looked less harassed. His gaze was alert, and his hair had been recently combed. He also smelled of soap and fresh laundry. "So, what can you tell me?"

Detective Noir paused. "Are you well?"

"As can be expected. The case?"

"Of course. You know most of the details, so I'll keep this brief. Hettie keeps asking me to pass on her apology."

"I don't accept it. She's only sorry because she was caught receiving money to lie about me."

Detective Noir nodded slowly. "Perhaps. Are you sure you are—"

"I am fine." My wellbeing wasn't his concern. "That day, when I heard Rupert threatening Hettie, I should have realized something was wrong, but I thought he was sticking up for me. What a fool I was. He was just scared about keeping someone alive who might reveal their deceit."

"Your cousin and fiancé—"

"Ex-fiancé. I have broken off the engagement. I want nothing to do with that man. And as far as I'm concerned, Rupert died years ago."

"That's understandable. Your former fiancé, then. Neither of them show remorse. And as we've looked into their association, it stretches back to just before Emory approached you and expressed an interest in getting to know you."

I should feel something at this news, but it came as no surprise, and my numb core accepted the information with barely a change in my pulse. My relationship had been false. Emory and Rupert didn't care they'd stamped on my heart and shattered it.

Detective Noir cleared his throat. "Hettie will testify against them. As will others."

"You mean me?"

"Not just you. We discovered Emory and Rupert conned two more women in a similar fashion. They were both older than Emory and not as wealthy as you, but they lost all their assets."

"Ah! They were practicing their skills, wanting to ensure they could get away with it before they came after me."

"It's possible. It took some convincing before the women agreed to testify. They were embarrassed at being tricked and didn't want their reputations tarnished."

"Of course. Reputation is everything. My parents taught me that."

"It helped when they learned what happened to you and that you were standing up in court."

I'd argued with my parents for days about testifying. They could have threatened me with any form of punishment or sanction, but I wasn't backing down. Let our reputation be smudged. These monsters would not escape justice.

"Anything else?" I said.

"Because of the evidence and testimonies we have, there is no way Emory and Rupert will get away with this."

"Good. And the paperwork I signed? Will I be able to retrieve my money?"

His expression turned sorrowful. "I'm sorry. It's gone. There was a long and complicated money trail that ended in a dead bank account. Whatever they did with that money, you won't see it again. It was withdrawn, so someone has it, but they won't say who."

"Would a visit from my corpses change their minds?"

Detective Noir inched up an eyebrow. "It might, but that's illegal."

My eyes narrowed. "And what they did to me isn't?"

"Two wrongs—"

"No! Save me the sanctimony." I ground my teeth and stared at the headstone of a white witch. Despite what Emory had said when I'd confronted him, he'd left me with barely any funds to live on. If it weren't for my parents ensuring I had a roof over my head and food on the table, I'd be destitute.

Detective Noir reached out a hand but didn't touch me. "Miss Digby, what they did to you was a terrible injustice."

"Murdering Molly was the injustice. Money can be replaced." I waited until my rage mellowed and I no longer had the desire to rain down corpse-induced terror on the world. "Do not worry about me. I won't use my corpses to do wrong. The money is gone. I don't have it, but neither do they while they're behind bars."

"That's one comfort."

"A very small comfort."

Detective Noir tugged at his jacket. "I owe you an apology. I made a mistake assuming the necklace we found on Molly had been stolen. I witnessed for myself how kind and generous you are to everybody, so I should have known better."

"You should. And I told you numerous times Molly was a friend. You didn't believe me."

"I put the evidence together incorrectly, and it's something I deeply regret. You should never have been arrested for her murder."

Again, it took me a moment of deep breathing not to go full-on evil corpse summoner. "You were using the clues you had at the time. They took you along a certain line of investigation. And while I didn't appreciate being put in a cell, at least I learned I can get out if I ever need to again."

His stunned expression almost made me smile.

I looked out across my now familiar environment. I'd spent all my time in the cemeteries since I learned the truth about Emory and Rupert. Only two weeks ago, I'd been thinking about how I could balance my life in the cemetery with dancing and marriage. I'd been so naïve to think I could have it all.

"I've brought you your necklace," Detective Noir said. "Your father mentioned it was valuable, and we no longer require it as evidence."

I looked at the necklace he held out. "Give it to someone else or sell it and donate the funds to charity. My work rarely requires me to look enticing. The corpses have no care about things like that."

"It's not mine to sell or gift."

"It is. I give it to you."

He rubbed the back of his neck with his free hand. "I'll leave it at your house."

"Whatever you wish."

Detective Noir pocketed the necklace. He didn't leave. "I wish things had been different."

"Wishes change nothing, unless you have a willing genie on hand. All I care about is your assurance Molly will receive the justice she deserves."

"That I can promise you." He looked around the cemetery. "Is she here?"

I nodded. Molly had been released into my care two days ago, and I'd found her the perfect resting place. "Would you like to visit her?"

"Yes. It would be good to pay my final respects."

I led him silently to a corner plot underneath a beautiful old cedar tree. Molly's freshly filled grave had been covered in her favorite yellow roses.

"She was happy to rest?" Detective Noir said after a moment of respectful silence.

"Molly went in peacefully. She'll be no trouble. But just in case, I'll always watch over her. Even when I'm far away, my bond with Molly will keep her safe and settled."

"You're becoming a full-time cemetery guardian?"

"Yes."

"What about your ambition to dance? Whenever you spoke about it, your face lit up."

The brief flash of bitterness I felt vanished into indifference. "That was a foolish idea. I'll look after the dead and accept my power."

"So that's it?"

I glanced at him, surprised by his sharp tone. "I'm not sure what you mean."

"Miss Digby, Silvaria, you have so much life in you. You could achieve anything if you truly wanted it."

"You sound like I used to. I once believed that. Not anymore."

"I'm sorry to hear that." He tugged at his jacket sleeves. "Even though you infuriated me beyond belief frequently, I admire your spirit, and you never gave up on Molly. You relentlessly pursued every lead."

"And got things wrong because of that. I accused three innocent people of her murder. Everyone was right. I had no idea how to solve a crime, proven by the fact I missed the one happening right under my nose. If I'd been more suspicious of Emory and Rupert, Molly would still be alive."

"No! You can't blame yourself."

I was about to protest but then shrugged. I couldn't change what had happened. It was just something I'd learn to live with.

"You were so enthusiastic and determined. You had to figure it out," he said.

"It was the right thing to do for Molly." And maybe I'd assumed I was better than everyone else and could do things the experts could not. Look where that had gotten me.

"Those actions make you a decent person. The very best of people. This work often leads me to those who don't have kindness in them. I deal with those who are looking for an angle and a way to get something out of a situation, often leaving others deprived or unhappy."

I simply nodded. I knew all about that.

"But spending time with you and seeing your pure heart, it changed me." Detective Noir paused long enough that I looked at him for a second. "I've grown very fond of you."

I returned my attention back to Molly's grave. "My heart doesn't feel pure anymore."

"If I can, I'd like to help you change that."

"What are you suggesting?"

"We could meet for dinner. I'd enjoy getting to know you when we're not hunting for a killer together."

I took a few seconds to study his face. Detective Noir was handsome, and when he hadn't been trying to keep me out of his investigation, he'd supported me and even encouraged me. I'd also appreciated when he'd stood beside me after I discovered the truth about Emory and Rupert.

"I want you to see there are still good people in this world, Silvaria. People who want to be kind to you and look after you."

Could I see a future with Detective Noir? One full of companionship, honesty, and maybe love?

The tiny flicker of hope I had died. "I don't need looking after. And I reside with the dead now. I have no time or interest in the living."

"You're giving up on relationships? On life?"

"The corpses are better company and always loyal. I never have to second-guess their motives, because I already know them."

"Silvaria, cemetery guardians live for a long time. Will you be content to remain lonely for the rest of your life?"

"I've been lonely for most of my life. Apart from brief flashes of friendship, a friendship that is now buried six feet beneath us, I'm more used to being on my own than being in company."

"One bad experience with a man doesn't have to mean the end of love."

I turned to face him, an unkind sneer on my face. "Is that what you're offering me? You'd be happy to live a life with an embittered, cold corpse lover? Because that's what I'll become. Death will seep into me and suck the life from my marrow. You can already see how it has affected me."

"Because you're shutting everyone out. It doesn't have to be this way. You can be a guardian and still find happiness."

"Not with you, I can't. It's easier this way, for both of us. Don't waste your time or thoughts on me. I shall not be thinking about you." With my heart closed to feeling, I'd never be hurt again. "Thank you for updating me on the case. Let me know when I need to testify, and I'll be there." I turned and walked away from my old life, my hopes, and my dreams. It was time to embrace my destiny with death.

I didn't look back at Detective Noir. There was no point. My corpses were calling, and I needed to be with them. I'd accept whatever guardian position my parents sent me to, tend to the corpses, and be at one with the dead.

My future mission was simple. Whatever I had to do, I'd become the most respected cemetery guardian that ever existed. And after I'd grieved for my old life and fully embraced this new one, I'd seek the power in Witch Haven and truly be what I was meant to be.

A queen to the corpses.

About Author

K.E. O'Connor (Karen) is a mystery author living in the beautiful British countryside. She loves all things mystery, animals, and cake.

If you want to be part of the Witch Haven crew, practice spells, solve a few murders, spend time with amazing witches and their talking familiars, and get a **free** book, join her weekly newsletter.

Sign up today.

Newsletter:
https://BookHip.com/QKGDWJW
Website:
www.keoconnor.com/writing
Facebook:
www.facebook.com/keoconnorauthor

Also By

Spells and Spooks
Hexes and Haunts
Curses and Corpses
Muffins and Moonlight
Cupcakes and Cauldrons
Pancakes and Potions
Hauntings and High Jinx
Hauntings and Havoc
Hauntings and Hoaxes
The Case of the Screaming Skull
The Case of the Poisoned Pumpkin
The Case of the Cursed Candy
Fire Fang
Silvaria

If you enjoyed

Silvaria

turn the page to read an extract from another magical mystery. This book features Juno, a unique talking cat, and Zandra, her troubled witchy sidekick, How will a plucky witch and a feisty cat with a big secret beat a dangerous gang, find a killer, and locate Zandra's missing mother?

EVERY WITCH WAY BUT GHOULS

ISBN: 978-1-915378-42-2

Chapter 1

"These prickled hogs are a pain in my behind." Zandra Crypt skulked beside me in the late evening gloom. The stars were out, and we should have finished work three hours ago, but these magically enchanted hedgehogs we tracked had a different idea. They weren't giving up their freedom without a fight.

"We're close. I can smell them." I lifted my perfect pink-tipped nose and breathed in the chilly evening air. It was tinged with eau-du-hog. Spicy with a bit of musky sweat. The faint sparkles in the air from the noxious gas they emitted when startled also helped with the tracking.

"They definitely came this way." Zandra slowed to inspect small tracks in the dirt on the path we followed through Crimson Cove woods. "These are the right sized prints for hogs."

I sniffed the tracks and nodded. My cute little booping snooter was excellent at picking up smells. "The scent is fresh. They must have been here less than five minutes ago."

Zandra looked around and sighed. "I'm sure we've come this way before, though. These critters are sneaky. It wouldn't surprise me if they're leading us in circles just for fun. Twisted little spiky monsters."

There was a scuttle of tiny feet up ahead, and we froze. My hackles lifted, and Zandra clenched her hands.

"Juno, did you see where that came from?" Zandra was crouched as if ready to pounce, but I'd warned her several times about not grabbing our prickled challengers. These magically enchanted hedgehogs had poisoned prickles that would shoot out. Get those stuck in you, and you were in a world of hurt.

"No sign of them yet." I didn't feel the cold, thanks to my magnificent white fur, but Zandra was shivering, and her breath plumed out of her. The last thing I wanted was for my witch to get a cold. She was a grump when sick.

"Let's keep moving. They must tire soon." She rubbed her hands together and blew on them.

I didn't like to point out we'd had four nights of endless tracking and hog hunting, and we'd yet to capture these critters. Who knew magically enchanted hedgehogs would be so difficult to detain? They were small, noisy, and indiscreet. This should have been an easy win.

But I was still deliriously proud of my witch, since this was the only assignment we'd failed to complete. Four days on the job in animal control, and everything was ticked off our list.

Our new boss, Barney Hoffman, had been giving us other tasks during the day, since these hedgehogs were nocturnal. We'd mainly checked households to ensure the families followed the familiar care rules and provided suitable enrichment for any tame magic creatures they kept. Animal control was particular about how magical critters were looked after, and sometimes, people got sloppy.

Other than the checks and reminders issued, Zandra had been learning the ropes of her job as an assistant animal control warden, and I was alongside her as her trusty familiar to make sure everything went smoothly. Apart from these pesky hedgehogs, it had been a perfect start to our new careers.

Zandra shivered again and rubbed her arms briskly.

"We could always try again tomorrow," I said.

"No way! These hogs are going down tonight. If I don't catch them, Barney will figure out we lied to get this job."

"We didn't exactly lie. We showed how excellent you'd be in this role."

"You pretended you were a crazed, possessed magical being, and I fake captured you. That's not at all lying."

"You'd have been able to do that with any magically crazed being. There just weren't any around when their services were required. I stepped up. Besides, Barney likes you. He won't fire you for one tiny fabrication."

Zandra ducked, shoving her dark hair tighter under her hat. "That bush moved! It must be the hogs."

She stalked forward before I could stop her, so I sprinted to keep up. "Ten more minutes, then we're calling it a night. Barney doesn't have the budget for overtime. He's always telling you that."

"There won't be any regular time if we don't pull this off." She pressed a finger to her lips. "They're so close, even I can smell them."

"It isn't hard with all that stinky, sparkling gas they keep parping out of their tiny behinds."

A small black blur shot out of the hedge and whacked the side of Zandra's head.

I launched into the air, my claws exposed and a murderous growl shooting out of me, but I was a second too late. The hedgehog pinged off Zandra's cheek, leaving behind several poisoned quills.

She went to touch her face, but I sprung up and knocked her hand out of the way. "Get on the ground. I'll extract the quills before the poison spreads."

"But... the hedgehog! It's getting away. This is as close as we've ever gotten."

"Down! Now! If that poison gets into your system, you're toast."

Zandra dropped to her knees, and I hopped my front paws onto her shoulder and grabbed each quill between my teeth, yanked it out, and spat it on the ground. It must have hurt, but my brave witch didn't protest.

She grimaced as the last one popped free. "You done?"

"One more thing. Think sparkly, happy thoughts." I latched onto the side of her face and sucked the poison from each hole.

Zandra shrieked, since there was nothing I could do about my fangs, so she got a few extra holes in her face. But poison bested cat fangs, so she'd have to endure the pain.

Only when I was certain the foul taste of rotten eggs was no longer present on her skin did I stop sucking.

Zandra gingerly touched her swollen cheek. "I know I should thank you, but that burned like dragon's breath after a spicy curry."

I licked her cheek, then trotted off and lapped from a slushy puddle to clear the foul taste of poison from my mouth. By the time I was done, Zandra was pulsing a healing spell over her cheek. It took a few minutes, but the swelling faded and the holes closed.

"I see now why Barney doesn't want to deal with these hedgehogs himself." Zandra got to her feet and brushed dirt off her knees. "Or maybe this is hazing. All the new recruits get the lousy jobs to see if they can handle the pressure."

"Barney wouldn't do that to you. He's a gentleman."

"The others might."

Zandra often reacted like a startled, magically enchanted hedgehog in circumstances she found uncomfortable. She'd fling out prickles and verbal barbs when trapped in an awkward situation. And when she'd met the rest of the team in animal control, things had been a little strained.

"They'll come around once they get to know you." I wound around her legs several times until she let out a sigh and petted me. "And although I'd rather these hogs were in their cages safely under lock and key, I admire their spirit. They've beaten us for days." I walked along beside Zandra, sniffing the ground and hoping to find a fresh hedgehog trail.

Zandra scooped me up and settled me on her shoulder. "I sort of agree. We need a new approach, though. This stealth tracking isn't working. The hogs must be able to hear us approaching. Even your delicate paws cause a vibration."

"What do you have in mind?"

"Automatic traps. The hogs come in different sizes and have different food preferences, so we'll need a variety of traps and treats. We'll place the traps around the woods, since this is their favorite spot, and wait for them to fire."

I booped my nose against Zandra's healed cheek in approval. "You're sure you don't want a break? There are snacks in the van and a thermos of coffee. We can get everything we need and come back tomorrow evening."

"Snacks and rest later. That'll be our reward once we've caught the hogs."

It took an hour and a trip to the local store to grab food the hedgehogs would eat, but four traps were finally planted around the woodland, complete with tempting treats to entice our spiky nemeses.

We hunkered down in the van at the edge of the woods and waited. Zandra had set up a four-way receiving camera linked to the mobile snow globe network to remote monitor the cages. She had her mobile globe open and was flicking between the images.

"Come on, hoggies. You must be hungry. All that running from me and Juno has burned up calories," Zandra muttered.

My nose was distracted by the meaty cat treats in the glove box. "Give them time. They'll be nervous of the traps."

"Not that nervous. I've got movement on one camera." Zandra grinned at me.

I gave her the cat version of a smile, which was more of a whisker twitch with a tail flick. If I tried to smile like her with my teeth, I looked like I was about to attack. When I'd been turned into a cat, it took me a while to unlearn how to smile and a good year to learn the fine art of cat body language. Use the wrong ear twitch at the wrong moment, and I could have all-out war on my furry paws.

"Look! A hedgehog is going to the smallest cage." She tilted her mobile snow globe so I could see what was going on.

I forced myself not to keep sniffing for treats and focused on the image. Sure enough, the smallest hog we'd been tracking was creeping toward the cage. It sniffed for a good five minutes before slinking inside.

"Is that a hat on its head?" I said.

"Not sure. It's got something on its head. Maybe it's a leaf? Any second now," Zandra whispered. "That baby is ours."

The hedgehog hesitated, then darted forward, mouth open, revealing sharp teeth. The second it got to the food, the trapdoor triggered, and it snapped shut.

The hog twirled around and charged at the door, but it was too late to get out. The critter hit the door several times, quills shooting out in self-defense and pinging harmlessly through the bars, but there was nothing the little prickled spud could do to escape.

"Woo-hoo! It's our lucky night," Zandra said. "Two more hedgehogs are going after the other cages."

"That still leaves three out there," I said. "The family unit. The mamma and her two babies."

"They'll go for the largest cage," Zandra said, surety in her voice. "I reckon the rest are males. We've got the boys, but of course, mamma hog will be cautious and smart. She won't lead her babies into danger."

"If only we could make them believe they weren't in danger from us, but they won't listen to reason."

Zandra petted my head. "You tried talking to them, but they told you to get lost."

"Their language was coarser than that. It involved sticking their prickles where the sun doesn't shine. Repeatedly. And sideways."

She grinned. "You did your best. Some critters just won't listen to reason. They think animal control is all about capture and destroy."

"Once we have them, they'll have a safe place to sleep and all the hedgehog food they can handle, and no one will report them as a nuisance once they're in a sanctuary." I leaned in for more pets. "Like many of the animals we've dealt with since starting this job, they don't trust us."

"Animal control hasn't got the best reputation. Someone needs to do a positive PR spin. It would make our lives easier."

I nodded as I watched the action via the camera. We'd been in this job for less than a week, yet had heard alarming prejudice about animal control. Sure, there was a misguided assumption that all we did was hunt innocent magical creatures and put them to sleep, but Barney was a decent boss and as animal crazy as Zandra. He advocated kindness first. The animals got compassion and understanding. Even the hedgehogs who poisoned Zandra got a second chance, and I was always unforgiving when anyone hurt my bonded witch.

We watched for another ten minutes before all but one of the traps was filled. The hedgehogs were raging mad about being captured, shooting out quills and parping sparkly gas, but eventually, they settled in and ate the food. And why not? Why fight something when you know you've been defeated?

Zandra bounced in her seat. "It's the family! They're approaching the largest cage. Any minute now, we'll have a full house of hedgehogs."

"Are they wearing hats, too?" The feed from the camera wasn't clear thanks to the magical distortion–magic and electronics did not play nicely together–but I was certain the family of hogs were wearing tiny pointed hats.

"Yeah, they are. Where are they getting those from?" Zandra tried to unblur the image, but it wouldn't get any sharper.

We watched in silence as mamma hedgehog tentatively approached the large cage and sniffed around. The two smaller hogs were eager to go inside, but she kept nudging them back with her nose and nipping them if they disobeyed and tried to dodge past and grab the food.

The view from the camera wavered for a second, then it blacked out before coming back online.

"What's wrong with this thing?" Zandra said. "Don't fail me now. I need to see when the hedgehogs are trapped. If we move too soon, they'll run again."

"It could be magical atmospherics." Barney had come up with a range of clever inventions to ensure most of the vehicles and equipment worked with minimal disruption, but they still weren't perfect.

"This feed runs through the snow globe network. There shouldn't be any interference." Zandra jiggled her mobile snow globe.

The camera image wobbled again and went blank, but not before I spotted a large shadow looming over the hedgehog cage.

Zandra jerked in her seat. "You saw that, right? Someone had better not be messing with my equipment or my hogs." She jumped out of the van and raced toward the largest cage, and I was hot on her heels.

We made it halfway to the capture site, when there was a roar, and a light lit the gloomy trees.

Zandra's eyes widened, but she kept running. We entered the clearing, where the large cage was located, and stopped.

Inside the cage was not only the three hat wearing hedgehogs cowering in one corner, but a magic user who looked to be part dragon. His red arm scales flared brightly, and flames flickered from his mouth.

His yellow eyes darted our way, and he roared again before emitting a jet of flames that burned through the cage bars.

"Hey! Stop that!" Zandra yelled above the roar of the flames. "That's the property of animal control."

"I don't think he cares about who owns the cage," I said.

Zandra didn't appear to have heard me. She stalked toward the cage, magic sparking on her fingers.

The part dragon looked at the hedgehogs. He grabbed each one and swallowed them without chewing.

"Oh, no, you didn't. You did not just eat my catch and ruin my cage." Zandra ran at the cage, her magic flaring in bright red, dazzling swirls.

I gathered my own ancient magic. Although my power was dull and reluctant to perform, I'd force it to life to protect Zandra.

Panic seized my silken tail and tugged it. Nothing happened. My magic refused to function.

My witch was about to go head-to-head with a smoldering, hog eating dragon, and I couldn't help her.

**Every Witch Way but Ghouls is available in
e-book and paperback
ISBN: 978-1-915378-42-2**